Shorty Gotta Be Grown

Shorty Gotta Be Grown

T.C. Littles

www.urbanbooks.net

Urban Books, LLC
300 Farmingdale Road, NY-Route 109
Farmingdale, NY 11735

Shorty Gotta Be Grown
Copyright © 2020 T.C. Littles

ISBN 13: 978-1-64556-061-6
ISBN 10: 1-64556-061-9

First Trade Paperback Printing July 2020
Printed in the United States of America

10 9 8 7 6 5 4 3 2 1

This is a work of fiction. Any references or similarities to actual events, real people, living or dead, or to real locales are intended to give the novel a sense of reality. Any similarity in other names, characters, places, and incidents is entirely coincidental.

Distributed by Kensington Publishing Corp.
Submit Orders to:
Customer Service
400 Hahn Road
Westminster, MD 21157-4627
Phone: 1-800-733-3000
Fax: 1-800-659-2436

Shorty Gotta Be Grown

by

T.C. Littles

By the end of this story, you're all going to have much respect and much love for Calvin Jackson, the same way I have much love, respect, and admiration for Rodney Jones—the man behind the character. Yendor, this one is for you!

CHAPTER 1

PORSHA

Eating a bowl of Frosted Flakes, which was my favorite cereal, I sat Indian-style in front of the television watching the *Ricki Lake* talk show. The episode was about couples who assumed their spouses were cheating and wanted them to take lie-detector tests. One dude admitted he was cheating and had a baby on the way with his girlfriend's best friend. Another one of the guests caught her boyfriend cheating with a decoy the producers had baited him with at the hotel all the cast was staying at. And one of the husbands on the show found out the set of twin girls he had been raising for three years were not even his. The petty drama had me all in.

"Ma! Hurry up and get in here. Ol' boy just found out he's not the father of those twins and tried to flip the wife's chair over with her in it," I yelled for my mother. She had gone to the kitchen to refresh her drink, which was Tito's and cranberry juice. We both loved talk shows and had been watching them back-to-back all morning.

"Oh, hell naw. I knew it, though. Ain't neither one of them li'l bastards have his nose, eyes, or complexion like she stood up on stage trying to point out. I swear to God, I will never understand why females go on national talk shows and put their business out to the world. That heifer knew good and damn well that man was not the father, so she should have kept that shit swept under the rug." Trinity would have made a great correspondent for the show.

"I wonder if they get paid to go on there."

"I am sure they get a few dollars, but you could not pay me enough money to fuck up my life for somebody else's ratings. Here, roll me up a few wraps while we are sitting here." She pulled a sandwich bag of marijuana from her bra and handed it to me.

I was so used to seeing drugs that I could eye the weight of the baggie and tell it was an eighth of buds. I came from parents who were in the streets heavy, broke a lot of laws, and pushed a lot of dope into the city of Detroit. My father, Calvin Jackson, was one of the biggest drug dealers on the west side of the city and even maintained control over a zone in Highland Park. And Trinity was the queen, partner in crime, and mastermind behind a lot of my father's hustle and grind in the game. Calvin was the head of our family, but my mom was the neck. She was also the eyes and ears around the house, which was why I could not wait until I was 18 and could move out.

My nose started tingling as soon as I broke the sandwich bag open. Each time I dropped a bud in the cigarillo wrap, I was itching to drop a bud off to the side to eventually gather up enough for me to roll up a joint. Me and my homegirl Imani had been sneaking and smoking for the last few weeks, but our other friend Nikola could not partake because she was in a certified nursing assistant program that made her take a drug test every month to maintain enrollment and the scholarship.

She used to be my skipping buddy before her mother pulled her out of school and made her start learning a trade that she could get a job with. Ms. Mack might've had a bunch of babies, but she promised Nikola she would kick a baby out of her stomach if she got pregnant before she had her life all the way together. I was glad I was too close to 18 for Trinity to shove that trade shit down my throat, although I had been thinking about going to cosmetology school once I snagged my high school diploma in a couple of months. Nikola's program came with too many rules, and I already had a warden on my back within Trinity. I had been promising myself I was going to look into some beauty schools since I knew college was out of the question, but I had been too busy putting all my spare time into checking up on my secret bae, Street.

"Porsha." I heard my mother dramatically snapping her fingers. "I do not know what you are daydreaming about. But hurry up and finish rolling that weed so you can bust down your chore list before your father calls up here needing your help. I did not let you stay home so you could lounge around and watch TV, running up my electricity bill and getting fat because your ass wanna eat everything in the damn refrigerator." And just like that, she had killed the good vibe with her alter-ego personality. Trinity did not have a diagnosis, but you could not tell me she was not bipolar.

My clothes would actually fit you if I gained a few pounds. I looked her up and down on the sly in my baby T-shirt and leggings, damn near biting my tongue off so I did not let my thoughts slip from my mouth. I hated that Trinity was always in my drawers and clothes but had a problem if I wanted to borrow one of her outfits or a pair of gym shoes. My mother was not old-fashioned about her style or her behavior. Of all my friends, I had the cool mom, but that did not always work in my favor. I sometimes wished I had an airhead for a mom, for no other reason than I could get away with a lot more. Trinity Jackson could be a muthafucka to handle, and that was putting it respectfully.

"Okay, Ma, what's on my slave itinerary for the day?" I turned the TV off before the preview for tomorrow's episode could finish playing.

"Slave itinerary? Oh, you wanna be cute? I can have your smart-mouth ass on the roof sweeping off the shingles if you want to do some real work. You think the light labor you do around here is equivalent to a slave's? Child, please."

I giggled. "Yeah, whatever, Ma. I am good on that. Just tell me what I gotta do." I got up to take my bowl to the kitchen but was shoved back down to the floor within a split second.

"I do not know what young nigga's dick you done sat on that got you feeling yourself, Porsha, but you are going to end up getting a helluva reputation through the hood for giving some gummy head. You have got one more time to say something slick to me, and I am sending you to the dentist with your teeth in a Crown Royal bag." She stood over me, braced to blow my mouth out if I tested her promise.

Scared to say the wrong thing, I nodded and dared to catch eye contact with her. I knew all too well how wild Trinity could go off on me.

"Ma, ma, ma, ma, ma." My little brother's voice broke through the awkward silence and took Trinity's attention off me.

"Here I come, Benzie," she responded to my little brother in a much calmer voice. Then she looked back at me and addressed me with a growl. "You, Porsha, clean up that milk before it sets in and starts smelling spoiled in here. Then get in there and see after your brother. You done pissed me the fuck off with your smart mouth, and I do not want to take it out on him." She scooped up the joints I rolled, then stepped over me on her way out of the room. "And by the way, I was trying to chill and be nice to you. I do not always like having to grow you up by beating your ass, despite what you think."

I made sure I did not mutter a word until I heard her bedroom door slam. Then I said, "Whatever. I sure as hell cannot tell." Episodes like that were why I could not wait to get out of her house.

By the time I finished cleaning up the milk and the broken bowl and getting Benzie some oatmeal and juice in a sippy cup, he was restless and whining. I tried hurrying up so he did not start having a full-blown tantrum and agitate Trinity even more. I loved my brother, although it was kinda hard to sneak around with my homegirls with him on my hip, but I started rebelling when I found out Trinity was pregnant. She taught me how to warm up ravioli in the microwave when I was in kindergarten so she did not have to feed me after school on demand. So I knew a younger sibling was going to be more of my baby than hers. Older kids always have to be overly responsible for their younger sibs. I had seen it happen with my best friend, Nikola. Her mother had been a vessel for life and a passageway for all babies waiting to be born until she had her tubes tied. Nikola had six younger siblings, and she'd raised the three who were ages right underneath her. Noel, Nyla, and Nicholas were no more than two years apart. I stopped complaining whenever I thought about how much shit she had to do for all three of them.

As soon as I opened the door and Benzie saw my face, he stopped crying and started jumping up and down in his crib with his arms spread wide. He was always happy to see me.

"Up, up, up." He reached for me. Benzie was smart as hell for a 1-year-old.

"How was your nap, li'l man?" I picked him up and kissed his forehead.

First, he fell against my cheek with a mouthful of drool and gave me his version of a kiss. Then he caught me off guard and headbutted me.

"Ouch, Benzie." I rubbed my head and exaggerated the pain so he would have some sympathy for me and regret for his actions, but that only made him laugh more. My daddy had been calling himself toughening Benzie up lately, and it was obvious it was working.

"I am going to give you a whoop-whoop if you headbutt me again." I knew good and well I was not going to hit him or let harm come his way. I was my brother's keeper.

After showering Benzie with kisses, I sat him down on his play mat with his favorite toys and got him a fresh diaper and laid out clean pajamas. He had been fighting a cold for the last few days, so he had not been leaving the house. That was part of the reason I got to stay home from school. Trinity did not feel like getting up this morning when he was fussy and coming down from a fever.

My mother's patience was burned out when she gave birth to me, so I did not know why her tubes weren't tied to prevent her from having another child she did not feel like strolling to the park or playing with. I spent a lot of my time as a kid watching soap operas over her shoulder and looking outside at the other kids playing because she did not feel like sitting outside with me. She did, however, buy me every toy in Toys "R" Us so I could entertain myself properly. It was hard to complain or say I had a bad childhood when I was in fresh clothes and gym shoes every time I went to school or left the house. I was the only kid in the neighborhood with a Sega Genesis, a Nintendo, a Game Boy, and video games galore. Benzie was going to be spoiled out of his mind the same way. He already was.

"Hey, baby girl, are you ready to come downstairs and work?" My father came into Benzie's room, kissed me on the forehead, then scooped Benzie up and tossed him in the air.

Benzie was laughing harder and smiling harder than he was when I walked in the room, but I was not surprised, because he loved being under our father. Calvin was a savage in the streets, but he was the best dad in the world. And although not all of his time was devoted to us, he made sure he was present and kept me schooled on street politics. Family was important to him. He felt, preached, and taught me that we were supposed to hold each other down no matter what.

"We're all we've got in this cold and cruel world, Porsha. You better ride just as hard for Benzie, your mom, and me as I ride for you. No one in this family should fail if we keep each other's backs covered. Do you understand?" My dad's words played over in my head as I watched him play with Benzie. The one thing I did not have in common with my homegirls was that I had my dad living in the same house, and a great one at that. I would not trade Calvin Jackson for anything.

"I am ready to help you, Daddy. I've just gotta grab my phone and headphones."

"Okay. I'll be downstairs. Hurry up, and make sure you do not get into no more shit with your momma." He shook his head and leaned back in the rocking chair with Benzie pulling on his beard. "Y'all two are worse than the knuckleheaded niggas I deal with in the streets."

Benzie was lost in his favorite cartoon when I walked past his door, headed to the basement, which was Calvin's man cave and where he and his crew met to hook up product. He had an eighty-six-inch television

mounted on the wall, a fully functional bar, and ten re-
clining theater seats. Half of the room was laid out as
a movie theater and the other as a living space that included a kitchen and bathroom.

Our house was big as hell because it was not built to
be a single-family home. It was originally a four-family
flat, but my father purchased it from a cokehead who was
in debt to him for a few sacks he had been fronted. The
guy signed over the deed to spare his life, and then my
father renovated the entire house and customized it to
fit his trapping lifestyle. We had eight bedrooms, four
bathrooms, and two kitchens that I had to keep clean.

"Hey, niece. I'm glad to see you are alive," my godfather,
Fame, joked when I walked into my dad's man cave to
find him, my dad, and one of my dad's workers.

"I keep telling her to stop playing with her crazy-ass
momma," my father jumped in, agreeing with his best
friend. "Fuck catching some heat from one of these young
niggas trying to come up through the hood. My own wife
and daughter are going to be responsible for dropping
me to the grave." My father always tried to get Trinity to
chill on me, but it only worked when he was around.

"Y'all won't be joking in a few months when I'm grown
and on my own." I sat down at the table across from
Fame and one of my dad's veteran workers.

"Girl, you ain't never going to be too grown to catch a
foot up your ass from Trinity."

"Naw, not at all. But enough about that, let's get to
grinding and get this weight packaged up and on the
streets. The drought is officially over." My dad took his
seat beside me.

Sliding my mask over my nose and lips, my gloves
on, and my wireless earbuds in, I turned on a hip-hop
playlist, then joined the guys on the assembly line. It was
usually me, my mom, or sometimes Fame's first baby

momma whenever he and she were getting along, but I was solo-dolo today. I was cool with the responsibility, though. My pops taught me how to operate within every position like a boss, even the chef. *"If you know how to feed a fiend, you will never be broke."* His survival teachings were embedded in my membrane.

My dad, Fame, and the other worker scooped the appropriate amount of grams into the baggies, and then I made sure the yellow baggies were sealed, in bundles of ten, and in Ziploc bags of one hundred. We never finished with fewer than ten bags, and no one dared to move from the work area until we were completely done. The only person to bend that rule was my dad, and only I or my mom were allowed to have bathroom breaks. Everyone else had to piss in cups with their backs turned to us. Calvin barely trusted himself, so trusting others was out of the question.

"Are you good, Porsha? Or do you want me to call Trin down for some help? This shipment was packed with more weight than the others since the streets been dry."

"I am okay, Daddy. You know I'm not trying to split my money." Calvin paid $50 an hour for this position.

"You are a mess, baby girl." He laughed.

"Dad, I'm not a baby. I am a few months shy of being eighteen. And I would really like that car I asked you for."

He laughed harder. "You are not mentally ready for a foreign whip, P. You are not about to get me sued for tearing up some shit in an accident."

I smacked my lips with attitude. "But let it be a drive-by, I can whip the Audi all day."

"Now I see why your momma wants to go in ya shit." He shook his head.

"Well, since I'm heading down a dead end on the car subject, let me know if I need to give you a list of things I like, Godfather."

Fame laughed. "I do not need a list. I'ma put a few bills in ya hand to set you straight, though. I swear, whatever nigga you be with better have some long money and deep pockets," he joked seriously.

"You damn right. Whatever muthafucka I let roll with my baby better be coming with more than that," my dad said, jumping back into the conversation. "We ain't playing with no lightweights. Ain't that right, Porsha?"

I giggled. "I don't know. I might have to if they have a car."

"Fuck around and get a dumb nigga murked, Porsha. You already know I am not about to let you bring no chump ass into the fold."

Calvin had no idea I had a crush on a dude who was already part of the fold, and I had every intention of keeping it that way. I would not make it to my eighteenth birthday if he found out I was creeping around with one of the dope boys from his main crew. Elvin "Street" Thomas had my young ass wide open, mind, body, and soul. I tried not even thinking about Street when I was around Cal or Fame because they would put a bullet in his dome, dick, and heart if they knew he was stroking their precious Porsha.

Finally, after two hours, the last batch of baggies was sealed up and ready for delivery. I was hella anxious to get out of the house, especially since Imani had hit me up an hour ago and said the field by her house was starting to jump. Imani lived on the same block as one of my father's main trap houses. And once upon a few years ago, the field housed three different homes. But after the homes were abandoned and stripped down for years, the city tore the blight down, and we all turned it into a hangout spot.

CHAPTER 2

PORSHA

Back in the day when my father stayed on the block trapping all day, Imani and I used to ride bikes and jump rope together. She was my first real friend. That was before Nikola moved to the hood and started at our elementary school. She made our duo clique a trio one day during fifth grade recess, and it'd been that way since. There weren't a lot of females I could tolerate, and Nikola was a lot like me. She and I got into more fights than Imani did.

Anyway, I knew the field was about to be jumping because the spring season was breaking through, and the sun was out. In bitter-cold-ass Michigan, we didn't need it to be ninety degrees for us to hang outside. We were used to the bitter cold. It was about to be like an amusement park for thots. Although I didn't fit in the category of a neighborhood freak per se, I could act little dehydrated at times, or a lot. I always acted out of character when I was around Street, though.

Street was 24, a certified thug, and reckless as fuck. His name fit him perfectly with his roughneck ass. He was gritty and straight gutta, just how I liked 'em. Day in and out, he hustled hella weight for my dad that helped feed my family. He moved more weight and made more pickups from my house than any other hustler from my dad's team. Calvin stayed bragging about Street's list of savage qualities and even labeled him a lionhearted moneymaker. My dad might've preached that he wanted a different type of man for me, but all I homed in on were Street's thug accolades.

"Daddy, can I go over to Imani's house after I give the last runner his package?" I lied, knowing the truth wouldn't set me free. My dad would clown hard if he knew I was one of the fast-tailed girls he talked badly about.

"Yeah, but be home by nine o'clock. You've gotta watch Benzie tonight when me and ya momma go out. Oh, and before I forget, you will be going to school come Monday. I'm tired of that damn attendance officer leaving me voicemails. They left one saying a home visit was next if your attendance didn't improve. And you already know I ain't having no type of muthafuckas poking around my house."

I rolled my eyes, sick of school altogether. I couldn't wait to walk the stage. "Okay, Daddy. I'll be back by nine and then up bright and early on Monday morning for torture. I'll even get the homework they gave in school from Imani when I go over there and get it done over the weekend. I'll play their little game since there's only a month left."

"Yeah, make sure that you do, Porsha. And even if the truancy office wasn't on your head, I never intended for you not to care about your education. Me and ya momma both got high school diplomas, and you're not about to fuck up the family tradition by not graduating. Getting a GED is a great achievement, and I'm not discrediting that, but do what you have to do to graduate. Are we speaking the same language?"

"Verbatim," I answered, knowing when I needed to be serious. I wasn't complying to shut him up. I actually

wanted a diploma, even though all the pomp and circum-
stance that went along with graduation didn't matter to
me at all. I was more concerned with my birthday than
prom, a senior trip, or even taking senior pictures. The
only reason I'd signed up for the lock-in was so that I
could sneak off with Street.

"Have you thought about what you want to do after
high school? Or do you think you're about to live off of
me and pimp me for an apartment, car, and paying all
your bills every month?" He leaned back in his movie
recliner seat.

"I was actually thinking about asking Nikola if her trade
school offered cosmetology, or looking into some schools
myself. Since I'm good at doing hair, I might open a shop
one day."

"That's what I'm talking about, baby girl. Do that shit,
and I'll front you the money you need to open it."

"For real, Daddy?"

"Yeah, most definitely."

"Yeah, and I'll pitch in with your father to make sure all
you have to focus on is getting you a gang of nappy-head-
ed clients," Fame chimed in, finally off his phone from
arguing with his baby momma. He and Scooter went at it
worse than Trinity and Calvin did on their worst day.

"With all this motivation, I'm going to start researching
cosmetology schools this weekend."

"Make sure that you do and you're not just telling your
old man what he wants to hear," said my dad. "You're
good at the family business, but this ain't gonna be your
retirement plan like it's been mine. Got it?"

"Got it."

"Okay, we're done here. Make sure you put my business
first before you go over to Imani's."

Right when I leaped up from my seat ready to break
from the basement, my hopes of leaving sank at the sight
of Trinity stumbling in with her glass of liquor. I froze
dead in my tracks, thinking she must have had the house
bugged with cameras and listening devices to always
show up right on time. No one's timing could be that
damn perfect.

"Where do you think you're about to sneak off to?" she
questioned with her hands on her hips.

"Dad said I could go to Imani's and drop these packages off." I threw him under the bus, trying to divert her
attention from me to him.

She looked at him, then back at me. "Naw, I don't
think so. You can dead that plan. We're about to go on a
mother-daughter date to the mall and out to eat. Then I
need you to do my hair so I can be cute for the cabaret me
and your dad are going to tonight."

I tried my best to hide my disdain while being respectful. I didn't want no part of a mother-daughter date after
how she'd slapped me up earlier. "Dang, Ma, can I go
over to Imani's for at least an hour? I'm not just trying to
hang with my girl, but find out what I missed in school
as well," I begged and lied all at the same time, pulling at
strings. I wanted to see the boy I'd been crushing on hard.

"Get the hell out of here, Porsha. I must look like
boo-boo the fool to you," she responded in reference
to me mentioning school. "Please don't make me think
we're revisiting the same problem I told you not to
muthafuckin' revisit. I'll be mad as hell if I've gotta waste
my good liquor by tossing it in ya face."

Tensing back up, I recognized her stance as the same
one in my bedroom and quickly backed down. Seeing
Imani or my crush wasn't worth the beatdown. "No, no,

no, no! We're good. I'll go get dressed." I dropped the shenanigans.

"That'll work. I'll be ready when you are."

"I swear I can't wait until my birthday," I mumbled with my head down, walking out the door.

"What did you say?" she called out, able to hear a ghost blow through the room.

"Nothing. I was just singing a song." I played it off, knowing she knew better but was letting me slide. Once I was on the other side of the door, I slammed it.

"Calvin, ya better get ya daughter. The li'l heifer thinks I'm playing." I heard her jump on my dad's back about me.

"Chill, Trinity. You be going too hard on that girl, for real."

TRINITY

"What-the-fuck-ever, Cal. I am not doing anything but making our teenage daughter show me some respect. I know how I was with my mother once I found out she wasn't gonna put her hands on me for real, and I refuse to go through that same shit with Porsha. You can bud-dy-buddy with her if you want and get burned." I justified my behavior because I believed it was a surefire way to outsmart karma.

He threw his hands up and surrendered to me and the argument. "I ain't even about to go back and forth with you if you're bringing up your mother, because when you bring up Ma Dukes, I already know you are somewhere else in your head." Calvin knew all too well about my past and how crazy it made me. "But I will advise you to remember that Porsha is your daughter and cut from a much rougher cloth than you were cut from."

"Don't you think I know that, nigga? Don't tell me how to be a mother." I poked my finger into his forehead and pushed it back.

Before I knew it, Calvin's hands were around my throat.

CALVIN

"What the fuck is really wrong with your crazy ass, Trinity?" I applied pressure to my already-tight grip around her neck. "I didn't want to beef with you. I tried falling back and giving you room to get the hell out of my space, and you're trying to put some shit together for us to disagree about. All you had to do was take your aggressive ass upstairs. Why do you always got some slick shit to say to me like I won't split yo' shit?"

"Bro, come on, man. You know I'm not trying to get in the middle of your personal shit, but I also can't let you muscle up Trinity in front of me." Fame put his hand on my shoulder, and I nudged it off of me.

"Then leave. This shit ain't got nothing to do with you. Period." I wasn't letting up on Trinity, because I was tired of her recklessness when it came to me.

"Damn, nigga, it's like that?" Fame questioned but was still suiting up to leave.

"All day. I'll holla at you later, though."

Fame got ghost without saying another word. I never got in the mix between him and his baby momma Scooter whenever he was beating her ass, because I knew within the next minute he would be eating it. You can't fight a couple, no matter how many muthafuckas you ride on in the streets together.

"I cannot believe you've got your hands on me, you bitch-ass nigga. You better go ahead and choke me out, because if I get free, I'm going to kill you," she barked in my face. I smelled the Tito's over the gum she was chewing, which made me loosen my grip. I knew my wife's weaknesses more than she did.

"You ain't gonna do shit but take your drunk ass upstairs, take a shower, and then brush the vodka you've been drinking off your breath. I thought you were going to ease up on that shit."

"And I thought I asked you to ease up off my neck." She peeled my fingers off of her and swung on me.

"Don't make me collar you back up, Trinity. I let you get loose because I wanted to, not because of your strength. I suggest you leave me alone and get the hell on to wherever you are going with Porsha."

"I swear to God and on my dead daddy that you better stop thinking you run shit around here, Calvin. And I dare you to put your hands back on me. You've already got to sleep with one eye open for that li'l fuck boy stunt you just pulled." She swiped one of the bundles of cash I'd just collected from one of the workers and walked up the stairs.

I couldn't do shit but laugh at my gangster boo. Her savage-ass ways were what made me check for her back in the day, and I was still madly attracted to her mentality. It did not matter what crazy shit we went through. Trinity was my soul mate. I would put a whole family on ice if she told me to. Watching her ass shake in the too-small shorts she was wearing, I grabbed at my bouncing dick and thought about going upstairs and fixing her attitude.

PORSHA

"I thought you said you were on your way over here. What's taking you so long?" Imani answered my call while I was picking out something to wear to go out with Trinity in.

"Unfortunately, there's been a change of plans. Trinity is up to her usual hating, so I've gotta go somewhere with her."

"Aww, damn!" Imani was disappointed. "You can't get your dad to get you out of it?"

"Nope, not this time. But I wish I could. Street hasn't hit me up all day. Is he around there?" I was kinda hoping Imani would say no, but she didn't.

"I think so, but he was on the porch with Pete Rock and Dantez when I walked past from school."

"There weren't any girls over there, were there?"

"Girl, bye! You know I was not looking that hard." She was not lying. Of her, Nikola, and me, she was the shy and timid one. Nikola always joked and said Imani only kept us around so the neighborhood hoes did not tear off into her ass.

"Okay, well, hit me up if you see him up in a trick's face." I started rushing her off the phone so I could get dressed before my momma barged into my room on some more bullshit.

Even though Imani was nervous around boys, she did not mind dropping a dime on Street. If Street did something in her eyesight, Imani was telling it in detail. I had caught that nigga up in about ten lies this month alone based on her recall/retell of the situation. I had come to the conclusion that Street was going to be Street, and that simply meant he was going to do what he wanted to do.

It didn't take me long to jump fresh. I kept it cute and simple in a pair of ripped jeans, a white tee, and boat shoes. My outfit matched the weather perfectly, plus it was fly enough to rock just in case I got back in time to go on the block. I could barely get dressed from Imani blowing my phone up over and over again with picture mail and messages. Super salty over how live it looked around her way, I temporarily sent all her calls to my block box to keep myself out of my feelings. Graduation and my birthday weren't coming quickly enough.

Trinity swore she would only be five minutes, but of course, it had been double that by the time I was done getting dressed. I opened my Kindle application to pass the time. I'd been reading urban fiction ever since I saw a social media post on a blog site hyping up a few titles. After reading one story about chicks from the hood, I was hooked. If I went to school more often, not clowned while I was there, and grasped English, I'd have been a shoo-in to write a novel. Without a doubt, I was sure my story about how I grew up would sell millions. I'd been through just as much drama as many of the characters I had read about, if not more.

Even though the book was hella good, I couldn't get into it because my mind was too wrapped up thinking about how I was going to spend the money my dad gave me. He'd filled my hand with bills to spend at the mall as a pre-gift for my birthday. I was happy to have the extra chicken, but he better be coming with more when the actual day arrived. I didn't care that I was running around here, screaming grown. *He and Trinity better have at least a parting gift for their only daughter.*

After I got deep into a juicy chapter, Trinity stepped out the door, dressed to impress. Unlike a lot of the raggedy, no-style-having mammies around here who wore pajamas all day, mine was a true diva. Everyone on the outside looking in could tell she had money.

After putting her red cup of juice and alcohol into the cup holder, she tossed her oversized purse into the back seat. Calvin must have broken her off with way more money than me. I wasn't hating, though. I was happy to have what I had. Plus, I knew Trinity wasn't going to take me to the mall and not buy me something. I could say she was a lot of things, but selfish with her money was not one of them.

"I hope you've got your charger," my mom said, plugging her phone in.

"Yup, it's right here." I dangled it, then buckled up in the passenger seat of her Ram truck. Trinity didn't believe in tiny cars and even ran them off the road if they weren't driving fast enough.

"All right, then let's be out." She threw the truck into reverse and backed out of the driveway with her favorite rap track bumping.

CHAPTER 3

TRINITY

Calvin and I weren't your average married couple with a kid, not even for one that was rooted within one of the worst neighborhoods in Detroit, Michigan. But what made us stand out was what made us stick together. Calvin was my soul mate, and I was certain that I was his Bonnie, his better half, and the voice in his head when it was time to murk a muthafucka. I made Calvin crazier. In spite of how much we bumped heads, we always bounced back together. I was glad he'd come and piped me down before I left the house so I could kick it with my daughter. Getting dick always had a way of calming me down.

My only daughter sat across from me, looking over the menu. She had not said much in the car, and neither had I, probably because of the events earlier. I wasn't gonna apologize, though. It was my job to keep my foot on her neck. I was from the school of hard knocks. Granny Ruby whipped my mom with a switch. My mom welted me up with belts. So I was following in line and continuing the tradition by two-piecing Porsha up when she disrespected me or attempted to. Wasn't no kid getting ready to square up with me or even get fooled by their imagination thinking they could fuck with me. Benzie would soon learn about me.

The waitress came, and we both ordered entrée fajitas with extra meat, Sprites with light ice, and bowls of our own queso. Mexican food was our favorite. As much as she and I bumped heads, we could always bond over a good meal. The only thing I ordered that Porsha couldn't was a Patrón margarita. I kept a drink to my lips. With me, there was never a line drawn or a limit set to say "that's enough." I didn't think I could function without alcohol in my system.

"What stores are you trying to hit to spend that fat-ass knot your daddy gave you?" I questioned Porsha, trying to get her attention on me and off her phone.

"I don't know. I'm probably gonna load up my RushCard and shop online. All of the boutiques around here that I know of have the same boring outfits at each one. What I might cop though are new gym shoes, a cell phone case, a purse or two, and another charm for my Pandora bracelet," she responded like a spoiled brat.

I wasn't hating, nor did I blame Porsha for her attitude. She got it honest and had been placed on a pedestal since birth. Calvin and I prided ourselves on giving Porsha what she wanted, Benzie too. Being stingy with dope money didn't make sense.

"You're lucky your parents sell dope. You should say thank you more often since we stay risking our lives to give you and Benzie the finer things in life. You see how them other kids be looking in the hood: rough, ratchet, and like li'l dirtballs. You got it good." I was being honest.

She smacked her lips, then turned them up like something smelled bad. "You and daddy been selling dope way before me and Benzie were thought of, so don't put y'all choice of careers off on us. We were born into the game."

Right when I was getting ready to read Porsha again for having a smart-ass mouth, I laughed instead. She made the adage "the apple doesn't fall far from the tree" seem alive, true, and well. Porsha wasn't acting out. She was acting like me. If I wanted her to act differently, I'd be beating the traces of me out of her, if ya get what I mean.

After the waitress brought out our food and drinks, we dug in and enjoyed our lunch as mother and daughter. I might've not wanted to lighten up on her since she'd tried to get gully with me earlier. Still, I chalked her behavior up as karma and moved on. I might've not admitted it to Calvin, but I knew my bark was a little too vicious, and I didn't want to push my Mini-Me away. In life, all we have is family. I might have had a funny way of showing it, but I'd lay my life on the line for all of mine, and I had. Once Porsha was grown with her own children or a family, she'd understand my stance and not keep a chip on her shoulder.

"Dang, Ma! You look fly as hell in that dress," Porsha complimented me when I stepped out of the dressing room.

We were finished with lunch and now at the mall. She'd done all the shopping she'd planned on doing, so now I was trying to find the perfect outfit to wear to the cabaret tonight. That was why I'd forced Porsha to come with me in the first place, to help style me, as the young kids these days called it, on fleek. I might've been her momma, but I still was fine as fuck and stepping on the toes of any of her other friends' momma's without trying.

Ring, ring, ring.

"Dig my phone out from my purse for me," I told Porsha. I was busy posing in the mirror, trying to see how my curves looked in the dress. I wasn't a flat-tummy, no-roll-having diva. I had meat on my skin and wore it well, along with clothes that fit me.

"It's Auntie Tanya." Porsha held my phone up.

I rolled my eyes. "Answer it and talk to her while I change."

Tanya was one of my older sisters. She and I were the most different of all my siblings. She was a teacher who dated an accountant and went to church every day of the week like Jesus Christ be at the service too. First of all, I didn't wanna be bothered with my own kids, let alone a bunch of snotty brats who got on their mother's nerves when not at school. Secondly, I wasn't never about to bust it wide open for a nigga in a Brooks Brothers suit. If a nigga wasn't a thug, I wasn't fuckin' with him. And lastly, I'd probably blow up into a million pieces if I stepped into the house of the Lord. I was a sinner who planned to keep sinning until the day I died.

The extreme differences between Tanya and me kept us at each other's necks like we were enemies with different blood. Yet and still, we'd link up in a heartbeat to beat an outsider's ass. That was how all my sisters and I were for one another. Besides Tanya and me, my momma had Tiana, Trish, and Ruby (the oldest and named after my granny), all by the same nigga. She wasn't a ho, but that didn't keep him from not being shit.

He beat my mom until she stopped breathing one day. While Tanya was busy trying to resuscitate my mom and call 911, I was busy breaking a mirror over our dad's head, then slicing his throat with a piece of the broken glass. I didn't serve time or no shit like that for murdering my daddy. However, child protective services opened a case on my mom to make sure the well-being of me and my sisters was intact. I also had to undergo extensive therapy that only made the visual playback of his neck squirting out blood as he died more in depth and constant. Yeah, you can believe it. I'd been coldblooded since I was a kid.

Tanya called because my mom was losing the house we grew up in. She was off her rocker, popping pills every day. All of us daughters were supposed to pitch in and save the house we grew up in, but I was like fuck that 'cause that house was nothing but a representation of hell for each and every one of us. I'd told them time and time again that I wasn't giving them one dirty dope dollar toward saving that house and that I'd feed her pill addiction instead, but Tanya kept calling me incessantly. Since we were kids, she'd been trying to boss me around because she was the older.

Fuck age. She knew good and damn well that, between the two of us, I wasn't the weak link. Besides, my momma probably wouldn't take the money if I offered it to her. She'd never said it, but I felt like she started disliking me the day I killed her husband. I wasn't pressed about carrying that monkey on my back, however. If Calvin ever raised his hand to strike me, I would send him to the grave too. I'd never been cut out to get beat on. My momma shouldn't have been either.

"Ma! Dang, what's taking you so long in there?" Porsha tapped on the dressing room door.

"Here I come, girl." I slid on the next outfit, then stepped out, grabbing my phone. "Hey, sis. What's up?"

"We only got a little more time to pay the taxes on Momma's house. Please tell me that you changed your mind about chipping in with the rest of us." On the topic I'd expected, Tanya was ruining my mood. I hated repeating myself, especially about this.

"Damn, Tanya. How many times do I have to tell you no? No, no, no, no! Y'all trifling as hell to wanna save that house of terrors. Matter of fact, I should go over there when Momma is gone and light that bitch on fire." I spat venom, meaning each word.

As soon as the words slipped off my tongue, my mind moved even quicker, trying to see if I could really burn the house to the ground and get away with it. I didn't want to commit too many crimes surrounding my mom but really pertaining to my dad. Luck runs out, and I'd already walked away without even a slap on the wrist with one murder.

"Sis, you're crazy as hell for one. For two, you're going to have to get over what happened when we were young. What are you planning on doing? Carrying that burden on your back forever?"

"Yup. It ain't nothing for me to do that, Tanya. What's known didn't have to be said."

She huffed and puffed, irritated by me not giving in and being an asshole in the process. "Argh, I swear, if you weren't my sister—"

"Yeah, whatever, Tanya. You better get off my phone. Goodbye." I didn't give her a chance to retort before hanging up.

"Here, put this back in my purse." I handed Porsha the phone after turning it down to vibrate. I didn't need any additional distractions while shopping. This spree was hella important.

Modeling back in the mirror, I was feeling myself the most in this dress. It showed the perfect amount of cleavage and half of my thick thighs, and it had a triangular dip in the back that showed my tramp stamp of Calvin's name. I thought that was the part that made it a winner to me. I loved showing hoes I was branded along with my man. He had my name tatted on his neck.

"Ma! Hello." Porsha snapped her fingers in front of my face. "Are you getting that outfit or no? We've still gotta hit the beauty supply, and the good one closes before dark to keep from getting robbed," she rushed me.

"Yeah, damn. My bad. Give me your opinion—do you think I'm on fleek? Am I killin' 'em? I'm trying to walk up in that party stunting hard," I said, using a mouthful of young slang.

She rolled her eyes at my choice of language. "Oh, wow, Ma! You swear you're the one about to be eighteen.

Yes, you look fleek. If you get a killer pair of heels and a handbag to match, you'll have the whole hood of ho . . . oops, I mean, women, talking about you in the morning."

"Oooh, for real? Hell yeah, that's what I wanted to hear. You know Momma likes to serve bitches nothing but the bomb dot com."

She blew out a long, exasperated breath of air like I was annoying her. "Please, Ma, quit being corny and get the dress. We've been in this store foreverrrr," she complained. "And you're killing me with your corniness."

"Shut ya ass up, I'm coming," I sighed, giving in because I knew how it felt to be a teenage girl out with your wannabe-hip mother. "Matter of fact, g'on to the nail shop and put our names on the list."

I heard her say thanks over her shoulder, but Porsha started heading out the door as soon as I'd said the word "g'on."

PORSHA

Being that school was out for the day and most people were done with work, the mall was swarming with people. The nail shop was really off the chain. Every pedicure chair bowl had some crusty feet in it, and every nail tech was filing or designing away. I put my and my mom's names on the list along with the services we wanted and sat down. I only needed a fill-in and maybe a polish change on my toes, but my mom needed a full set and pedicure. I texted her a picture of the waiting area so she'd be prepared for the long wait.

My phone was dry since it was still set on restricting Imani's texts. I was, however, kinda salty that Street hadn't called or texted me. Since we weren't on our way back to the hood, I left the restriction on and stayed off social media, too. Imani was probably posting pictures there too.

All into my phone, I'd tuned out all the background noise and movement going on around me. When I finally set my phone to sleep and looked up, my mother was coming in with a sour look on her face. She hated being cooped up in a room with a bunch of women. I didn't think we were going to stay, but she ended up giving the manager a few dollars extra in exchange for moving us up the list.

Another woman spoke up. "Um, excuse me! But I had an appointment for over an hour ago and have been waiting patiently. You can either seat me in a pedicure chair before or along with that lady and her kid or lose ya job. Don't make me call the owner of this establishment on you. I don't think Miss Woo will be too pleased about you running a loyal client away," she threatened and complained.

Of all the words the disgruntled customer said, "that lady and her kid" was the phrase I saw my mother's eyes rise to. I knew my mother was seconds away from popping off. Politely taking her purse from her hand, I took two quick steps to the side and waited for the situation to play out.

"No, no, no! You not have to call Miss Woo. I get you seated now," the nail tech promised, spinning around to find a resolution to the suddenly urgent problem.

The woman was busy feeling herself since she'd rushed the li'l Korean lady along. She had not even noticed Trinity walking from the pedicure chair back toward the waiting area, or me right on her heels. "Good idea. I like my water on the piping hot side."

"Hey, Miss Lady, are you good now? I couldn't help but overhear how upset you were about me and my daughter getting seated before you." She was mimicking the woman's high- pitched and proper voice.

The woman looked up, halfway frowning, and then rolled her eyes before responding. "Yes, I am. Just like you valued your time enough to cut in front of me, I value mine to do something about it."

"Oh, okay. Well, since this is the day to stand up for ourselves and shit, I didn't like how you made a reference to me and mine. I'm gonna act like I'm a lady and not smack the shit out of you this one time, but if ya do it again, my hand will fly toward you without warning. I'm not trying to make you have an unpleasant day, so don't make yourself have one." Taking her attention off the woman, she then checked me. "Give me my damn purse. I'll tell you when to hold my shit. I might've had to whip my buddy out and put a hot one in her impatient ass."

As Trinity nonchalantly marched back to the pedicure chair, the whole nail salon sat in awe and fear behind her blowup, the last statement especially. I was used to her clowning, but they hadn't known what to expect. A few of the customers were disgusted enough to get up and walk out, including the disgruntled woman, while those cut from the same cloth as Trinity praised her for giving them a show. My mom fed off people kissing her ass, which was where I got the drive from.

It took me a few minutes to pick out my polish, but after I did, I climbed into the pedicure chair beside my mom and found the perfect massage speed. By age, I wasn't old enough to have kinks and stress. But it felt like there were weights on my shoulders and someone was relentlessly pinching the nerves in my back and neck. The vibrations from the chair were soothing.

"There's the thug right there. That wannabe lady in the black jogging suit," I heard the lady's voice yelling out, making me open my eyes. "She said she had a gun. Arrest her!"

Two mall security guards were coming into the nail
salon with grim expressions. Behind them was the lady
my mom went tough on, telling them verbatim what
she'd said. The manager dropped my mom's feet into
the bowl, splashing water everywhere, and rushed to
intercept them from trapping us in the back of the salon.
It wasn't that she was going hard for us. She didn't want
the shop shut down, resulting in the owner being called.
Her "dirty deed" would then be exposed. Too bad for her.
The guards didn't back down.

"Ma'am, we need to search your bag. We don't allow
firearms on the premises," one of the officers growled,
pushing past the manager.

Oh, shit.

CHAPTER 4

CALVIN

Being one of the biggest drug dealers in Detroit, I rarely had time to fall back and chill with my family. Hell, I rarely got a moment of peace to think. Either a worker of mine was out of line, there was some drama from another squad, or I was simply in the mud hustling with Fame. Making money by living dangerously was the only way I knew how to live. So I was enjoying the small window of chill time I had with Benzie. All his toys were spread throughout the living room, and we had been watching clips off the sports channel all day. I did not watch cartoons with my boy, because wasn't nothing funny about the world he was about to grow up in. Plus I wanted him to like all the hobbies and sports that men liked.

Li'l man's real name was Calvin III, but I got the nickname Benzie from my love for the Benz brand. As much as I loved having a daughter, I really loved having a son I could groom into a soldier. He would carry on my name. I wanted to make sure Benzie had a bond with me just in case our time together was shortened. I was not living to die or planning on death, but I was a realist. I lived a dangerous life, and now that there was a new breed of goons stepping onto the streets, I had become more of a target than ever before.

"Yo, li'l man, are you hungry?" I grabbed us some snacks and a beer for me from the kitchen and came back to someone knocking on the door.

"Who is it?" I called out, reaching for my chrome-plated piece that sat to the right side of me.

"It's Spider. Can I holla at you for a second, C-Note?"

I raised the window and told Spider to come off the front porch so I could see him. "Yo, nigga, I'm spending some quality time with my son. Don't waste my time coming down the muthafuckin' stairs if you're about to ask me for some credit." I'd been hustling back and forth all day, but Spider was one of my regular customers who begged for credit on the usual. Mr. Nice Guy was not available for his bullshit today.

"No, I don't have any money, C-Note. But I was trying to see if I could work it off. I can sweep your porch, wash your car, or do whatever odd job you got around here."

"A'ight then, Spider. You got it. I cannot and will not hate on a man willing to work for his. I don't want to see a speck of dust on my porch when you knock back on my door. Do you understand?"

"Yes, yes, thank you. I'm about to run down the street and get a broom." He was tripping over his feet.

Falling back on the couch, I popped the top off my beer and guzzled down a fourth of the bottle. There had been a slow and steady flow of customers since Porsha and Trinity hit the streets for their mother-daughter date, but I was about to shut the trap down. It was a good thing Spider was going to be outside in the yard, because I was going to have him send away anyone else who wanted to cop a baggie.

I wanted to take a nap, then take Benzie out of the house for us to have a father and son playdate to the Riverwalk. I never knew my father to do corny shit like that, but that did not mean I wasn't trying to create a new trend with my own son. I wanted Benzie to have memories of us playing at the park and playing catch, and I even wanted to coach him if he played Little League when he got older. I was proud to have plans for my li'l man.

My phone rang and interrupted my thoughts.

"Yo, are you outside?" I answered it and was straight to the point.

"Yup, yup. I am walking up on the porch now," my top worker replied.

Elvin "Street" Thomas was one of the hardest-working hustlers on my squad, which was why I'd called him to meet up with me. He had been my protégé since he was a teenager and held major respect among his peers. Street was the first man in charge at my trap house on the block, the very first dope house I opened up years ago. It was the first house Trinity and I got together as a couple.

"What up doe, nephew?" Street spoke to Benzie, then shook his hand and addressed me. "Li'l fella is getting big, boss. He's gonna be knockin' clowns out around here."

"And making his old man proud." I hoped Street was speaking the truth. "Is everything moving smoothly on the block?"

"Ain't nobody complaining about not eating, and we keep selling out, so I'ma say shit's all good," he confidently replied.

"No news is always good news." I liked his report.

"I heard that, boss. But being that the block is slow and steady money, why don't we branch out and start serving product in another territory? I've already got a few li'l niggas who wanna come push weight with me, but there ain't no room on the block." It was obvious Street had not waited for the green light from me to start fleshing out his business plan.

I nodded and rubbed at my chin, letting what he put onto the floor soak in. It had been a minute since I'd studied Street with a critical eye, but his tenacity had me wondering if it was time to clip his wings or let him fly. I might have trained him a little too well.

"Okay, son. You've got my ear. Tell me what you've been thinking," I strategically quizzed.

"Nothing major, but a li'l, low-key spot. Me and Pete Rock can run in on an abandoned house that ain't been stripped down yet and set up shop."

"Do you really think you are ready to run two spots?" I questioned condescendingly, knowing I was getting ready to shut his plan down. His plan came with too much risk, and I was comfortable sitting on top.

"No disrespect, boss, but I've got the hustle in me, and I'm hungry. I've got a big appetite, and I've gotta eat. I've gotta get out here and put my foot to these nigga's necks and make a name for myself that will hold some weight." I saw the savage mentality Street had embedded within him bleeding through his eyes. Running one trap house was not good enough for him anymore.

"Look, son, what I'm about to say is not going to be what you want to hear, but it will be what you need to hear. There are levels to this shit, and you are not at the level where you can run shit in two different spots." I watched him slouch into the couch.

"I can respect that, Cal. But I do not agree with that. I'm a beast in these streets."

"I know that, which is why I put you in charge of the block in the first place. Don't mistake my carefulness for doubt. Make no mistake about it, you've got my eyes and ears open. I am definitely thinking about what you've suggested, but that doesn't mean I'm getting ready to give you the green light on shit past taking a li'l bit more off the top for ya pockets. We've all got set positions that must be played for a little while longer. Are you good with that decision for now, or do we need to have a different conversation? Are we good?" I questioned, knowing I wasn't getting ready to compromise or bend with what I already offered. I wanted to see where his head was at.

"Yeah, boss. We're good, no doubt." He dropped the subject, then was saved by my ringing phone.

Swooping my cell off the table when I saw Daddy's Princess on the screen, I dismissed Street. "A'ight, son. I'll be on the block in a few to see how shit is lying."

Already knowing I put my family first, he got ghost without another word.

"Hey, baby girl, what's up?" I answered Porsha's call.

"Calvin! I'm caught up in some shit and need your help." My wife's voice came through the headset.

"Say less. Where are you at?" I slid my pistol in my waistband and picked up Benzie. Hesitation was not a word in my vocabulary when it came to me seeing after mine.

PORSHA

"I want this woman arrested. Call the Dearborn Police," the loudmouthed lady said, making a scene.

"Ma'am, we're not going to keep telling you to calm down and let us do our jobs," the security guard warned the lady again. Then he turned to my mother. "Ma'am, I need to check your purse," he demanded.

"Oh, hell naw! You can miss me with that search shit you are talking. Y'all ain't got no warrant, and y'all aren't the police," my mother responded.

"We've got a complaint, and that is all we need," the guard responded, stepping toward me. "But the lady's right. I can call the Dearborn Police and let them handle it."

Moving quickly, I leaned between the chairs where both our purses were on the floor and grabbed her bag like it was mine while pushing mine closer to her chair at the same time. Although my heart was racing and my palms were sweaty, I had been in enough sticky situations with my parents to know how to think efficiently under pressure.

"I don't want to be in the middle of all this. Let me get out of the way," I said, playing like I was disgusted and wanted no part of the drama. But I was plotting to get out of the nail salon and the mall with my mom's gun.

People within the shop saw me, but their mouths stayed shut as I switched our purses and pulled a fast move on the security guard. I was not about to let my momma get locked up behind her concealing a pistol without a license. My personal grievances or how we bumped heads had nothing to do with me having her back. I was going to hold my momma, my daddy, and Benzie down until the world ended.

As I tiptoed across the floor with wet, bare feet, my knuckles ached from clutching her purse as tightly as I could.

"Ma'am, pass me your purse. Please do not make me request it again." The guard's voice shook the room.

Looking over my shoulder, I saw my mom handing my purse over to him with a shocked expression painted on her face. That was when I exited the nail shop as quietly as I could and walked as quickly as I could in the opposite direction of where the guard and loudmouthed lady were standing. I was walking so fast that I was damn near tripping over my own two feet. I did not want to run and bump into people and bring attention to myself. But as soon as I walked out the mall's exit, I broke out like a track star in a track-meet race. I was running so fast and hard that the bottoms of my feet were starting to burn from the pavement.

Ducking in between two cars, I rummaged through the big-ass duffle bag my mom called a purse for her keys. I did not want to get caught holding the dirty pistol.

Pulling out wads of cash, the pistol itself, and a bunch of paperwork about my grandma's house, I still could not find the keys. I was about to scream out from frustration until her cell phone started ringing, vibrating, and lighting up.

My baby P was what the screen read, which meant the call was coming from my phone.

"Shit," I whispered, not knowing for sure that it was my mom and not the guard.

My mother presenting him a purse of teenager items and an identification card that did not have her picture on it was reason enough for me to fear that my trickery had been exposed. I had never been so nervous. Nor had I ever felt such a strong nauseating feeling in the pit of my stomach. Having a dirty pistol in my possession without Trin and Cal around to protect me had me shaken the fuck up. I could not resist sending the call to voicemail.

Finally fishing out her keys, I bit my lip and peeked over the hood of the car I was hiding behind, making sure the coast was clear to take off. The truck was parked a few rows over. A few people going into the mall saw me creeping through the parking lot suspiciously, but I did not have time to worry about their reactions. Getting to Trinity's truck was my only concern.

Trinity's phone rang and damn near made me jump out of my skin. I completely froze when I saw Husband on the screen. It was my daddy.

"Hello! Daddy, oh my God! Ma got into trouble! We're out at Fairlane, and some stuff happened, and I got her—" I was trying to run off what was going on but was out of breath. He had cut me off anyway.

"Hey! I already know what's up. Ya momma said pull up on her at the bus stop and answer the phone. You've got this, Porsha. You're a Jackson. Cut all that coward shit out. Fear will get you caught, and you need to make sure you and your mother get out of there," he said, getting me back on my A game.

I listened to my dad give me a pep talk while I jogged the rest of the way to the truck. With him coaching me over the phone, I felt in control and like everything was going to work out in my and Trinity's favor. My daddy always made me feel safe and secure.

By the time I climbed into the driver's seat and revved the engine, my mom was beeping in on the other line. I was not able to finish clicking over before she was screaming.

"Where the hell are you at, Porsha? What's taking ya ass so long?"

"I just got in the truck. I'm not a track star. I had to run damn near all the way around the mall," I shouted with attitude, pissed that she was acting ungrateful when I'd just put my neck on the line for her. I was tired of her acting like I hadn't been holding my own.

TRINITY

I heard the attitude in Porsha's voice and wanted to jump through the phone and strangle her wannabe-grown ass for yelling at me. Fuck that she had just taken a risk for me and could possibly catch some heat behind having a gun in her possession if she did not get out of dodge with the quickness.

"Well, hurry up. That ho-ass guard told me to be gone before Dearborn Police show up. He called out a squad car when they realized I had a teen's purse, but that wasn't enough of a reason to hold me. I don't know what slick shit they've got planned, but we need to be out of this city, ya dig?"

"Oh, wow." She gasped. "I'm almost there, Ma. I'm coming around the bend near the restaurants now."

"A'ight, cool," I replied, trying to sound like I was in control, though I was panting and looking around nervously like every vehicle speeding into the mall's entrance was a squad car.

I was usually never off my square, but racism was alive no matter who said different. As diverse as Dearborn was, they hated black people. I was not trying to have my body ripped with bullets and the fatality report reading like I unloaded first.

"Get out of the way! What'cha gonna do? Not shit, so keep driving." Porsha was honking the horn and yelling at pedestrians. I heard the horn blowing not only over the phone, but close by. Porsha was coasting around the bend on two wheels.

"If you tear my muthafuckin' truck up, I swear I'ma kill yo' ass," I yelled, rushing toward the road to meet her. The quicker we could get on the freeway, the better.

Slamming on the brakes, she threw the truck in park and hopped over the console to the passenger seat so I could drive. Seeing Porsha in action was like looking at the younger me when I used to ride out on missions with her father. He and I used to set the city on fire doing dirty before he knocked me up.

"Ma! Come on," she cried out, visibly shaken like she was ready to break from the pressure she was under.

"We're straight. I got you, baby girl," I said in a calming tone so she'd chill out. I gave her her shoes, which she'd left at the shop and I'd managed to grab. "You did good. Hella good." I sincerely thanked her, knowing I owed her big time. I would have been cuffed in the back seat of a squad car facing five years for having the pistol.

"Ma, this shit is crazy. I can't believe this is happening." Porsha was frantic, looking back and forth between the mirrors and me as I drove as cautiously and quickly as I could.

"Keep ya eyes out of the rearview mirror. We ain't looking back. We're pushing forward," I barked at her. "This ain't ya first time riding shotgun or at least in the whip behind some crazy shit me and ya father got into. You know I'ma get you home in one piece. Don't doubt me. Matter of fact, dial ya daddy up and hand me the phone. Then get ya'self together."

Swooping down onto the freeway, I slowed down to the speed limit until I crossed into the city of Detroit. The last thing I needed to happen was for us to get flicked.

"Here, Ma. Daddy wants to talk to you." Porsha passed me the phone.

"Man down, nigga. I know yo' ass got my baby and is riding dirty on your way to save me, but I am straight now. Porsha actually saved me. I will tell you about it when we get home, but I'm going to make a quick stop first."

"Um, don't you think you should take yo' hot ass to the crib and tuck that pistol before you somewhere else?"

"Naw, I'm straight. We will be in the city. Plus, you know I'm not going nowhere without my heat."

"A'ight, man. Can't nobody tell your thick-skulled ass shit. I'll see you when y'all get home. Don't call me no more if you get in trouble." I knew he did not mean that last line before he hung up.

"Ma, where are we about to go?" Porsha asked.

"It is a surprise. I was going to wait until closer to your birthday, but your display of loyalty today is worth giving it to you now."

I saw her beaming out of the side of my eye. It felt good making my daughter smile since I was always swinging on her ass.

CHAPTER 5

PORSHA

It felt good as hell hearing my mother praise me to my daddy, and even better when she thanked me. I loved it when she gave me props. It felt a lot better than beefing with her. I spent so much time getting smart, and she spent so much time keeping me in check, that the "good job" moments were rare. The more details she gave about the story, the more at ease I felt. Today wasn't turning out to be that bad after all. My mom and I had gone from enemies to aces in less than a couple of hours.

With so much going on and for me to gossip about with Imani, I unblocked her calls and messages. She was the only friend I had to kick it with for real, but I wasn't able to get the first text message typed before my phone was blowing up with picture mail. Imani had been texting me the whole damn time she'd been restricted. There were photos from ol' boy I was crushing on and photos from this bottom-feeder chick who was crushing hard on him too.

My mood turned sour again. In almost every picture, the girl was either all in his face or draped all over him like a down blanket in the wintertime. I wanted to throw up in my mouth. I wasn't his girl, so I couldn't technically check ol' boy, but I'd be making sure Jamika gave him fifty feet the next time I wasn't around. All I needed was a li'l more time to lock him down for all these hoes to know who he'd really been creepin' up behind on the low. I'd never given Street the pussy within my panties, but I knew he wanted it. And true story, I wanted him to have it.

As I was all into my phone, staring at the pictures and trying to figure out how to respond and if I should, my mother's voice snapped me back into reality. I almost fumbled and dropped the phone to the floor.

"Ay! Yo! Earth to Porsha. Quit running ya damn mouth and let me get ya attention for a second."

I looked up and gasped. "Ma! For real?"

We were parked in the lot of a boutique that sold not only one-of-a-kind pieces but custom-designed pieces as well. I'd been following their page on Instagram for a few months and always liked their pictures. I even entered a contest and was blowing up everyone's timeline, trying to win a custom dress for my birthday.

"Ma, come on and answer me before I pass out. Are we here for me? What'chu know about this place? Huh?"

"Girl, shut the hell up. Yeah, we're here for you. I know everything you think I didn't know," she replied, throwing her hand up playfully. "But for real, I appreciate you looking out and stepping up at the nail shop. You've redeemed yourself one hundred percent from earlier for sure. The shit you did shows you're 'bout ready to be an adult." Her voice cracked. She was trying to lighten the mushiness, not wanting to wear her emotions on her sleeve and seem soft. "Anyway, coming here now is an early birthday/thank-you gift. Order you a custom outfit, and then I'll buy you a couple of thangs, too."

I jumped across the middle console of the truck and was damn near in her lap, hugging her. "Thank you, thank you, thank you!"

"Yeah, after all that shit you were talking earlier about not giving me a thank-you, I see ya ass taking a cop now."

"Yup, I sure am. And with that being said, I'm about to go in before you change your mind." I leaped out of the truck and busted through the boutique doors. I swore I loved growing up with so much fast cash.

Trinity ended up flexin' on 'em in the boutique, spending almost a rack. She let me order two custom dresses and get a few of the stoned-out bras to wear underneath certain shirts for the upcoming summer and a couple of pairs of ripped jeans. I was too excited. I was about to be fly as hell stepping into adulthood. Any chick who had eyes on Street were gonna have their eyes on the baddest bitch on his side—me.

Trinity thought she was simply getting me together so I could be fashionable, cute, and envied by all the girls my age, but she was really helping me be a fast ass at the moment. I'd sent ol' boy at least five pictures of me in the bras, and one with my nipples showing. I was intentionally trying to steal whatever attention he was still giving her way. When he responded with a dick pic with a caption reading, Let a nigga know when u ready 2 hop up on it, I fumbled the phone, having more attention than I knew what to do with.

"Humph, maybe I should've taken ya ass to the damn clinic for some birth control," Trinity blurted out, making me do more than fumble the phone, but drop it.

Like an FBI agent, she'd snuck up and was this time over my shoulder into my cell's screen. I was shaken, completely silent, and still, especially when she picked my phone up off the floor.

"Let me find out it's too late and you've already fucked up, Porsha. You already know I'll run a hanger up in ya twat myself. I'm too fly to be a grandma. Shiiiiiit, I was too fly to be a momma." After pausing like she was having an epiphany, she spoke again. "On second thought, scratch all that. A pussy's gonna do what a pussy's gonna do. So if you wanna play grown, you're gonna be grown, and there's nothing I can do about it. You're about to be eighteen, so hey, do you. Hurry up so we can hit the beauty supply and get home. You've still gotta do my hair, and in exchange for me keeping that trifling-ass picture a secret from ya father, I'ma need something super sweet."

"Turn the damn blow dryer off before you burn my scalp," my mom shouted, throwing her hand up, almost hitting me and getting black nail polish onto my clothes.

Being that we had not gotten serviced at the nail salon, she was getting her own hands together but doing a piss-poor job. My mom wasn't really the prissy type.

A stream of marijuana hit me in the face. I inhaled it and held my breath on the low. "My bad, but I'm not about to send you out here looking crazy. If I didn't add enough heat to the glue and spritz, the tracks won't hold to your head as tightly as I need them to. You ain't about to come home screaming at me 'cause your tracks done sweated out to the floor." Repositioning her head as gracefully as I could, I got back to work.

As gangster as my mom was, she was tender headed as hell. That was why she couldn't get a sew-in. She'd have died from me French braiding it, then stitching the wefts down to her head. Therefore, I was only doing a quick weave. When I got done, I'd iron it since she hated curls, and I'd clean her eyebrows with a razor. At least twice a month, her room turned into a beauty shop, and I'd be in here getting her together. After the drama that unraveled earlier, I was sure I'd be filing and polishing her nails, too.

"If the streets don't work out for you, Porsha, try your hand at being a beautician. I've gotta give you your props. There are bitches in the shop who can't fry, dye, and lay some hair like you can. For real."

"Thanks, Ma. I appreciate it." I was really happy behind my mom complimenting me again. "The thought crossed my mind, especially after Imani's mom said I had skills, but I'm almost done with the torture of school. I don't know if I wanna jump back into someone's classroom." I was being honest.

"Well, as far as Imani's mom goes, you better have charged that sludge rock. Don't let me find out you're through the hood passing out free styles or giving folks credit because you run with their kids." My mom was always schooling and warning me. "And in regard to school, I was never a star pupil to teach you how to be one. But I've always been a hustler and about my money. With that being said, do what you've gotta do to keep money in ya pocket and food in ya mouth. Doing hair is a good skill to have because there's always an ugly chick in need of assistance. Me and ya daddy won't be around forever."

I sighed. "I've got it, Ma. You didn't raise a fool. I never touch a head without my cho' first."

"That's what I'm talking about, Porsha. Good girl. As long as you keep that attitude up, you'll never fall from the throne your father and I have created for you. You're a Jackson, and Jacksons never get cheated up outta our coins." By now, she'd spun back to the mirror and was admiring herself while talking to me.

Whenever Trinity started talking about my family's greatness and how I was blessed to be a product of her and Calvin, I spaced out. I'd heard the same speech in several variations and could recite it backward. I didn't need to keep hearing I was on a pedestal for me to know it. I'd accepted that I was better than most people. No other family I knew of in the hood was driving luxury cars in real name-brand clothes.

"A'ight, Porsha, it's been real hanging with you today, but girl time is over. I've gotta take some time to zone out and get my mind right before this cabaret. Pass me my blunt from the ashtray, then skedaddle. Your brother's probably looking for you anyway."

"Okay," I quickly replied, all too eager to get out from under her. Today's impromptu mother-daughter date wasn't my idea in the first place, so she could save her flip-flopping-ass attitude for the cougars, young hoes, and even the tiny-tot thots who were gonna be checkin' for my daddy tonight.

"Ma, is it cool for Imani to come over and kick it with me and Benzie while y'all are gone to the cabaret?" I held my breath, hoping she didn't remember the dick pic she'd seen over my shoulder earlier.

She sighed like I was getting on her nerves. "Yeah, Porsha. I don't care. Ya think I can get a li'l peace now?"

"Yup, I'm out of ya way. Have fun tonight." I turned and left her room, not really caring if she had fun, because I knew for sure that I would.

Me: Come through when you're ready. I got the go.

Me: Tonight. Don't play me. I'm ready.

The first text was to Imani. The second was to Street.

Unlike the wild adventure-like day I had with our mom, Benzie had a much different experience with our dad. They kicked it, playing with toys, eating, and watching TV, which consisted of Calvin exposing him to sports. Dad never said it out loud, or at least in my presence, but I knew he loved having a boy, just like I knew my mom really liked having a girl, especially when it came to helping with cooking, cleaning, and tending to Benzie.

The whole house was a mess. My dad was a good dad, but not a great keeper. Like every boy I knew of, he was a slob when it came to cleaning up behind himself. There were crumbs all over the floor from the snacks he and

Benzie ate, sippy cups of spoiled milk on the table, and old diapers scattered in a few places, which could've easily been thrown a few feet away in the trash. I didn't know what my parents planned on doing when I moved, because that meant the maid would be moving too.

After I got the living room put back together, I burned a few candles to help with the spoiled milk and diaper smell, and I sprayed the furniture down with Lysol. I made sure all of my chores were immaculately done, cleaning the kitchen and bathroom as well as sweeping down the hallway stairs. I was able to get a load of clothes in before Benzie started shutting down from the sugar rush he'd been spinning on.

Li'l man had been shut off in his room, locked in by a gate, so he could still roam around but see inside my or our parents' room if our doors were open. He couldn't really walk yet but could crawl and pull up on stuff. Right now, though, he was flipping out, screaming and laughing at the same time. Because Daddy used to let me get Kool-Aid wasted and sing along with Zoe on *Sesame Street* until passing out whenever my mom was gone, I knew Benzie was only a few minutes from passing out. Sugar will take you high, then drop you low.

With red stains all over his shirt, sticky fingers, and a face covered in all the candy, ice cream, and chips he'd gotten to snack on, he was about to sleep good and be out for the night. That'd work out perfectly for me . . . well, Imani, since she was the one who'd be here babysitting him. To make sure of it, I gave him a bath, dinner, and a warm bottle of milk before laying him down and saying good night.

With the whole house fresh and clean, I locked myself in my room and did a search for some porno videos on YouTube. I was a virgin, and Street wasn't. So I needed to school myself on the art of straight fuckin'. Girls were doing some of everything, taking it in the asshole, eating the asshole, and twirling like gymnasts on the dick. I didn't know what Street was expecting, but I wasn't planning on doing anything more than missionary, doggie style, and maybe a sixty-nine-dine if he was lucky. I couldn't go from a freshman to a graduate in a couple of hours. *He better hope I don't back out on all the shit I've been talkin'.*

After scrolling through a few videos that either weren't exciting or were too much for me to even think about trying, I found one where the girl was cute and the guy was kinda built like Street. In my mind, it was us, and I was trying to put myself all the way in the girl's shoes. When that night came and I was put on the spot, I wanted to be able to perform. I paid attention to how she sucked his dick, took his dick, and threw her pussy back on him when she wanted more of his dick.

When a text alert interrupted the porno, I had to hurry up and wipe the pre-cum from between my legs with my panties and then put on a new pair.

Imani: Open the door. I'm coming up the block.

Me: Okay. Be down in a sec. Don't ring the doorbell.

The fact that I'd gotten moist meant I was really ready to have sex . . . well, at least to me. Even if I didn't perform like ol' girl, I was sure I'd still give it up without telling him to stop out of fear. Clearing the browser history on my phone, I hurried out of my room and to the door to let Imani in.

Imani's mom didn't care that my parents were unconventional or that my dad trapped from the first level of our house. As long as I promised to do her hair for free, she let Imani come over without a problem. I was cool with that, especially since I'd made a few dollars off her coworkers from her modeling my styles at work. It hadn't been much, but if I kept hooking her up with freebies, I thought I might build up a real good clientele.

"Damn, you weren't playing about getting out of the house," I greeted my girl.

"Yup, you know it. Your house is a vacation spot from my boring-ass house. My mom got so many rules that I don't know if I'm living in a halfway house or the Army," she joked but was dead-ass serious. "She said she wants three free styles for letting me come early, by the way."

Trinity might've gotten into my ass on several occasions, but she didn't ride me hard like Imani's mammy rode her. Imani could barely go places, didn't have name-brand clothes, and was talked down to on a regular like she wasn't shit. The only reason she got to come over here was because her mom benefited. I did her hair, and she'd borrowed a few dollars here and there from my mom before. Now that Imani could work, though, she'd be the one chipping in on the bills when her momma was short. That shit right there I most definitely couldn't relate to.

My ass whippings came with gifts, shopping sprees, and money. The only reason I was waiting on the 18 mark like a junkie in need of a hit was because I wanted the right to tell my parents no without consequences. I had a rebellious soul that was waiting to break out. Imani, however, was passively waiting on her eighteenth to disappear. That was where she and I differed. I wasn't groomed to run.

"Hey, bae. I got a big bag of stuff together for you. Remind me to give it to you before I leave later," I reminded her. I always gave Imani my hand-me-downs instead of throwing them in the trash. And if we were at the mall and I was in a friendly mood, I'd cash out on her a few outfits to walk out of the mall with, too. Me looking out for her had always kinda been my thang. You couldn't put a hashtag of stinginess behind my name, especially when it came to my best friend.

"Aw, thanks. But don't be trying to sweeten up because yo' ass gonna be out gettin' the dick while I'm watching your li'l brother. I'm cool. There's a *Sisterhood of Hip Hop* marathon coming on in an hour."

"Great. Now I really don't feel bad. Fair exchange ain't robbery."

My mom kept a fridge of food, thanks to the government. They gave us $500 a month for the three of us, plus we stayed buying stamps from custos who couldn't pay for their drugs with cash. There were three kitchens in this house, and each pantry, shelf, and fridge was stocked to capacity. After grabbing us some snacks and a soda pop each, we retreated into the living room and watched TV. Cable was another thing Imani's momma couldn't afford for them to have. I swore I couldn't survive with Netflix and Hulu alone, and she wouldn't have even that if it weren't for me giving her my login and password.

While she flipped through the channels trying to find something to watch, I busied myself, texting her how things were gonna go down ahead of time. Once my parents left, I wouldn't have time for much talking. My boo was on standby only two minutes away and ready to pull up. After I'd texted him that we were on for tonight, he'd anxiously responded by sending another dick pic with the caption, We'll see. I wanted every second I was secretly stealing to be dedicated to showing him how ready I was. I didn't know why, but I felt like tonight was my time to shine or to step the fuck back and grow up a li'l bit more.

CHAPTER 6

CALVIN

I'd been in the basement hooking up a few bags for Porsha to sell tonight while the wife and I were at the cabaret when I heard her little friend scurrying up the driveway. Imani was so consumed by her phone that she had not noticed me coming from the side door. I waited until she went inside with Porsha before moving from behind the dumpster and taking a seat on the porch. I didn't like dealing with my daughter's friends. Because little girls could cause a lot of trouble for a man like me, I never gave them the chance.

"Five dollars, Cal. All I need is a five-dollar credit until the first of the month." One of my regular custos begged for me to give him a credit on the cheapest packages of rocks I sold.

"You know I don't do credit, nigga. Either come with my money—and it can be in all pennies if you got it—or stay the fuck from around here and outta my face, rollie." I called most of the heavy-hitting fiends around here rollie because they stayed high. In the hood, once you were stone-cold gone off the drugs, you were always rolling anyhow.

"I'll have it when my check comes. You can be on the porch waiting for the mailman with me," he pleaded one more time.

"Ay, on the real, rollie, quit mafuckin' talking to me about credit before I silence ya ass for good. I already told you what it was around here, so be gone with that shit. I'm done talking." Whipping my heater from the waistband of my pants, I loaded one up in the chamber, then looked him square in the face. "Five, four, three . . ." He ran away before I finished my countdown.

Terrified of feeling the heat of a bullet ripping through his flesh, he pissed his pants before being able to leap up and run away. I didn't care about scaring a regular away. He wasn't doing me any good today, and if I gave him credit, he'd never want to pay again. I didn't get into the dope game to make friends. I got in it to make money.

Sitting back down on the porch, I set my pistol by my side and lit up a blunt. I'd been with Benzie all day and hadn't smoked once. Though I'd put my piece in a nigga's face with my li'l man strapped in the car seat and sold dope underneath where he slept, I didn't want him mimicking me getting high. I wanted to raise a li'l monster, not a young 'head.

When I first got in the game, I was a young OG who had the stamina to bang with niggas twenty-four hours a day. I built a kingdom from a few grains of sand. I was seeing my family eat and live better than I did as a child and could have even imagined. At the same time, I kept the law off my back and bullets out of my body.

But every man has their day if they stay in the game. Old men were supposed to retire and live off the fat of the land at some point in life. I wanted to live out my life to spend my riches. My goal was to oversee my operation from another angle—out of the hood. I wanted to give my wife some peace out in the 'burbs with some wealthy wives, walkin' a foo-foo dog or some shit. I wanted to give Benzie a big-ass backyard, playscape, and maybe a pond with some ducks in it. And I wanted to give Porsha her own li'l spot in a gated community away from all the bullshit the hood could bring to her life.

There was only one large hole in the plan, and that was that my team lacked the strength they needed to stand without my hands-on leadership. Though Street was trying to take a step on his own, coming at me like he wanted to grow my team and our revenue, he did not make me feel like he was going to be a strong fallback if I wanted to fall back out of the game. He was already hungry for power. Our conversation earlier made me realize that I had to remind the whole squad of niggas working underneath me that I was still the king of this dope shit.

"Hey, Daddy. Ma said for you to get your ass in the house to get ready. Her words and not mine." Porsha came onto the porch, relaying my wife's message.

"Okay, baby girl. But sit down for a second so we can chop it up."

She sighed. "Right now, Dad?"

"What's really up? You ain't got time for your father all of a sudden?" Looking up at Porsha as she stood with her arms crossed and her hip thrown to the side, it was then I realized how grown she really was. Not only was she a mini-version of Trinity, but she had grown body parts that I couldn't even look at. I wished I could turn back the hands of time to when she was running around with a sippy cup and a baby doll.

"Your mother told me what happened today, baby girl. I don't want to hold you up, but I did want to tell you that I am proud of you for thinking on your own in that nail shop. Regardless of how worried you were when I called, none of that fear crippled you from outsmarting a muthafucka. Keep that shit up."

"Thanks, Daddy. Now maybe you can stay off my back some because you know I've been listening." She cut her eyes at me with a smile on her face, already knowing my praise didn't mean I was about to be any less of a professor when it came to teaching her the politics of the drug game.

"Nope, I don't think so. I don't wanna bust the bubble I just gave you, but you've still got a lot of breast milk on your breath. Don't fuck up, thinking you know everything. Stay humble and pay attention to what I tell you. You need to know everything that I'm telling you and more. There's so much shit out here, Porsha. I'm really trying to build something big for you and your brother so y'all don't get swallowed in the hood like I did."

She smacked her lips. "Daddy, you always be talkin' like we live in a slum."

"We might not be slumming, but we can do better, Porsha. A whole lot better. The fact that you think this ain't slumming lets me know I need to show and expose you to more. But I'll preach at you later about that." I temporarily dropped the subject. "Other than the shit that popped off at that nail shop, did you and your mom have a good girls' day out?"

"Yeah, it was cool. I had not expected to since she'd checked out on me earlier, but I did."

I chuckled, then poured out a few sips of beer. "Ya momma stays checkin' out. That's a big reason why I'm so in love with her. And also why I've been keeping bail money with her name on it on reserve since I made her my wife. I see I'ma have to start keeping a few racks set aside for you too."

"I guess, but I hope I don't ever have to call on you to use it."

"Me neither, baby girl. That's why you've gotta know how to pick your battles. In addition to thinking smart and staying out of the way of the law, not everything and everyone needs a reaction. I'm not gonna be around to watch your back forever." I kept it real with her, as it was my job to do.

"Don't worry. I know. I know I'ma be straight out here."
I pulled her in for a hug. "I'm sure you will, baby girl.
I'm sure you will." We shared a father-daughter hug for
a few seconds, and then I started breaking down the
rules for tonight. "Make sure you hold the trap down
while me and ya moms are gone. Don't open the door for
nobody, and make sure you serve every fiend who comes
knocking through the mail slot. Money first, sack last.
Understand?"

"Dad, I've got this, don't worry. This is not the first time
I've sold some baggies while y'all were gone." She eased
my unsettled nerves.

I feared nothing, and Porsha mimicked that. Sometimes
it was scary looking at her because it was like looking
into my own eyes. Trinity and I had been on a wave of
craziness with her since she was old enough to speak her
opinion.

The front door opened, and Imani came out. I'd forgotten Porsha had company.

"Hi, Imani," I said, acknowledging her friend.

"Hi, Mr. Jackson," she responded, blushing and batting
her eyes at me like she was flirting and wanted to fuck.

"Oh, hell naw, little girl. You better check that bullshit
real quick." I raised my voice, scaring her and getting her
together super quick. Her body instantly tensed up. "I'm
a grown-ass man, and you're my daughter's buddy, a
little-ass child to me. I stopped being interested in pussy
y'all age when I was thirteen. If you bring that disrespectful shit around here again, you ain't gonna be welcome
around this house or Porsha. Understood?"

I was grim with her and in front of Porsha on purpose.
For one, I had to embarrass Imani so the shit wouldn't
happen again. Secondly, I needed my baby girl to be a
witness for me just in case Imani's li'l heifer ass wanted
to lie on me later down the line because she was bitter

about getting embarrassed. With all the illegal actions unfolding on a daily basis in my life, a hot-in-the-crotch teenager was not going to be responsible for taking me down.

"My bad, and I'm sorry," she stuttered, seemingly scared straight. "It won't ever happen again, Mr. Jackson." She'd transformed back into the teenage girl she'd always presented herself as.

"That's more like it, Imani."

Porsha was standing to the side, fiddling with her fingers, tight-lipped. She knew I didn't play with li'l rats, just like she knew I didn't allow her to run with rodents. I wasn't waiting until her fast-tail friend was out of earshot for me to put her on blast, or for me to warn my daughter about her affiliation and how she best be on her best muthafuckin' behavior or else.

"Ay, baby girl, you already know what I'ma say, but I'ma say the shit anyway. Birds of a feather flock together. Let me find out that you out here chasing cheese, and I'ma fuck your rat ass up without asking a question," I warned her. "If you ain't in no shit, then a muthafucka can't even lie on you. So I'll say it one more time: don't let me find out. If there's some smoke, you better clear that shit before it lingers this way." I stepped off and left to get dressed because there wasn't shit else to talk about. I meant what I said and was planning on standing by my words if and whenever I needed to. If Porsha broke my rules, all bets that we ever had were off.

PORSHA

I was in awe just as much as my pops was when Imani fluttered her eyelashes at him. Imani and I were aces, best friends, right-hand girls and all. I couldn't wait to tell Nikola how far over the boundary line this bitch had crossed but was always playing the shy role around the young niggas we fucked around with.

"You just flirted with my father right in my face. I don't know if I should smack you on behalf of my mother or say fuck sneaking out of the house and take you down to the hospital for an emergency psychological evaluation." I shook my head, thinking about everything that could've gone wrong behind Imani's inappropriate behavior. "You just dodged two bullets. One from Trinity if she had overheard you, and one from me if my plans had crashed and burned. In other words, if I weren't desperate to get out and about with Street, I'd probably beat your ass on principle alone."

"Yeah, yeah, yeah. I get it. It won't happen again," she nonchalantly responded, then tried pushing past me to return upstairs.

I threw my arm up and blocked her. "No, no, no. You don't get it. Sit tight right here on this porch and hang tight until I come back down. Yo' stupid ass done put us on the radar, and now we've gotta stay off of it until they are damn near walking out the door. We're about to walk to get a pizza and then some bullshit from the store." Pushing her backward and down until she was seated, I then slowly stepped upstairs, hoping Calvin wasn't sitting in the living room about to check the dog shit out of me again.

CHAPTER 7

TRINITY

"You better swear on your life that I am not about to have any drama with that ugly trick you were banging behind my back, or I am going to air this bitch out," I warned my husband as soon as we pulled into the parking lot of the banquet hall. It was crowded, and cars were blocking other cars in, so I figured the home-wrecking ho was in the building.

"Look, Trin. Do not get in there and get on dumb shit. I cannot control what that broad does. So if you will be purposely looking for a reason to pull your red clown nose out of your purse, we might as well grab a carry-out of Coney Island and go home." Calvin casually pulled on the leaf of Kush we had been sharing.

"Ha! I got something to pull out of my purse, all right." I snatched the leaf from his hand and took my own hard pull. "And I already told Porsha to have some bail money on standby."

"You are doing too much, Trinity. I know I fucked up by cheating, but do you plan on fighting that girl every time you see her?"

"Nope. One day I am going to end up shooting her," I casually responded, wishing Calvin had kept his dick in his pants. It was taking everything in me not to reach over the console and smack the spit from my husband's mouth.

Every time the topic or thought of Calvin cheating on me came up, I got amped up and ready to react erratically, just like I day I found out there was another woman. I could not erase the day from my memory bank, no matter how hard I tried. I was seven months pregnant with Benzie and as big as a house. I had been irritable since the day the doctor told me I was pregnant because me conceiving was a fluke of science. I did not want another baby, and I fo' damn sho' was not trying to give up smoking weed and drinking on a daily basis. The only reason I did not abort Benzie was because Calvin was at the emergency room with me when the doctor gave me the news. But I made sure my black ass signed up for a tubal ligation while I was pregnant so I would not get surprised again. Calvin did not lose a wink of sleep whenever he murdered someone, but he was not about killing kids, at least with me. After finding out about ol' girl, I was sadly certain Calvin had sent a few women to the chop shop with a mistake baby and some collateral cash to soothe their loss.

The bitch he was banging was brazen and slick enough to post a picture of her and my husband with the hashtag WithMyBae. Although she quickly deleted the evidence, she'd purposely started the fire knowing that I followed him. Where she studied long and wrong was assuming I had some sense. I was a special type of crazy that was very vindictive. I was beyond going back and forth on social media and throwing subliminal messages back and forth on my status. After doing a little digging on the internet, I charged my phone and packed myself a hospital bag in case I went into labor early, then drove to ol' girl's house.

"So are we going in this cabaret or what, Trinity?" Calvin impatiently questioned.

"Maybe we will. Maybe we won't. Why don't you roll up and give me a minute to see?" I snapped at him, pissed off that he'd even given me the thought to dwell on in the first place.

"Yeah, whatever, crazy lady. Fuck a nigga's past. I don't know if you been creepin' with some lame-ass clown lately, but I'm not he, and he ain't me if he let you talk like that. Don't get ya split." Calvin thought he was cleverly checking me.

Rolling my eyes quicker than he could finish his sentence, I went off. "Don't play with me, Cal. You and I both know you're the one with the creep card, but I'd better not find out it's in good standing and being swiped again," I warned, shaking with the thought. "It's gonna be off with ya head!"

"Whatever." He called himself blowing me off.

"Whatever my ass. You're more than welcome to try me if you're tough, though," I mocked and dared him confidently, feeling just as antsy and angry as I did the day I popped up over at his trick's house. Time hadn't healed my wounds.

I was ready to pop off. I was ready to stir shit back up and beef with Cal because I'd never gotten over him stepping out on me in such a major way. He and I had too deep a history for me to say fuck family all over another bitch's pussy and his weakness, but payback comes in all forms. He had one coming regardless of how right now played out for sure.

Calvin snickered a few times, then responded, "I'ma let ya have ya nut, ma. There ain't shit for me to be worried about up in that cabaret anyway. So keep working yo' crazy ass up for nothing." Turning the radio up, he waved me off and grunted some more smart shit I didn't bother asking him to repeat.

I sipped a little from my cup, then got back into the memory of the day I gave one of my best performances as a crazy wife. Before ol' girl got to delete the message, I'd already clicked on it to get her location. Like I said earlier, I didn't like basic reactions. I liked to change lives with how I retaliated.

If you teach a cat how to piss in litter the right way the first time around, you'll be saving yourself the trouble of scrubbing up the same mess time and time again. That was why I plugged in my phone, so it could get some battery juice, packed a bag for the hospital just in case I went into labor while performing, and gunned my truck all the way to ol' girl's house.

Knowing that she was looking for a tweet, I gave her one. It was real simple. I'm here.

My fat ass waddled up her walkway, held the rail walking up one stair at a time, and then pounded on the window until it felt like it was about to shatter. I was screaming at the top of my lungs for Calvin and his bitch to come outside. I had not given either of them any indication that I was coming, and given the neighborhood the side chick resided in, I knew nobody was calling the cops. They were too busy scrambling around trying to get closer so they could get a better view of what was going down.

As soon as ol' girl swung the door open, she started popping off at the mouth like she was tough. She made the mistake of thinking the pregnant belly I was carrying put her at an advantage. Phrases recklessly fell from her mouth like, "Ya pussy ain't good," "That's why he's over here ripping my walls out and leaving yours dry," "You could learn a few stunts from me," and, "Be happy you got Cal's kids, 'cause I got first call on his dick." Foolishly throwing her hands on her hips to stunt, she should have blocked her face, because I sent my fist straight into it and rocked her shit open. On impact, blood poured from her nose and mouth.

Then I took my wedding ring off and told Calvin's

ass to buy me another one in the morning because I
didn't want one that had her blood on it. I wasn't going
nowhere, and neither was he. Calvin was my man, my
partner, and my husband. He'd go to the grave before
I allowed him to rest peacefully in the arms of another
bitch.

By the time he crossed the threshold of her door, she
ran from behind him, trying to attack me from behind.
I'd spun around to give her the business, being that she
wanted to try me, but Calvin had caught her by the hair
and was flinging her down before my fist flew toward
her again. Since she'd gotten my adrenaline pumping
again, I threw the punch at Calvin since he was the
culprit who started this madness in the first place. I
was only upset with the side chick because she had the
audacity to be cocky.

After landing the first punch and feeling better, I started throwing haymakers on him like Money Mayweather.
I took advantage of the fact that he wasn't going to
hit me back because I was pregnant. The only reason
I stopped was because I didn't want ol' girl to see us
divided even more. That didn't mean I wouldn't make
his life hell when we got home.

Rubbing my hands together with a satisfied grin on my
face, the feeling of trampling her then, and again tonight,
made me feel undeniably good. I was particularly eager
to get at her because, unlike a year ago, ain't got no
waddle in my two-step. Plus, Calvin and I were stronger
than ever, because he knew my loyalty level was at one
hundred.

"A'ight, Trin, here's ya blunt," Calvin said, turning
down the radio. "Now I'ma ask you one more time before
I make the executive decision on my own. You walkin' up
in this muthafucka or naw? With all that liquor piled
up in the back, I'll have the trap rockin', so don't test
me," Calvin said, cutting into me with an ultimatum.

Putting the lighter to the tip of the blunt, I flicked the flame on until the Swisher Sweet started smelling sweet and strong. Taking a long hit, I blew the smoke out right in his face. "Gimme a minute. We're going up in there, but I've gotta make my buzz just right."

Despite me still harping on drama from the past and wanting to smack my husband's face, we interlocked arms and stepped into the banquet hall with our fronts up. That was how real boss couples moved: effectively, in silence, and as a unit. What I never did was let a muthafucka see me without my game face on.

Calvin was dressed like a Detroit player, with big block gator shoes on his feet and iced-out Cartier glasses on his face. And me, baby, my whole style was flawlessly put together from head to toe. Thanks to my Mini-Me giving me her young advice for flair, my hair, makeup, and accessories were all on point. Plus, I was rocking the shit out of my dress with a pair of gator pumps that perfectly matched my husband's fly. The picture man was gonna make at least $100 off us tonight. I was feeling our look, but really myself.

"You are a lucky man, Calvin Jackson," I whispered in his ear so he could hear me over the music.

"Nah, Trinity Jackson, luck runs out. I'm blessed." He leaned down and kissed me like no one was watching.

I let my tongue explore his mouth as I kissed him back just the same. In his arms, I always felt secure. It was times like this that made me weak in the knees for Calvin. I loved public affection like every other woman.

Once we got settled in at the table, folks from the hood started flocking toward us, trying to see what drink they could make from our spread. Every year at every cabaret, me and Cal laid it out with bottles of liquor and champagne, and of course, Cal had weed and dope on deck to be sold. Neither of us was selfish when it came to popping bottles with the hood. You've gotta give a little to get a little in return, and we had been moving around comfortably for years.

The menu for tonight's cabaret was chicken, rib tips, spaghetti, mac and cheese, and a bold salad that was mostly lettuce. I started trying to wave the waitress over to put in an order for a greasy plate of chicken to coat my stomach before I got pissy drunk and all the liquor settled on an empty gut. I did not know what they used as seasoning, but their special ingredient left a bitch licking her fingers each and every time.

The DJ threw some old-school songs on and had everyone with their arms up and waving, reliving whatever moment they were caught up in when this song first released in the nineties. I wasn't the friendliest of bitches, although I hosted parties at the trap, but even I got live and turned up to the throwback. I knew how to have associates and walk a fine line with women who were too catty for me to fuck with on a regular. My sisters were enough friends for me. With all four of them, I had enough turmoil to last a lifetime. But with the bass of the music bringing all of us women together, we got a hustle line going and were stepping hard in our heels.

The memories of how Calvin and I were when we first started being players in the drug game were the fuckin' best. That was back when muthafuckas had pagers and burner cell phones, and moved dope with the Feds on their payrolls. My other half and I were one of the first couples to have ever done it together, and I'd do it a million times more if he got his shit together.

As quickly as I'd gotten happy going down memory lane, I got pissed as fuck thinking about where Calvin was trying to take me and his family. The only place the Jacksons deserved to be was on top.

CHAPTER 8

PORSHA

Imani and I were chilling in the living room and watching the *Sisterhood of Hip Hop* marathon, of course. She was all in, stuffing slices of pizza down her throat like she had not eaten all day. But I couldn't finish the first slice I'd taken out of the box. My stomach was too full of butterflies to fit another morsel of food in it. And since I was planning on taking a large dose of something else in my mouth later, I didn't want to set myself up for failure now.

Me: What are you doing?

Trying not to watch my phone, I did. If Street didn't hurry up and text me right back, I'd think the worst. It took him three minutes to respond.

Street: At the card game. U ready for this dick?

That tingling feeling I got in my coochie earlier returned. I bit my lip and crossed my legs.

Me: Almost. Trapping. Send some my way. Lol.

Street: U doin' too much. Hit me up when u ready.

Feeling dumb, I already knew what he meant. I'd texted too much within our conversation. The Feds stayed watching, so I shouldn't have said one word about trapping.

Trying to distract myself from fuckin' up and not wanting him to think I was an amateur, I checked on Benzie, then got a blunt from my mom's stash to smoke on. If nothing else could, weed would do the trick.

Imani had not even paid attention to me being gone.

"Yo' ass is all in that damn TV."

"Girl, yes. When you turn eighteen and move out, you better get some cable so I can come over there and watch TV too," she joked.

"Uh, yup. Okay. Whatever. You wanna hit this?" I ignored her, revealing the blunt and what my intentions were. I started lighting it up.

"Damn, you ain't playin' tonight, I see. Okay. Yeah, I'ma hit that. Light it up."

One puff and the session I was getting ready to get started was stopped.

"Yo, C-Note." I heard a man's voice yelling my father's nickname outside. "Yo, C." He was persistent as I tried catching the last few seconds of the show before it went to commercial. My parents could not have gotten up the block before the first customer came banging on the door to get served, and the flow had not let up since. My dad and his team must have had that one-hitter quitter.

"He won't be back until later tonight, boss man," I hollered down off the top porch.

"Can you help me?" he desperately asked.

"Yup, yup, here I come." I passed the blunt back to Imani and grabbed the Ziploc of baggies I was serving out of. I was supposed to take the customer's order at the door, along with their money, then go upstairs for their package, but I had gotten too buzzed to keep running up and down the stairs. I could not wait until I sold out so I could stop trapping and do what I had been planning to do all day long.

"Yo, what'cha want?" I swung the door open, checking my surroundings just in case somebody was trying to creep on me and using the fiend as a decoy. My vision was not as on point as it needed to be because of the weed. My eyes were heavy as hell.

"Lemme get a dime bag," he requested, looking like he was about to lean into a nod while talking. He was dressed in tattered clothes, in need of a haircut, and I could smell him through the cracks of the door. Yet and still, he was spending his only $10 with me.

"No problem, I've got you once you come up outta that ten spot." Being respectful to my elders was not a rule I had to abide by when slanging. I could talk as harsh, gritty, and out of pocket as I wanted to. I popped open the mail slot. Once the ten was in my hand, the baggie was put in his.

"Are you for real, li'l Calvin? You know your pops holds me down during the month when I run out of my social security check." He was running me the truth, but it did not matter. That was his and my dad's deal, and that did not have anything to do with me.

"Not that I need to explain myself, ol' head, but whatever understanding you got with my daddy ain't an understanding you got with me. When he is not here, baggies are full price. Period." I was getting impatient because the commercial run was going off, and I heard some drama popping off. I had been watching reruns and now the season premiere was on, so I was not trying to miss a minute of the much-anticipated madness.

"Li'l Cal—"

He was gearing up to beg again, but I cut him off. "G'on and get the fuck off my porch. If you do not, I'ma call my daddy up and let him know you are giving me a problem. I already told you what it is, so say no more and bounce." I did not want to call Cal because I did not want him coming home messing up my plans, but the threat would work on the custo.

He backed down the steps without saying another word until he got to the last step. "I'm 'bout to go to the store to see if I can make a few dollars for a five-dollar bag. In case I cannot hustle up on it, though, can you call ya pops now and see if I can get that credit? I will be right back." He literally ran up the street. He better hope he pitied himself up $5 because I was not about to jump on Cal's radar for no bullshit.

As soon as I got ready to slam the door, a new snowflake white Charger sitting on chrome wheels pulled up in front of the house, blasting its music. I stopped and stared hard.

"Imani! Oh my God, Dread just pulled up. Look outside." I started fidgeting and feeling froggish in my dingy jogging pants and T-shirt. Since I had been chilling in the house with my homegirl, I had not gotten dressed.

"What is he doing here?" Imani asked, coming to the top of the steps.

"I do not know, but pass me that blunt real quick so I can calm my nerves." I ran halfway up the stairs and hit the blunt harder than I had all night. Dread was fine as hell and intimidated me more than Street did.

Hearing the music from Dread's car get louder, I saw the door was open and he was climbing out. "Okay, disappear, but stay close. Here he comes." I pushed the blunt back into Imani's hand, then ran back to the door.

"Yo, li'l momma. What up?" He walked up on the porch. "I didn't know you were C-Note's seed. He here?"

"Yeah, I am C-Note's daughter. But no, he is not here. Were you trying to get some work? Or holla at him about working for him?"

He snickered and pushed a few dreads that were dangling in front of his face behind his ear. "I do not work for nobody but myself, sweetheart. I was trying to cop some weight from your pops because I heard his shit is pure as hell, if I can be honest." That meant his customers were leaving him bold because his package was bold, but I let Dread maintain his cockiness.

"Oh, okay. Well, I can help you with that. Exactly how much were you trying to cop?"

"What do you have access to?"

"I got what you can spend." My comeback was quick and catchy.

"A'ight then, li'l boss." He smirked, then pulled out a wad of cash. "Let me get a grand's worth of the finest."

When the cash slid through the mail slot, my attention shifted from it to eye fucking Dread hard. If he was coming through with chicken like this, I was curious to know what his pockets looked like for real, for real. Ya know, on a day-to-day basis when he wasn't trying to cop. Street never pulled out chedda like this, and he rolled for my moneymaking daddy. This nigga had my attention.

Breaking the rules, I unlocked and opened the door and let him into the small hallway while I counted the hundreds and to let him stuff the product underneath his clothes. The truth was that I wanted to check him out a little more closely and see if he wanted to low-key holla. It would be nice having a dude to throw up in Street's face, or at least one to take my attention off of Street when he tripped. I ended up having egg on my face when Dread-head didn't give me a second glance or a compliment after getting the baggies. All he was concerned about was getting his weight and pushing the fuck on, and that was just what I let his ass do.

I shook that shit off, figuring something had to be wrong with him. I was a bad bitch in my own right. I didn't need him or no other nigga to build me up. When it came to my self-esteem, I was cockier than Amber Rose walking the slut walk. Besides, I had plans with Street, and he should've been the only hustler on my mind.

Once the transaction was done, I let him out and slammed the door behind him, ecstatic as hell. Not because I had a grand's worth of hundreds in my pocket, but because I'd sold completely out of baggies. With that being the case, I could slide up outta here on the sneak tip sooner rather than later. Making sure the door was bolted, I also put all the chains on to make sure no one ran in on us. This was a nightly precaution I, my dad, and my mom always did. You can never be too safe living in a trap house. After stashing the money for my mother to count in the morning, I texted Street to see if he was ready, then caught Imani up on the slight change of plans.

"A'ight, girlie. My dude is on the way. Make sure you keep the TV down so Benzie doesn't wake up, and keep the blinds closed. If anyone comes knocking to get served, ignore 'em. They'll eventually go away. If you get scared or need me, call me," I shouted over my shoulder at Imani, rushing to the bathroom. My phone was going off, and it was Street texting back saying he'd meet me in fifteen minutes.

Even though I was pressed for time, I slowed down to wash between my legs. The prettiest bitch can easily be the ugliest bitch if her coochie smells tart, so I didn't play when it came to keeping a clean monkey. To make sure I never became a "Smelly Melly," the "talked-about girl," I freshened up and changed my panties twice a day. Washing up twice, then a third time just to feel extra fresh, I then sprayed some feminine spray on my thighs because it only seemed right to do so. I loved my juicy thighs, I swore I did.

My hair was already fixed into a messy bun, so all I did was untie the sides and make sure the baby hairs were laid down with some edge control. Finally, I slid on the purple pajama lounge set I'd picked out earlier, which was a pair of loose-fitting shorts and a T-shirt. I'd purposely covered up my curves because I was totally exposed underneath. Street loved getting freaky, and I loved giving him easy access.

He was texting me to come on by the time I finished sneaking from my mom's bedroom with a pre-rolled blunt. Street said she always had the strongest shit. Sneaking one we could smoke was worth the risk of her finding out and me getting in trouble. However, if she asked me who I blew it down with, I'd lie and say Imani. Fingers crossed she'd never find out though.

"I'm about to go, Imani. Don't forget what I told you, and I'll be back before my parents." I spoke over my shoulder again, this time on my way out the door.

"Ya ass better be," I heard her scream back to me.

I had to walk down a block then around the corner before getting into Street's car. He was parked with the lights off by an abandoned house we'd randomly picked another night I'd snuck out. Even though he knew my parents were turning up at the annual hood cabaret, Elvin "Street" Thomas knew better than to pull up in front of my house. Why? 'Cause my pops wouldn't hesitate to put a bullet in his dome.

Street was the exact type of nigga my daddy told me to stay away from, yet he was the prototype of the man my momma schooled me on snagging. Elvin was a hustler with money, swag, and clout in these streets. What they'd probably agree on if they knew about my sneaky behavior, though, was that Street was too old for me. I wasn't trying to hear none of that with my birthday coming up. I was damn near grown, so I needed to be on a grown man's arm.

CHAPTER 9

TRINITY

"Yeah, that's what I'm talkin' 'bout. Y'all got me in here sweating, and I ain't doing nothin' but spinnin' tracks," the DJ announced, then put a slower record on. "For the next few songs, I'm going to slow it down, giving my lovers a chance to two-step. You're partying with DJ Beats, the man of music. Come by the booth with your requests."

Calvin and I were dancing our asses off. Instead of dwelling on the problem I had with him, I decided to keep my fronts up and enjoy our night, especially with his old trick continuously checkin' for us. It felt good having the man she lusted for and got dissed by draped all over me, winning in her face, while she sat salty, wishing she were in my shoes. It felt hella good stunting on her now that I didn't have pregnancy pimples and a flared nose. She couldn't juice her ego up with jokes now. As hardcore as I was, I ain't gonna lie and say she didn't fuck with my self-esteem a little bit back then. How the tables had turned, though.

She kept looking me up and down from head to toe with her face frowned up with hate, probably mad 'cause I wasn't the ugly duckling she'd sized me up to be. From my flawlessly laid MAC makeup down to the polish on my toes, I was feeling myself and fucking her up at the same time. You couldn't tell me nothing, and if you did, I wouldn't listen. This was only the calm before the storm, though. I was the type of woman who liked to bark and bite.

Every time I looked her way, she was already looking in mine. Calvin peeped it too, because he kept me calm and still with his hand firmly braced at the arch of my back. That didn't mean my blood wasn't boiling, however. I hated not being able to leap for a bitch with her boldly asking for some attention. I didn't think that'd change with age. Like wine, I'd get better with age.

"Sup, sis." Fame came out of nowhere, hugging me.

Calvin and he did a secret handshake, which was a man thing, followed by a manly hug that lasted for only a split second. We three were like family, being that we'd been breaking bread together since the day we broke down our first kilo. My momma didn't have but five girls, so Fame was like the brother I never had. He and Calvin were so close that it wasn't even a question as to who would be Porsha and Benzie's godfather. And trust when I tell you Fame stepped up helluva for them both when he was called upon, and sometimes when he wasn't. He was good people.

"Hey, bro! Everything is all good," I lied through my teeth with a smile.

"That's what's up, sis. You lookin' good, by the way." Fame was trying to butter me up.

"A'ight, nigga, put ya butter knife up before you spread the margarine too thin. You know a bitch can read bullshit in any language." I picked his compliment apart.

He laughed, knowing he'd been called out. "Damn, Trin, let a nigga at least think he slick," he replied all in fun. "No wonder my partna stays on his toes."

Now it was my turn to snicker. Rolling my eyes only, I kept what I really wanted to say about Calvin being on his toes to myself. Not everything you know needs to be said, so I used my discretion. "Anyway, Fame, what's up?"

This time around, he got straight to the point. "I was trying to sweeten you up before I took Cal away for a second. I see y'all partying and shit, but I really need to holla at my partner about some business if that's cool with you."

"No doubt it's cool. Do y'all thang," I blurted out almost too fast. The quicker Calvin got out of my face, the quicker I could put my fist through ol' girl's face again. Like I told her when I was pulling off from her house that day, the shit wasn't never gonna be over.

CALVIN

Watching my wife walk over toward Nette to order some chicken, I gripped my dick, watching her fatty jiggle. I couldn't wait to get her fine ass back home. With a firecracker like Trinity, I didn't have time to be out here checkin' for young girls and cheating. Well, not anymore. She was bodied. Ol' girl I'd banged didn't have nothing on Trin. She'd just come around when wifey was slowed down with Benzie's pregnancy. When I made love to her tonight, I'd try to fuck the memory of my thoughtlessness out of her mind for good. I checked my hip for my heater before walking out the exit, then held the door open for Fame to walk out first.

"Yo, that's my bad if I created some friction between you and Trin. It wasn't my intention. I just wanted to holla at you about what we kicked it about earlier," Fame apologized, then spoke in code about me wanting to back up some from the game.

"You good. It ain't no thang. You already know Trin takes it to the max, and it didn't help that ol' girl I fucked when she was pregnant with Benzie is here."

"Aw, hell naw! I told you to buy that bitch a li'l crib, a used whip, and a one-way plane ticket to somewhere warm. Had you listened, she'd be on the beach in a bikini, trying to get the attention of some other pimp, instead of in there about to fuck up ya life," Fame said, giving his advice.

"Shiiit, real talk, I said fuck it after Trinity found out I was creeping. Ol' girl is lucky I paid that high-ass dental bill I know she had altered. Didn't no two front teeth cost no five fucking grand when you've got Medicaid. She got her come-up though, simply 'cause I figured that's the least I could do."

Fame burst out in laughter. "Dog, I swear, Trinity ain't to be fucked with. She had ol' girl running around the city, looking like a toddler by the mouth. Her thotting ass was probably giving some hella head though, tickling a nigga's dick with her tongue through the gap and shit."

A ho was a ho, so Fame's direct disses about ol' girl didn't faze me. Yet and still, a nigga could live without the constant reminder that he and Trin kept hitting me in the gut with. "A'ight, Fame, we cool and all, but what's up? You ain't drag me up out of the cabaret from my wife to kick it about my ex jump off."

I wasn't a playboy. I was a man. Cheating wasn't the norm for me. Unlike a lot of cats who took pride in doing their women wrong, I didn't. I loved Trinity and the kids she gave birth to for me. Me fucking ol' girl wasn't because she was lacking as a woman, a partner, or even a mother, although she was rough around the edges. I cheated on Trinity because I thought Benzie wasn't mine. Yeah, me and my wife shared some helluva secrets that we spent the same amount of time trying to cover up.

"You're right, the liquor and the backwoods got me tripping. That's my bad, Brodie. Anyway, down to business." After taking a cop, Fame looked over my shoulder, then reached underneath his shirt, whipping out his trusty heater.

"What the fuck?" I murmured, confused, slightly buzzed, and slow on the draw.

My drunken-induced disability didn't stop shots from firing off and rocking the room.

CHAPTER 10

PORSHA

Seeing a pair of headlights coming up the block, I peeked around the bush I was hiding behind to see my boo pulling up in his black-on-black Impala. He looked oh so fucking fine to me, bobbing his head to whatever rap track he was blasting. I couldn't help myself from liking him. He had a powerful presence that turned me on. My pussy had a heartbeat whenever I was around Street. I was gonna have to make good on all the stuff I was texting him earlier. Shaking a few branches, I made my presence known so he wouldn't be startled to shoot. Then I came from behind the bush.

Street didn't drive the flashiest car like most of the other hustlers from the hood, or even Dread-head from earlier, but it was clean and decked out with a sound system and rims. To me, Street was a winner. I didn't have a car and barely had access to the three in my driveway. Calvin and Trinity only came up off the keys if they wanted me to run an errand. I was going to be pissed if I didn't get at least a piece of a car for my birthday.

"Hey, baby," I sang to him, sliding into the passenger seat, greeted by a cloud of weed smoke. I caught a contact on instant.

The leather interior was cold on my thighs because he had the air bumping. I felt my nipples harden and swell on instant. Regardless of the season, hot or cold, Street kept his whip cold and the windows slightly cracked to keep the smoke circulating. He always had a cigarette, blunt, or even a joint up to his lips. If not there, then behind his ear, waiting to be lit.

"What up? You looking good." He looked at me, licking his lips, and at the same time smacking me on the thigh and squeezing it tightly. Street had big hands. His touch had me squirming in my seat.

"Thanks, bae. You do too," I replied, blushing and meaning the compliment.

Every inch of his entire body was cut and sexy to me. His hands were rough, but it didn't matter. He'd been hustling all day. I wouldn't have liked him if he were a straight and narrow, nine-to-five, working college boy. It was his thuggish ways I was attracted to.

"Thanks, shorty. But I'm good on all that small talk if you are. What'chu tryin' to get into?"

"You tell me. You already know I'm down for whatever." I wasn't timid to be his hot girl.

He chuckled the type of chuckle that makes you know a nigga ain't taking you seriously. "You been talkin' a good game all day to a nigga, P. We'll see what that mouth really be like when it comes down to it, though."

Not waiting for a response from me, Street turned the music up loud enough to blast our eardrums out, then pulled away from the curb. I held on to his words, knowing I'd have to make good on mine. If I even tried to backpedal, Jamika would surely step into my place in a heartbeat.

I didn't necessarily know where we were going, nor did I care. As long as he made me feel good when we got there and made good on his word to get me back home before the cabaret was over, I was good and comfortable. And since we both could die if Calvin or Trinity caught us together, I knew I could settle in and enjoy the window of freedom I had.

"You trying to sip, or are you on that kid shit tonight?" he questioned, pulling up to the liquor store.

"If you're buying, I'm drinking," I replied boldly, trying to act grown since he'd called me out.

He laughed sarcastically like I had him twisted. "Don't ever play me close, shorty. I ain't no suck-a-dick-ass nigga who puts his hand out to a female. Never have and never will be. Now is ya drinking on something or what?"

Street wasn't on the same level as boys my age were. I couldn't run him in circles with my games. Each and every time I tried to, he shut me down and let me know I didn't have the mentality to fuck with him on his level. And this time was no different. I quit playing and answered, "Yeah, I'm sipping. Can you get me a bottle of green apple Cîroc, please?"

He snickered as if I might've been a handful to deal with. "I swear to God you're just like your momma. A nigga gotta get nutty with you before you act right. But I got you. Lock the doors when I get out."

I did more than that. Trained to be a thug's girlfriend because I was raised in the trap by thug parents, I watched his back until he disappeared up an aisle of the store. Instead of getting lost in my phone on a social network full of chickenheads posting their whole life story, I kept checking my surroundings to make sure no one was lurking or creeping. If something even looked suspect, I'd be letting my dude know any way I had to. I wanted Street to know I was loyal, a rider, and resilient to the streets, in spite of me being immature sometimes. The way I figured it, he'd be quicker to wife me knowing I wasn't going to be easily broken.

There was nothing going on around the store. In the night, everything was still but the few bums standing right outside, waiting for folks to give them change. I paid them no attention because I didn't have any intention of giving them a dime from Street's cup holder. They could get it how they lived.

Just when I thought Street and I were getting ready to make a clean break from the store without running into anyone we knew, his homeboy Pete Rock pulled up. I rolled my eyes so hard at him that my head started hurting.

Hate was a strong word, but it was perfectly appropriate when describing my feelings toward Street's best friend. He was tall, lanky, weird, and always had something smart to say when he saw me and Street together. It was always something referring to my age, followed by statements about my dad. That hating shit was on purpose, so I hated being in his presence. I couldn't wait until I was 18 so I could quit living with a lie and having simple muthafuckas hold it over my head.

"What up, young P?" Pete Rock's annoying ass approached the car, putting emphasis on the word "young." He could've kept his greeting if all he was gonna do was irritate me.

"Nothing," I dryly responded, not extending a question back of what was up with him. I didn't care nothing about Pete and didn't want him thinking I did.

"Where that man at you fuckin' with, baby P?" He boldly snuck one in.

"Oh, I see you're in rare form tonight with ya weak-link ass," I clapped back. "Get the fuck on up outta my face, Pete. I ain't in the mood for your tainted ass trying to ruin my night." Born addicted to drugs, Pete Rock knew I was referring to him being a crack baby and having a nutty personality because of it.

Cackling like a hyena, he wasn't the least bit fazed by me calling him out. "I ain't the one you need to be worried about ruining ya night. It's ya daddy Cal you should be focused on finding out, li'l creeper."

Knowing this back-and-forth battle could go on and on without either of us letting up, I rudely ended it. "Speaking of daddies, yours is in the store. Bye-bye." I rolled the window up, turned straight ahead, and dismissed him. *He better hope his hate game is strong, 'cause if not, I'll be dismissing him as Street's lackey in a few weeks forever.* I didn't want Pete Rock nowhere around me, let alone tagging along like the third-wheel loser he was.

Through my peripheral vision, I saw him mean mugging me with hate in his eyes. I knew he was salty about me calling him out as Street's son, but it was not my fault he couldn't be controlled and must have an overseer. Street monitored every move Pete Rock made because Pete was out of his rabbit-ass mind. I'd seen him go ham on females, men, and even grandmas. A filter never existed when it came to him attacking a muthafucka.

Pete was like a mangy mutt, especially when he'd gone off them pills. But I was not worried about him laying one of his psychopathic fingers on me. If he kept staring or making threats, though, I would put a bug into my daddy's ear that'd have him murked. Matter of fact, I might do that anyway just to get rid of his irking ass. My hate for Pete Rock was through the roof.

After a few more seconds of staring me down with his nose flared, Pete flicked me the finger and mouthed the word "bitch" before walking away. I watched his booty closely to see if it switched or jiggled with his steps, instead of checking him for calling me out of my name. I swore he had more female tendencies than I did.

First kicking it in the store for a few minutes, Street and Pete Rock finally walked out, continuing their conversation in front of it. I rolled my window back down a little on the sneak tip so I could try ear hustling. I wanted to know what they were saying.

As expected, Pete had my name in his mouth, hating. He wanted Street to "put me back into the playpen" so they could shoot some moves. His words and not mine. I had to sit on my hands, bite my lip, and close my eyes as tight as I could to keep from jumping out and going ham on Pete. Like I said, I had no qualms when it came to saying I hated Street's lackey.

My boo put him in his place before sending him away with a mouthful received about minding his business, not ours. On the inside, I was grinning like a kid. If Street was taking up for me, he and I must've been as serious as I hoped we were. When he turned to walk my way, I hurried and dropped my head into my phone, acting like I was all in the gossip on a celebrity blog site.

"Here." He opened the door, handing me the plastic bag with our stuff in it from the store, then slid in. "I was gonna take you back to the crib and see those pics you sent in person, but there's been a change of plans. I've gotta trail this nigga while he makes a few runs."

I smacked my lips hard, twisting all the way around in my seat to face him. "Are you serious with me right now? Is that nigga my age or something? He can't never say nothing to me about being a baby if he need you to trail behind him like a fuckin' little boy," I snapped, disappointed because I didn't want to part ways with Street so soon.

"Whoa, whoa, whoa! Chill out with all that rah-rah shit, P. I ain't with the drama, and you know that." He called himself putting me in my place.

"And I'm not trying to go home." I huffed and puffed again, gearing up for a full-blown tantrum. "I hate when you put other people before me, Street. Like you tried to do with that Jamika trick. I hate it. I hate it. I hate it!" I fussed, stomping my foot like a little kid.

Street flipped on me, exposing a side of him I'd never
seen. Reaching over the console, he covered my mouth
with his hand, then forced me to lean back in the seat. My
breathing deepened when he put his face close to mine.

"You better give your daddy a hug and kiss when you
see him. If it weren't for that nigga Cal, you'd have the
imprint of my hand across your face instead of it over
your mouth. Now make the decision to either chill the
fuck out or get the fuck out and walk home. I won't be
saying 'calm down' again." Uncovering my mouth, he
leaned back over the console, staring at me.

I stared back at him, trying to figure out how to play
my next move. Even though I wanted to go ham and
give him a taste of what I'd learned from my momma, I
sucked up my ego and sat still. However, this was the last
time I'd be on record as bowing out gracefully. The shit
was killing me to be quiet and compliant. Turning the car
back on, he cranked the radio up on full blast and started
rolling a blunt. Me not being the focus of his attention
was really pissing me off.

Street ended up getting me a bottle of water, a Sprite,
and a half-pint of apple Cîroc. I cracked the liquor
open and called myself guzzling it straight down from
the rim. Taking it like an amateur, I almost choked as
it burned my throat, and I only managed to swallow a
few mouthfuls. I was grumpy as hell over him not caring
about me being grumpy as hell, so much so that I sipped
another mouthful, this time only choking on the burn a
little bit.

"I see you over there in that passenger seat trying to be
grown and shit. You know good and damn well you can't
handle liquor yet, so slow it down," Street said, reaching
over and taking the bottle from my hand. "And you can
fix your spoiled-rotten attitude, by the way, P. I'ma let
you ride with me to take care of business," he gave in,

lighting his blunt. "But as soon as we hit the freeway, drop ya head in my lap. I ain't trying to hear you talkin' the whole ride to the east."

I smiled, glad to be getting what I wanted. All I was trying to do was be by Street's side and prove I was the girl for him. He had a few chicks down to ride, Jamika being the ring leader of the rat pack, so I was about to make my time with him most memorable. It wasn't enough that I was the daughter of Calvin and Trinity, because he wasn't fuckin' with my parents. Holding my own was what mattered in the grand scheme of thangs. As soon as he said to drop it, I was going to fill my mouth up with spit and give his sexy ass the wettest and sloppiest blow job a girl had ever blessed him with. Just like the freak did on the porno.

Pete Rock had to grab the packs he was selling before we could head east. I was apprehensive as hell about going on the block even though my dad wasn't supposed to be there trappin'. He'd kill both me and Street with his bare hands if he found out about our secret relationship. Me for fuckin' the help and Street being disloyal. I was his most prized possession and wasn't supposed to be touched by a nigga from the hood. If I could be honest, my dad was foolish as hell for thinking I wouldn't get sprung on a thug when it was the only type of man I knew.

"Hey, do ya mans a solid real quick and re-bag these couple of bundles," Street addressed me before tossing one of the Ziploc bags I'd just filled up with baggies earlier into my lap. I wasn't sure what he meant.

"Huh? Re-bag 'em? What's wrong with the way they're already bagged up? Me, my dad, and Fame ain't make no mistakes when we was weighing and packaging them. I can do that shit in my sleep," I bragged on my trapping abilities. I didn't care how many girls threw themselves at Street. I was the only one who could match his level when it came to hustling. He never seemed to give me my props, and this time was no different.

Blowing out all the smoke he'd just sucked in, he threw his hands up, frustrated. "Damn, why yo' ass just can't do what you're told?"

"All right, all right, just forget I even asked," I backed down, not wanting to argue.

"Naw, this shit needs to be spoken on before we go any further. When I tell you to do something, do it simply because I said so. I don't give a fuck how you and your daddy run thangs. That's y'all dynamic, and that ain't got shit to do with me." He laughed, showing his true colors. "You gonna either be my girl or a daddy's girl. You can't be both, li'l P."

Sinking farther down in my seat, I looked at Street with a closed mouth and wide eyes. I was itching to pop off on his ass for disrespecting me and my daddy like it wasn't shit. I felt slightly sick to my stomach. Here we were, not far from the house I was brought home to as a baby, with the dope that provided for me and my family in my lap, next to a disloyal nigga who basically worked for me but I was emotionally wide open for. Yup, super complex . . . and messed up!

If it weren't for my family, Street wouldn't eat, but I fell back and played the role of a basic bitch. I knew better, and it was tearing me up on the inside to be acting so dumb. The game was fucking me raw dog and without remorse. To soften the blow to my ego, I kept telling myself that following his lead was part of the territory of being his girl. I thought this was what my momma meant about me finding out when it was too late that I was young and dumb.

"Well, what's your answer? I ain't got all day." Street put me on the spot, blowing another cloud of smoke in my face.

I refused to verbally say I was going against the grain. That meant I should've jumped out of his car and walked home like fuck him. That didn't happen, though. Instead, I slid on a pair of surgical gloves, then opened the Ziploc bag I'd personally sealed earlier. Street stopped staring when I started moving the rocks from one baggie to the next.

Whereas my dad's baggies were green, the ones Street had me putting the dope in were miniature manila envelopes stamped with the word "Thriller." It didn't take a fool to figure out what Street was doing. He was slanging my dad's product as his own. It took me approximately seventeen minutes to help a muthafucka come up off my flesh and blood's back. This was the type of dick-sprung shenanigans my momma warned me about.

After I finished putting all the tiny envelopes in the Ziploc bag, Street gave it to Pete Rock and then told me to hop out and throw my dad's no-name baggies into the trash. I snickered to myself, wanting to tell Street that this was the part of the game where he needed to listen to me and get schooled. My daddy didn't have a particular color for his baggies or a name that he called his product because those things were easily traceable. Cal wasn't about to give the cops puzzle pieces for them to make a picture out of, and now that I was in the position to see things done differently, I completely understood my dad's logic. Even knowing better, I continued playing dumb.

I had not gotten my lips wrapped around the rim of the Cîroc bottle before Street was back at my head. "Oh, you can drop that bottle and throw that mouth in my circle in my lap. Don't act like you forgot." He reminded me of the sexual favor he'd bluntly requested.

Being that I'd just been disloyal to my dad, which meant my mom and Benzie too, I really wasn't thinking about anything sexually related. Matter of fact, the thump in my panties had completely vanished without me even noticing. However, when he reached over and grabbed the back of my neck and started lowering my neck, I sprang into action.

CHAPTER 11

PORSHA

Glad to be up for air, I wiped my mouth and tried fixing my messy bun from where Street was grabbing in my hair. It was no use. No longer was my hair cute, but a bunch of flyaway strands ruffled on top of my head. Combing it up with my fingers into a basic ponytail was the best I could do.

My mouth game had him swerving and flooring the gas pedal more than a couple of times. All that did was make me lock down and lick on it more. He swore he was a boss ass nigga with his big mouth wanting to control a bitch, but all that mouth did for miles west to east was moan my name. Street was lovin' the shit! My edges were on fire from him holding on to my strands for dear life.

Sitting back in my seat, I took a sip of the Cîroc again, then put it underneath the seat so I could stay alert. I felt uneasy as hell riding through the east. It was unfamiliar territory to me. From the many stories I'd heard, muthafuckas didn't hold 'em up around these parts. And just from the stance and glare of niggas I saw in passing, wasn't none of the venomous stories I heard lies. Shady was an understatement for how these dudes were out here looking. I didn't even blame Pete Rock for wanting Street to follow him at this point. The area we were bending blocks in looked worse than our hood, and that was saying a lot.

Street was in serious mode with his jaw locked, his stare game on steroids, and his eyes moving back and forth around the angles of his car. Never seeing him this focused, I could easily tell he was just as uncomfortable as I was. Seeing him seeming to question his control made the butterflies in my stomach swarm around even faster. Either that or the liquor wasn't mixing well with the leftovers remnants of pizza I'd managed to eat earlier.

Street didn't even put the car in park when Pete made his first two stops. The third stop was what had my young head slightly fucked up, though. Pete pulled on the side of a gas station that looked like a death trap. Half of the pumps had signs covering them, saying they were out of order, and half of the overhead lights weren't working. The ones we'd parked underneath spooked me by flickering every few seconds. It was like some shit out of a scary movie. In the scene I was in, there were two dudes posted up like this was the hangout spot: one sitting on the trunk of a Tempo that was on bricks near the alleyway, and the other right beside him but standing up. They were in the middle of a conversation and sharing a cigarette when we'd arrived, but dropped all that, making us the center of attention shortly afterward.

Click-clack.

That was the sound of Street loading a bullet into the chamber. I had not even seen him whip his gun out from the holster on his hip.

"What the fuck?" I blurted out before I could catch myself.

"Be chill, P. This ain't shit but protocol. You see how cruddy them niggas lookin'." He called 'em right.

"No doubt I do."

Pete Rock hopped out of the car and walked over to the two dudes. After exchanging a few words, he waved at the car for Street.

"Slide down and reach underneath your seat for my extra pistol. If you see one of these dusty muthafuckas go to draw, send some fireworks their way," he commanded, sliding his pistol into the waistband of his jeans instead of in the holster. "Make sure your aim is on point, by the way."

Before I could respond, Street was out of the car and heading over to them. I did as I was told, but not before cracking the window some so I could hear what was said. I might've ridden shotgun and been the watch girl for my mom and dad before, but never with a gun in my hand with orders to shoot if need be. I didn't know if this was a test to see if I was thuggish enough to be his girl, but I was gonna pass with flying colors if it was, I guessed.

"These the cats I was telling you 'bout earlier," Pete Rock told Street. "Nuggs and Lenny."

"Yo, what up doe?" Street greeted them how Detroit niggas greeted one another. From east to west, the lingo was the same. How the two sides banged, however, was totally different.

Nuggs nodded and remained silent, while Lenny gave Street a plain and simple reply. Immediately after that, my finger started sliding up and down the handle of Street's pistol. I didn't like the way Nuggs was looking. I didn't know if Street peeped his ill-mannered demeanor, but not shaking his hand or speaking was a red flag of disrespect. Still and all, the conversation continued.

"Pete says y'all be moving units around here." Street's statement was open-ended for them to answer.

Once again, Nuggs fell back, and Lenny answered. "You heard right."

"Good, 'cause I've got some units that need to be moved. The first run can be a seventy-thirty split, but sixty-forty thereafter. Does that sound like some shit y'all willing to float with?" Street was straight to the point, which was good because I didn't like the unsettling vibe I was catching from Nuggs.

The whole time Street was breaking down the proposition to sell baggies under him, Lenny was focused on the particulars, and Nuggs was throwing looks back and forth between me and Pete Rock. Speaking of him, he must've blown a blunt or popped a pill on the ride over, because he was looking spaced out and cross-eyed. It was a good thing I was here to watch Street's back, 'cause his partner in crime sho' as hell wasn't suited up for the meeting among men.

"Yo, fuck all the particulars of ya little contract if ya product ain't hittin' like fire," Nuggs finally spoke out, making my skin crawl. Lighting a cigarette, he leaned back on the Tempo and kicked his foot up on the bumper. "So, boss," he laughed, being blatantly disrespectful again, "what that work be like?"

"It be that type of work that'll feed some hungry-ass niggas. It be that type of work that'll keep diapers on some bastard baby's ass. It be that type of work that'll make eviction notices go away. Ya feel me?" Street sounded just like Calvin did in the streets, which should've been the case since he'd been shadowing my dad for years. He was calm but going hard.

A lump settled in my throat when the thought of Street's deception reemerged. I didn't let it choke me up, however, seeing that I was in the middle of a drug transaction that I had to make sure I got out of. Gripping the pistol's handle, I was ready to go full throttle if need be. Street had bested Nuggs and was standing firm in his face without blinking. I held my breath.

Turning his head, Nuggs blew out his cigarette smoke before looking Street up and down. "I hear you talking, but um, ya words better be adding up on the back end of thangs. The first bad I review I get on ya product, you can bring ya red-bottom-shoe-wearing ass back 'round here to pick it back up. And no matter what, I does seventy-thirty. Take it or leave it."

"Leave it," I whispered, almost too loud. After I said it, I bit my lip, hoping none of them heard. Since they didn't look my way, I figured I was safe to keep ear hustling.

"Your cockiness is admirable, but my contract, as you call it, ain't flexible." With or without Pete Rock, Street was holding his own.

Nuggs opened his mouth to say something I'd never know, because Lenny jumped in and accepted my man's offer. "I'll get at Pete after the units are moved. We're good with sixty-forty after this, chief."

"You do that, and holla at ya nigga before we meet again. I ain't for all that back-and-forth bullshit. Pete, give them they work and let's be out." Now the one feeling cocky, Street turned his back and walked back toward the car.

I didn't take my eyes off Nuggs until he was completely out of sight. There was so much I wanted to tell Street, but I chose to remain quiet, given my experience with opening my mouth and getting cursed out about it.

Taking a sip of my drink, I let the concoction soothe all the built-up tension riding shotgun with Street had created. My momma was a straight gangsta for being my dad's partner in crime for all these years. It was a thrill for me being a kid in the back seat, yet hella intense experiencing a similar experience as an adult with a role to play.

"You good, P?" Street asked, finally caring about my mood.

"Yeah, I guess I'm as good as I'm gonna be. I wouldn't fuck with that nigga Nuggs, though." I couldn't help blurting my opinion out.

"See, that's how you supposed to have ya man's back—with your mouth closed and your eyes wide open. That means you were watching like I told you to. I got shit under control, though, li'l P. The only thing you gotta worry about for the rest of our time together tonight is how you gonna take this dick."

He didn't have to say a word more.

On our way headed to the hotel of my choice, I danced in my seat, popped my tits out for him to feel on, and let him flick my clit. I even tried bending back over into his lap for a repeat blow job, but he said he wanted to save his nut until I was sprawled across the bed. As I was mentally sprung off this nigga, Street was like my keeper at this point. He could and would get whatever he liked. Real talk, he already was.

"You got a nigga feeling ripe. I'ma stroke that pussy to sleep," his dirty-talking ass was turning me on.

I giggled. "That's on you, nigga. I've got Kryptonite in my pussy." The alcohol was talking for me, but I liked what it had me saying. My hopes were to lock him down for good after throwing this virgin pussy on him once. Anything else would be a smack in the face.

Street claimed he was waiting for me to turn 18 before we had sex. I kept showing him articles on Google that proved my case of me being of legal age, but he kept calling it a setup created by the system. Him not taking me up on my offer to give him some pussy told me he was getting it elsewhere. He fa'damn sho' wasn't being celibate. All that did was make me want to put it on him more, especially since he was finally breaking his rule. The second after I gave him my virginity, he was gonna be exclusive to me from all the hoes he'd allowed to be privileged. I couldn't wait until we pulled up to the hotel.

CHAPTER 12

TRINITY

"Hey, Trin, honey. Are you enjoying yourself tonight?" Nette questioned, ready to take my order.

"Yup, yup. The DJ has been doing his thang since I hit the floor," I replied, wiping a few beads of sweat off my forehead. "I can't wait until Calvin comes back in from with Fame so we can start back up right where we left off."

"Okay, okay! I heard that. I saw you and your hubby out there cuttin' a rug. You don't be playing about keeping his attention." Nette called out the obvious.

"Hell naw, I don't. You already know how I'll get down on a broad." Nette had been a witness to more than a few of my wild attacks.

"Yeah, I know it. But what can I get for you, babe?"

"I know this sounds crazy, but lemme get one wing with a whole lot of lemon pepper and extra chicken crack," I joked about their special seasoning. "Y'all got a better hustle than me and Cal."

"Everybody gotta eat, and don't nothing sound funny about making money, boo." Nette laughed, then filled my order. "That'll be a buck."

Every Friday, they had fish fries jumping, and every Sunday, they cooked soul food meals. Nette and her people were the point of contact whenever there was a hood function, church function, or even when a lazy homemaker didn't wanna cook. When she pulled out a

wad of cash to peel my change from, it confirmed just
how profitable their grind really was. I took my fried
chicken, then tilted my head and hand to Nette, giving
her my utmost respect. It wasn't nothing for me to pay
homage, just like it wasn't nothing for me to teach a ho
how to pay me mine.

With Calvin outside with Fame, I was about to make
my move. Picking up the neck of a Sutter Home wine
bottle, I waltzed my fine ass right across the room toward
ol' girl while tearing up a piece of chicken. I wasn't the
type of bitch who barked but didn't bite. Being that I
killed my daddy, anybody in the whole wide world could
get it, particularly the bitch my husband lay down with.
Without a doubt, Cal was wrong for cheating on me and
making her an issue in the first place. But that still didn't
stop my obsession for hating her. I know that I was
gonna have to get over him cheating, why he did, how
it made me feel, and so forth at some point. But tonight
wouldn't be that night.

Halfway across the hall, the music stopped abruptly.
The loud static from the speakers made us jump. I then
froze, keeping the bottle behind my back and making
sure to move with the people around me so ol' girl watching couldn't square up with a weapon like me. At the
same time, I looked to see what was going on along with
everyone else. I also finished my piece of chicken and
dropped the bone to the floor. It had been so tasty that I
wanted to run across the room and order enough to take
home. Some other shit was about to happen, however.

The DJ was talking to the owner of the banquet hall,
Mr. Marciano. I'd just given him a deposit on this place
last week for Porsha's eighteenth birthday party. Unlike
that day, when he was pleasant and smiling very profes-
sional-like, Mr. Marciano's face was ripped, and he was
yelling, but I couldn't tell what he was saying.

"Party over! Gunshots have been fired outside. You ain't gotta go home, but you gotta get the fuck outta here," the DJ yelled into his microphone.

There wasn't a body in the room that didn't scramble. I was included in that count, but for a whole different reason. I wasn't leaving this banquet hall without hollering at ol' girl. I was true to my word. This problem would've been heading her way whether she'd been gawking at me all night or not. Come to think of it, she might've been scrutinizing my moves as a way of watching her back. Whatever the case might've been, Calvin was right in saying "luck runs out," because hers had.

Sliding between a clan of girls, when I barged through the last two, I came out swinging the wine bottle at ol' girl's face.

Wop!

I'd heard through the grapevine that Calvin got her teeth replaced after I knocked them out. I dared his ass to pay for a muthafuckin' stich behind this bottle crackin' her face open. Her eerie screams filled the banquet room.

"Stupid, mutt-face, home-wrecking ass, fallback pussy, trash bucket! As hard as you been watching me, you should've seen it coming. I'ma tell you again, dummy, it ain't gonna be a time a problem won't come yo' way when you see me. Checkmate!" I was feeling real cocky. Standing firm in my pumps, I wanted to grab another bottle and break the glass in her face again. The celebratory feeling was short-lived, however.

Her girl, who'd I'd underestimated, charged at me like a bull. She was dominating me at first by pushing me backward and into tables. After getting damn near thrown over the first one, I regained myself, then attacked her back like I was trying to give her a death date. It was admirable that she was trying to be a savior for her girl, but she wasn't part of our beef and wasn't above catching it either. Therefore, so be it. Who was I not to give a bitch her fate?

I wouldn't take all the credit. The two of us had set off pandemonium within the banquet hall. People were already off the chain about shots being fired outside. Now they were falling over one another, not knowing whether to run, duck, or what because me and ol' girl's homegirl were going head up. I ain't gonna lie and say she wasn't loading me up with a few strong shots, but I literally had my bare foot on her throat by the end of it.

The shit was crazy how it all went down. Calvin's ex jump-off tagged herself back into the match and made shit even worse than it already was for them both. I'd already blacked out to an "I don't give a fuck, let's rumble, wait until I get to my purse" mind zone. She wasn't nothing but dead weight to her homegirl, but she was an advantage to me. With a bloody face and stammering steps, she was in the way as her friend tripped and fell over her to the floor. That was when I got my muthafuckin' bop it on again and swung a chair like Babe Ruth at both of their asses. I couldn't draw a W for the win until I left one of 'em limping at least.

Feeling someone's hands on my shoulders, I turned around, swinging and yelling. "Get yo' hands up off me! Where my husband? Where's Calvin Jackson at?"

"Sis, yo, come the fuck on and up off the bitch. Cal is by the door waiting. There were some niggas shooting outside, and we got to busting too! Let's go," Fame shouted at me, snapping me out of the bitter trance I was stuck in.

I had not given the DJ announcing the gunshots a second thought with my bitterness for ol' girl taking over. I ain't have time to feel foolish, though. I kicked her neck back as I took off toward the exit, grabbing my purse.

I had my pistol out with one in the chamber aimed in front of me when the outside air hit my face. For every bullet I heard, I shot back, because that was what I was supposed to do. Ride or die: that was the type of life you lived when you signed up for the dope game. I knew the rules and played them well. For the hell of it, and because I could be extra petty, I put two bullets into ol' girl's windshield. I remembered her car and plate from whipping up in her driveway that day.

Calvin started cursing me out as soon as I jumped into the front seat. Apparently, people told him and Fame I was in there scrapping as they ran for their cars to get out of dodge. He wanted to know, rightfully so, what would make me do some shit so unthinkable. My response was simple, because he did some absurd shit by cheating on me.

"Yo' ass is psychotic, Trinity! The first thing you think about doing is busting a nothing-ass trick over the head with a bottle when you hear gunshots are being fired outside? You didn't think you needed to see if ya husband was good? Basically, you was just like fuck me." Calvin felt some type of way, evidently. He'd said a mouthful, but I didn't care about one word. He still wasn't getting the point.

I smacked my lips. "Come on now, Cal. You know that trick was irking me all night. And you had to have known I was gonna walk up on her once you and Fame went outside. Now was it like fuck you intentionally? Of course not. However, you can quit trying to read me and drive. You ultimately created the monster that came out of me anyway. So I'm not about to be berated about it," I popped back at him, nonchalant about the shootout. Me, him, and Fame were in the car and alive without wounds. My family was good, so I was good. He should've been too.

"Both of y'all are crazy as hell," I heard Fame interject from the back seat more to himself than to us, but too bad because I heard it anyway.

"Oh, um, you can shut all the way the hell up, Fame. Ain't neither of us talking to you, so don't insert yourself into this conversation. Okay? Thanks," I rudely cut into him, never giving him a chance to respond one way or the other. He didn't have a choice anyway. If he didn't like how I laid it to him, he could get out of the truck and find his way to wherever.

Fame was fam. I loved him like the brother my mother didn't have. And I'd probably apologize tomorrow. Matter of fact, I was sure I would. Yet and still, tonight I was infuriated, and it was whatever the fuck when it came to how I served it. The alcohol, the weed, and me going head up with two hoes had me amped and feeling myself, quite frankly.

"Wow, sis, my bad. Damn, you just slammed yo' bro like I'm some sucka-ass nigga, but it's cool. I didn't mean you no harm. I see you're in rare form, so I'ma be on silent mode 'til y'all drop me off at the crib." Fame took a cop without hesitating, then tried rubbing me on my shoulder to calm down.

"Getcha hands up off me, Fame. I know you chill. I know you love me, too. But ya bro got me fucked up and in a helluva mood. Speaking of that, hurry up and get me home, Calvinnnnn." I carried out the last consonant of his first name, making my husband even angrier than he already was.

"You on that petty shit, Trin. Quit talking to Fame sideways before I pop off on yo' ass in a real rude way. That nigga saved me from catching some hot ones. He was outside pushing me to the side and busting shots at the same time while you was in there fighting a broad over some dick."

"Fame might deserve an apology, but you don't. So quit campaigning, Cal. Fuck you."

He swerved, then reached over the console and grabbed me up by the material of the dress I was wearing. I was shocked quiet. Fame yelled for Calvin to get a grip and drive, and Calvin growled for me to say another word so he could rip my neck off. I knew when to shut up. I nodded and fell back. Tonight, he'd mysteriously get some laxatives in the food he was gonna have me cook since we couldn't make the usual restaurant stop. I ain't gotta always announce when I was getting retribution. I practiced moving in silence with and without Calvin.

CHAPTER 13

PORSHA

And just like that, my virginity was a blurred memory. "Damn, you sure as hell worked my young ass out." I could barely speak as Street rolled off my body. My legs felt like spaghetti strings, and my heart was racing faster than dough boys running from the Feds. If I wasn't in love, my tingling pussy sure was feeding my heart lies. You could call me young and dumb. Fuck it, I was. I'd be that and more for this grown-ass nigga.

All the porno watching in the world couldn't have prepared me for the sex session Street and I just came out of. My young ass had not been ready. But he'd thugged, fucked, and taken me like a savage. I was now a grown-ass woman. And from the way my body was feeling, I wished I had given him my innocence sooner. His stroke game had me dizzy. I couldn't wait to tell Imani about my first time.

"Yeah, and as long as you keep it tight for me, I'ma keep working it out. The wetter the better." He laughed, wiping his manhood off with a towel from the hotel.

Chewing at my bottom lip, I giggled, blushed, and grinned. I liked it when Street talked nasty to me. Staring up at the ceiling, I swore I saw stars. There weren't any rose petals, candle flames flickering, or soft love music playing in the background when his first stroke broke my virginity, but he'd surely fucked me into a fantasy.

Wasn't nothing about nothing on my mind but cuddling up closer to him.

Tossing his shirt to the side of the mattress, he lay back on the pillow, then pulled my head down to rest on his chest. "It's sexy as hell that you've got your own hair, P," he said, touching my scalp. "It means you won't be in my pockets for no bundles."

"Yeah, whatever. Thanks for the compliment. But bundles or not, I still like my shit done once a week."

"Well, if you keep ridin' with a nigga and holding me down like you did earlier, you ain't gonna have time to get ya hair done. I'm gonna be busy fuckin' it up. I love a down-ass bitch. That shit turns me on."

"Oh, well, in that case, let's ride to the east one more time before you drop me off." I was playing but knew he'd get the point. "But for real, if you have my back, I'll have yours too, Street."

I smiled, seeing myself waking up and falling asleep doing this every day. In my mind, this was what real couples did. I couldn't wait until I was grown so I could do this all day and night.

Half my body was draped across him with my moist vagina pressed against his side. Street's breaths started deepening when I started rubbing on his manhood again. As soon as I touched it, it hardened up, and pre-cum started oozing from the tip of it. Just like he'd told me to stroke it earlier, nice and slow, but with a firm grip, I was gonna be a pro in no time. Now that I'd gotten a taste of dick, I didn't think I was gonna ever get enough. I went down to taste it, but he pulled me up with something else in mind.

"Shiiiiiit, roll over and brace ya'self up on ya elbows. I'ma spread that fatty and climb up in that one mo' time."

"Hmmm, do it then, daddy." I was quick to roll over and prop myself up. Biting my lip, I buried my face in the pillow while he started tickled my booty hole with his finger. Never when I watched the porno earlier did I think I'd be letting him play anally, but I was. Still, though, I squirmed, slightly uncomfortable with the feeling.

I let Street do his thing. I wasn't about to give him a chance to complain or bounce from this hotel room sooner than we had to. The view of the Detroit River along the boardwalk and Canada was really nice. I really wanted to do it in the window. After a few more sips of Cîroc and maybe his Rémy, maybe I'd work up the nerve.

"Tell me you want some more of this monster, girl." Replacing his finger with his stiffness, he ran the tip of it up and down the slit of my booty. Street was obviously an ass man, because he had not paid too much attention to my breasts.

"I wa . . . want some mor . . . more." My lips vibrated as I spoke. I couldn't speak in a straight sentence if I wanted to.

"You want it up in you now?" Rubbing his finger gently up and down my walls, he then tapped on my clit, which drove me insane. He was stimulating me in too many ways at the same time.

It felt like electricity was flowing through my veins. I threw my head back and moaned, feeling hot all over. "Yes, yes, yes," I shouted my response, panting from a simple touch. "Oh my God, yes!" So far, what I'd learned was that sex felt good, and so did getting teased. I was ready to climb up the wall. If he weren't gripping my hips like a wino does to a whiskey bottle, I probably would've.

"You wanna feel it raw? I know I do. I wanna see how warm and wet ya pussy can really get around this muthafucka." Street wasn't playing fair. The tip of his dick was already pushing its way inside of me without a condom on it.

I started wriggling so it wouldn't go in, but not enough for him to think I didn't want him sexing me at all. "Stop, no. I don't wanna get pregnant," I finally spoke out with some sense after catching my breath from panting.

"I'ma pull out," he promised, a lie my dad said all niggas told.

Going forward with what he wanted to do, he pushed it halfway in. I gulped a big ol' gulp. My pussy muscles contracted on their own, letting Street know that I liked it in spite of my mouth saying otherwise. With him pushing it in slowly, one centimeter at a time, and me easing away like a crippled snail, Street and I were having peek-a-boo sex.

Even though Trinity wouldn't necessarily approve of me having sex, she didn't keep me shaded from the details of how boys and men talked good games. I got schooled about hormones, sex, and even how boys got wet dreams about girls when they hit puberty. She wanted me to know how frisky they really were so I'd know how savage-like they'd be when it came to some real poo-poo kitty.

What she didn't lecture me on was that my whole body would sync up with a nigga once I felt him raw. I didn't know how good my juices felt on Elvin, but feeling his dick with a condom on it fa damn sho' had me about to pass out. It did feel different. In a very good way. It was hard to pull away, but when he slammed into me, howling because I twerked and it squirted, I reached back, pushing him out.

"Naw, you can get preggers off of pre-cum, nigga. You can hit this again, but you gotta put a condom on," I demanded.

For the first time tonight, I'd spoken up for myself. The thought of Trinity's reaction if things went far wrong and I did get knocked up pushed me to make sure the accident didn't happen. Even if I was 18 by the time I delivered the news, she'd calculate from my due date back to the gestation date and deliver her own grandchild on site. She'd make me miscarry, then pour me a drink to drown my sorrows in.

Bzzz! Bzzz! Bzzz!

When I heard my phone vibrating, the grip he had on me didn't mean shit. I jumped damn near to the ceiling. I knew it was one of three people, because the only other person who called my phone had his hand on my behind.

"A'ight, I'll throw a rubber on. Get back over here." He tried pushing me back down and raising my cheeks back up.

Bzzz! Bzzz! Bzzz!

"Get off of me, Street! Back up! It's either my dad or mom calling." I was panicked.

He grunted, then fell back on the bed. I paid him no mind. I leaned over, scared to look at my phone for good reason because it was my mom. I was praying I didn't pick up the phone to her saying she was home. In a rush to get booed up with Street, I had not even thought about Trin and Cal getting home early and finding Imani and Benzie there without me.

Bzzzz!

With a shaking hand, I finally slid the bar over, answering the call. "Hey, Ma," I muttered, half groggy for the play off.

"Wake yo' ass up to open the door when me and your father get home. Some fools were shooting outside of the cabaret. We're on our way dropping Fame off now." Her words sent me in a frenzy.

"Okay, Ma, okay." Panicking, I leaped out of the bed and started putting my clothes on. I was so nervous and rushed to get out of the hotel room that I'd slipped on my shorts inside out. "Street, come on and get up! I've gotta get home like five minutes ago," I yelled at him.

He grunted, then climbed out of bed, still jacking his dick. "This is what the fuck I get for fucking with a kid. You either gonna take this nut while I'm speed racing you home, or I'ma hit Jamika up."

"Nigga, don't play with me," I yelled even louder. "Cumming is the last thing you need to worry about. If you don't get me back to the crib, Calvin is gonna kill me after making me watch him kill you. And if you call Jamika, I'ma make good and damn well I tell my daddy you popped my cherry." I didn't care how much of an immature little girl I sounded like. I was serious about throwing both of us underneath the bus if he called my nemesis after dropping me off.

I saw how he was looking at me, like I was disloyal by nature, so I paused and corrected him. "Well, I don't know what the hell you expect me to do. If it's fuck me, it's only right for it to be fuck you, Street." I put things into perspective.

In response to my reasoning, Street cut me a menacing expression I'd never seen him give anyone other than cats in the street. I felt like I'd said the wrong thing, or he'd taken it the wrong way, but I wasn't taking a word of it back because I could and would drop a dime on him if he called Jamika. I said what I meant, so he ought to respect it.

He finally broke the cold stare with words. I was sure they weren't the ones he really wanted to say. "Bring ya ass, little girl," he growled, sneak dissing me like Pete Rock. Swooping his keys off the nightstand, he put the blunt I'd snuck from my mom's room behind his ear. It had not even been lit.

Walking out with his jeans on, no drawers, and putting his white undershirt over his head, the thought crossed my mind about him calling Jamika for real, and my mood got sour. He wasn't shit for throwing the comment into the air after I'd just given him my virginity. It haunted me our whole silent ride to the place he'd picked me up at. Although I'd been texting back and forth with Imani that I was on my way, as well as asking her if anything happened that I needed to know about, my mind was too caught up in Street playing me like a random bitch to truly think straight.

After breaking every law put in place about speeding, yielding, and abiding by traffic lights, Street pulled up to the same spot he'd picked me up from, then looked over at me like I repulsed him. "What the fuck are you waiting on? I got you back on time, right? Now you ain't gotta go snitching to ya daddy." This time, his words were probably dead on as to what he was thinking.

I smacked my lips. "Stop tripping, Street. You are the one who said you'd call that thirsty, broke ho. That was wrong, especially since we just had sex for the first time," I explained, hoping he'd stop being a baby about the situation. I saw my mom was right: a nigga's age didn't make him grown.

"Yeah, whatever, li'l P. Like I said, hop on out and get on home. We oughta be good, so I don't expect to hear shit different from Cal." Street was firm on making me eat my words.

So I did. I didn't have a choice. Racing against time, I had to beat my parents home. Me and Street would have to pick this conversation up later. When I hopped out of the car, I tried saying one last thing. "I'll call you in a few so we can talk. Don't blow up what I said, Street. Not tonight. Not after what just went down between us."

"You should've thought about all that before you got to runnin' ya mouth. Please shut my door. I ain't cuttin' up on you, 'cause I don't wanna give you a reason to tell on me and shit." He had jokes at my expense, several of them. From the screwed-up expression on his face, though, he wasn't playing.

"Street! Don't flip this on me. You mad, fine. But you're the one who brought Jamika up in the first place, not me! You know how I feel about her." I was wasting my time, because he wasn't trying to hear a word I had to say.

"Cool. Close my door, Porsha." He was impatient yet calm, which was irking the shit out of me.

"You better answer and not be making plans with that bitch, Street. I mean it," I barked, then slammed the door, determined to have the last word. Unfortunately, my grandstanding meant nothing.

Elvin did the unthinkable and pulled off.

CHAPTER 14

ELVIN "STREET" THOMAS

No sooner than Porsha climbed out of my passenger seat pissed, Calvin called about the shootout and the moves he wanted to make behind it. He wanted me to inform our crew, make sure I kept my eyes open, and keep my ears to the streets for any buzz about some dudes whipping a red Trailblazer. I was kinda mad that I wasn't still grinding up in his daughter while he called himself runnin' orders to me and being a boss. It was a waste of time listening to his old ass tell me shit I already knew to do.

"Cal, yo, chill." I was cool with it. "Like I told you earlier, I've got shit sewn up and under control. That's what you've got me over here for."

"A'ight then, Street. I hear you. And sometime in the very near future, we'll revisit our earlier conversation. I recognize ya hustle." He was trying to pacify me.

"It ain't no thang, Cal. Holla at me when you're ready. I'll be trappin' and tappin' this trigger finger 'til then." I let him think his li'l manipulation was working. Whether he picked up on it or not, my whole tone and demeanor wasn't as passive as it usually was to him.

"My boy." Calvin sounded proud. "You got it."

"No doubt, C. No doubt at all." Grabbing my cock, I smugly grinned, wondering if he'd sound just as proud knowing his daughter's virgin pussy juice was still drying on its tip.

"Then I'ma pull it in with the fam and holla at you in the morning. Do ya thang." Calvin was mistakenly at ease, a quality he taught me never to feel about another nigga in the game.

"Yup, yup. Holla."

Trust is a weak quality that a man in the game should never portray. Cal and I didn't share the same blood. That was why he never referred to me as his family, but some low-level shit like boy and son. I ain't had nobody but me. I'd looked up to his let-a-nigga-down ass long enough.

The moment I'd stepped foot out of Calvin's house earlier was the moment I stopped needing his confirmation or green lights. I'd gotten tired of being forced to stay stagnant. He wasn't about to control my money, the way I lived, or the way I started my own monopoly in these streets. Too bad for him that he trained me to be a boss instead of a lackey. Even if Nuggs and Lenny didn't come through on that sack or started hustlin' up underneath my reign, I'd still do my own thang. I wasn't worried about coming out on the other side or on top.

As I made a sharp turn on to the block, my cell started jumping again. It was Porsha calling, and when I sent her to voicemail, she texted. Shorty was desperate to get a response from me. The messages went from her apologizing about threatening to bump her gums to her father about us, which I knew she'd never do, to messages about how I ain't shit but a dog because she was salty over me threatening to call Jamika after taking her virginity. Porsha wasn't texting me nothing different from any other broad I'd gotten with who'd slipped up and caught feelings.

Up top, being honest, I knew li'l chicks got emotional about dudes popping their cherry. Even still, I didn't give a fuck and never had. Girls didn't speak out of turn to me just like men didn't, and Porsha's spoiled ass was not on the throne in my life. She could run circles around her aging pops, but I wasn't warranting Porsha to spit reckless to me on no given day. She could play like she was Trinity with her peers and Imani. Just like I'd whipped off on her ass a few minutes ago, I ignored every call and message Porsha was blowing me up with. I'd take her off punishment when absolutely necessary. Maybe like when I needed someone to break down Cal's baggies or when I felt like climbin' up in something tight. As I grabbed at my cock again, my grin got wider. I was feeling mighty arrogant.

Real talk, ego speaking for me or not, I had her exactly where I needed her to be. Especially since I was her first. If anything, my plan was to have her scheming and scamming for me more. She'd already shown me she was down to ride. Since Calvin didn't want to break me off with a chance to expand, his daughter would. Porsha might be a sweet parting gift if she bowed.

I didn't have much of nothing as a kid. The soles of the worn shoes my mom got me from the Salvation Army were superglued down, and the raggedy stitch job she had my arthritic grandma patch up my holey clothes with always came apart. It was the constant teasing and suspensions I received from beating up on my wannabe bullies that turned me into a ferocious nigga. I might've been poor, but my pride was always rich.

Once I earned the title of being the troublemaking boy who'd knock a sucker out, I didn't waste any time building my reputation up as being the kid who'd steal the clothes off your back as well as the shoes off your feet. My momma got tired of cursing other parents out for coming to her house about me. However, when one of the other drunk moms went over her head with a beer bottle because I'd snatched some high-priced frames off her son's face, I spent my last night under her roof. After

I slept on the porch, fanning off insects and with one eye open for ruffians or rodents, I found my permanent place in the streets, becoming an around-the-clock menace to society.

Being a delinquent but getting what I wanted from those a little more fortunate was a better way of life anyway. I broke into houses, robbed old women as they left church Sunday morning, and stole mail from people's mailboxes every first of the month. The backdoor thieves at the scrap yard, who knew I was snatching copper pipes and furnaces up outta damn near every vacant house in the hood, put me on to stealing valuable home furnishings from occupied homes while folks were at work, on family vacations, or even on simple store runs. A slumming nigga like me didn't have a phone, but I had a pair of wire cutters and a back built muscular and strong like an ox. In seventy seconds flat, I'd clip a fence to scrap and be hauling ass with on my back to the yard. I survived, in spite of how I did so. The streets fed me. That was how I got the nickname.

When I was a few months into being a terrorist, Calvin crossed my path. He thought he was using me to his advantage in the streets, yet I was using him to some degree. The dough I made grinding kept me from stealing, moved my notches of respect up, and even had me sitting on a bankroll of cash stashed. As thankful as I was to him for helping me off my knuckles, I couldn't help but bang his daughter off with good dick. There was something about my ego that could never be controlled. That was probably why me and Porsha kept bumping heads.

To some degree, I owed her dad for breeding me to become the man I claimed to be today. Yet and still, I was a muthafuckin' monster at heart. I ain't have no qualms about biting the hand that fed me. That was why I'd so easily concocted the plan to pass off Calvin's product as my own on the east, open up a trap house independent from him, and then have his daughter steal my needed supply from underneath his nose. You can't turn no field rat into a pet.

"What up, nigga? What'chu doing back on the block? I thought you and shorty got a room," Pete Rock questioned as soon as I pulled up on him and some random chick I'd seen him around the hood with.

"I hit that off then dropped her off." I spared him all the details, not in the mood for his opinions on my and Porsha's relationship. Pete was my manz and all, but he didn't need to know why Porsha was so appealing to me.

He cut into me with them anyway. "That nigga Cal gonna have his right-hand goon cut ya dick off if he doesn't put a bullet in ya hard-headed ass himself. You might as well tell a nigga which casket you wanna get buried in for fuckin' with that old man's daughter." Pete Rock stated what I already knew but wasn't trying to hear, especially since I'd just heard an earful of threats from his daughter. I was starting to have a love-hate relationship with the Jackson family.

"What Cal doesn't know won't hurt him." I shrugged Pete's comments off. "I thought we agreed upon that." I spoke in code, reminding him of our side business on the east.

He chuckled. "Yeah, nigga! Whatever! I see you using that shit when it's convenient, but it's all good. I ain't stickin' with ya dick, so let me get up outta ya business."

"That's more like it. I fuck my hoes, you fuck yo' hoes, then we meet in the middle to handle business." I reminded him about how we needed to operate while throwing a cheap line at ol' girl.

He chuckled again, then took another sip of his beer. "Brodie, my nigga, you can say what you wanna say to and about this broad. I ain't her man or protector. I'm her employer. I paid her for some pussy."

I burst out laughing. Ol' girl, however, turned her face up like she was ready to cry. *She had better get some thick skin if she's going to be out here thotting.* I kept my advice to myself, however. She wasn't no family of mine to care about.

"Dog, you nutty as hell, but whatever. What's popping 'round here?" I questioned to get an honest reaction out of Pete before I relayed Calvin's message. I didn't want him thinking too deeply into what he might've seen or the normal bumps of the night.

"Shit, I can't call it, but it's been slow motion since I got back from the east. Muthafuckas probably still at the cab partying and bullshitting," he said.

"Probably so, but they should be 'bout to flood back to the hood in a minute. Cal called not that long ago and said somebody started shooting. They shut the cab down, of course."

"Bet nobody come on the block with that madness! I know that much! My heater stay with one in the chamber while it's on my hip, you cocksuckers," Pete Rock yelled out into the night to no one while pounding on his chest with one fist. Pete was in rare form with his behavior, the exact reason why I watched him with one eye almost all the time. If he wasn't popping pills, he was simply acting crazy 'cause normal wasn't in his blood.

Me and Pete Rock had been friends for years. In elementary school, we ran the playground together and refused to do homework, do chores, or mind our manners when it came to respecting elders. When my fed-up moms set me out, he was the only cat who had my back with what little scraps he was tossed per month by his moms. We were rebels, the best type of hustlers. Our bloodlines were where we differed. My mom drank like a fish, and his mom hit the pipe like she was a welder.

Word on the street was that he was conceived and born off the rock. Although I never cut into him sideways about it, because it wasn't my business, a part of me believed the story because he always showed signs of being kind of slow. If it weren't for me leading the way and bringing him aboard ship to hustle, he probably would've been addicted to the other side of the game like his mom. Regardless of all that, though, Pete had always been one hundred with me and loyal to what we called a friendship, so far, anyway. That was why I'd pulled him in on my plan.

"Yo, Pete, chill the hell out. You can save all that energy for if and when the opportunity presents itself. 'Til then, finish up with ya girl, then meet me in the trap." I gave him his orders, then whipped into the driveway and straight into the garage.

Calvin had his house decked the hell out before he moved to what we all joked was the mansion of the hood. Hate it or not, no families were doing it like the Jacksons. They weren't *The Cosby Show* parents, Trinity and Calvin, but they were two parents still together, raising their kids. If Calvin had taken me in as a son instead of putting me out on the streets, I wouldn't be a beast, turning on him like every other young nigga in the hood was plotting on doing.

Moving throughout the trap, I stashed all the product but a few baggies in a secret spot in the attic ceiling that only me, Pete, and Calvin knew of. The ones I left out were in plain sight and underneath the kitchen sink cabinet. That way, if someone did run in, they'd at least be pacified with a small lick versus nothing at all. In order to survive in the game, ya gotta be able to efficiently think on ya toes. I was always trying to outthink a muthafucka.

Pete had come in and secured the side and back doors with two-by-four wooden slabs. A muthafucka wasn't gonna run in on us without us knowing. If they did, they'd catch bullets galore because every dirty pistol up in here was loaded and ready for firing. On any given day, on guard or not, we kept guns stashed in various places so we'd never get crept on without having a weapon nearby. I'd come from nothing and wasn't letting a cat as hungry as I was take me down.

"What happened to ol' girl?" I questioned Pete as soon as we'd gotten done taking care of business.

"I sent her on her merry way. It ain't take me but a minute." He clowned himself but didn't care. "That's why I only paid her ass ten bucks."

I laughed. "You a fool, Pete."

"Hell yeah, but fuck it." Plopping down on the couch, he tossed me one of the Xbox controllers. "Let me win a ten off you real quick so I can call her ass back. Square up on dis *Madden.*"

CHAPTER 15

CALVIN

As soon as Fame hopped from the back seat to go in his house, I reversed from his backyard, going off on Trinity again. Did she have a legitimate reason for being upset with me? Yes. Had I been disloyal to her by breaking the vows of our marriage? Yes. Should me and shorty I'd stepped out with still be catching heat behind our li'l affair although I'd apologized time and time again? Yeah, I could be a man and admit that as well. A woman scorned ain't never a woman you should try reasoning with, especially when you're the one who caused her heart to ache in the first place. Yet and still, Trinity had chosen a bad time to retaliate.

"Trin, I can't believe you let that insignificant-ass bitch cloud your judgment."

"Calvin, sweetheart, you're not in the position to tell me about my judgment calls," she sarcastically replied. "My bad, because you said y'all was in the middle of a shootout or whatever, but you're not getting any more sympathy than that. So please, please, please stop talking to me," she huffed, threw her hand up, and then got back to rolling up a blunt. "We need to be focused on who was shooting and why. Real talk, yeah, focus on that."

As she antagonized me with a condescending voice, I was itching to pull over and hash it out with my wife, as physical or critical as it might get. Her mouth, although I loved it wrapped around my meat, was too damn vicious at times. It was a great weapon when working against others, but it worked as the force that drove me crazy at the same time.

"Yeah, lemme take yo' advice before I catch a domestic violence case and beat on you like Spade did that girl Jakia."

"Uh-huh, whatever. I know you must be coming down off yo' high and can't function to be talking that asinine bullshit to me, Calvin Jackson. Spade wouldn't have lived through the first night if I had been wearing that poor girl's shoes. I love you, but that's that *Graveyard Love* drama that T.C. Littles writes about. Believe it, and I'm sure you already know it. Let me hurry up and roll this weed up so you can hit it and get ya mind right."

Ring, ring.

"Let that be that ho calling you, and I swear before my Lord, you're gonna drive this vehicle straight to her house," Trinity threatened, getting hyped in her seat.

I was infuriated by my wife's performance tonight. She could have been the government's special weapon in a war, I was sure. She was going hard, but for nothing. "Chill yo' terrorist ass the hell out. That bitch ain't called me since you knocked her teeth down her throat, so you wasting all yo' energy for nothing. I keep telling your silly ass that. It's Fame."

"Oh," she responded nonchalantly, then waved me off with her hand. "Then answer it and leave me alone." Trinity seldom admitted when she was wrong.

Knowing I wasn't going to win the battle with my wife, I rubbed my face, trying to gain my composure, then answered Fame's call. "What up?"

"Yo, that nigga Mack ain't make it. I just got the call a minute ago that the ambulance showed up, but he was pronounced dead before they pulled off. Solider had a son." Fame sounded distraught. "Man, shit is hot out here, so I gotta turn the heat up on my end to make sure I stay living." In the same breath, he was back on some street survival shit.

"I heard that, and I'm with that, but I'ma have to get Trin to hook up a li'l care package for his girl and their li'l one regardless." I heard Trinity smack her lips in the background, being real merciless. I shook my head at her like damn, then tuned back into Fame.

"That'll be what's up. I'ma have my baby momma slide through here real quick and shoot me over there to tell his girl what went down. I know she probably heard the 411 by now, but she needs to know that her nigga was murdered on purpose. Whoever was in the back seat of that Trailblazer whipped out and blasted Mack directly. His murder was intentional."

"A'ight, holla at me when you leave from over there. As you know, Street is already on guard, so the trap is good. Plus, he got his ear open to anyone talking like they know something." I reminded him of the conversation he'd listened in on from the back seat. After Trinity got off the phone calling Porsha, I'd gotten in touch with my crew.

"Fa'sho. We gonna stay good. I'll get at you. If not tonight, in the morning. Peace," he said, and then we ended the call.

It had been a minute since a life from the hood had been claimed. Something in the pit of my stomach told me his was about to be the first of many this summer. That unsettling feeling didn't get to linger for long, though. As soon as I set my phone in the cup holder, Trinity snatched it back out, ready for round three of our argument.

"There better not be one call, text message, correspondence, or picture of anything I didn't approve of, Calvin."

"And if there is?" I taunted her.

"Let's just say Mack won't be the only nigga getting carried by six other niggas in a few days."

PORSHA

"Imani, hurry up and open the door! I'm here," I shouted into the speaker of my phone, then hung it up.

Since Street pulled off, leaving me in the dark and not even making sure I made it home safely by lurking a safe distance behind me, I'd been running like the force was with me all the way home. For one, I needed to beat my parents, and for two, I couldn't get caught on these dark Detroit streets alone. As tough as I thought I was, or Trinity and Calvin actually were, none of their strength or hood cred would matter if I was snatched up by a menacing muthafucka unknowingly. I knew better than to be out here this late without a nigga by my side. But for some reason tonight, I'd been acting all out of character, even before losing my V-card.

Not missing a step and managing not to trip over my feet, I made it up to my porch and through the front door, almost running Imani down, trying to get up the steps. My dad's headlights had turned onto our street when I was just getting on the porch, but he was two blocks down. I knew it was him because of the blaring rap music. My mom and Calvin rode the same way.

"Hurry up, Porsha." Imani was panicking.

"Uh, duh! What do you think I'm doing? Is Benzie in his room asleep? Is there anything I need to know about?" I questioned her real fast.

"Naw, other than a few people knocked and whistled up here for somebody to serve them. They left after a few minutes."

"Cool." I was glad nothing happened. Meaning there was nothing for me to tell Trinity and Calvin.

Ring, ring, ring.

My phone was vibrating across the floor. It was my mom. I knew she was gonna be yelling for me to open the door, but I couldn't until I was out of these smelly-ass clothes. Not only did I smell like weed because we'd been smoking in his car, which already smelled like an ashtray, but I also smelled like like open ass and sex. Not having time to wash my coochie or body, I used a few of Benzie's baby wipes, hoping the powder-fresh scent was enough to mask my unpleasant odor for now. Once my parents were tucked away in their room, hopefully having a drunken lovemaking session of their own, I could take a shower. The only good thing was that I could still smell Street's cologne on me. The quick thought of him made me hope he wasn't still acting like a crab.

"Imani, put these in the bag of clothes I gave you and tie it back up tight," I told her, then tossed my cum-soiled shorts and shirt her way. "I'll get them back before you go home."

She looked like she didn't want to take them, but grabbed them anyway. "You're lucky—"

"And you're lucky I gave you my hand-me-downs. Please don't try it," I snapped at her, even though there wasn't a real reason to. Not only was I in a rush, but I was also caught up in my feelings about how Street was suddenly acting. Imani had not done anything but do me a favor by staying here while I was out being hot. She was catching it simply because I'd caught it, fair or not.

Tonight was all of a sudden on fast forward, but I needed time to slow down so I could get my mind right and process everything. Finally grabbing my phone, I answered before the call went to voicemail. I was sure

Trinity would be coming through the phone if that happened.

"I know you hear us outside honking, and I know I called ya ass twenty minutes ago saying be up and at the door," she went off on me before I said hello. "Did you think I was playing?"

"Naw, Ma. I know you weren't playing, and I'm coming. I had to pee real bad and didn't want to open the trap back up," I lied, rushing toward the front and back down the steps.

"Then you should've squatted on the porch. When I say do something, find a way to make sure it's done. Now please, open up the damn door," she barked, then hung up. Even when using the word "please," Trinity wasn't asking nicely.

CHAPTER 16

STREET

The block was banging hella hard since the shootout shut the cabaret down. People weren't ready to stop partying just because Mack's body got riddled with bullets. Matter of fact, me and my team were slanging baggies left and right quicker than we did on a regular night. We mourned every nigga from the hood the exact same: we'd drink, build liquor-bottle memorials wherever the body dropped, and shoot for the stars while getting high so we could kick it with our homies in the clouds one last time. What we didn't do was sit still dwelling over what another man's struggle was.

Mack wasn't necessarily hated or loved. He didn't slang extra-strong weed or some type of magical fairy dust none of us couldn't get our hands on. He was just a young nigga from the hood who was always in the middle of something. I didn't run with the lame, so I didn't care one way or another about his death. What I did care about, however, was knowing who took Mack's life. I needed to know who was out here murdering muthafuckas to make sure I wasn't next on the list.

Shortly after me and Pete secured the trap and the product that was stashed inside, we'd joined the block party in our own ways. It was a little after two in the morning. I might've been among the hood, but my eyes stayed open to anything out of the ordinary. Wasn't nothing going on but the same ol' same, though. Cars had their radios synced and blasting the same tunes, the drunken dances were taking place, and I smelled nothing but drugs in the air. Even the hot young girls with no parental supervision who'd been too young to attend the cabaret were trotting around looking for trouble. It was too late for Porsha to be around here even if she could have been, but Imani . . . yeah, I was missing her cute and shy self. She always found a reason to be outside in my view when I was serving fiends late at night.

Whereas I was on the porch smoking the blunt Porsha snuck from her mom's stash, Pete Rock was out front being a hypocrite, being entertained by a group of young and tenders. For him to have so many jokes about me fuckin' around with Porsha, he sho' looked thirsty enough to drink from the fountain of youth too. All but one of the shorties dancing around Pete went to school a little more infrequently than li'l P did.

Rae Sremmurd and Nicki Minaj's song "Throw Sum Mo" blasted through the speakers of someone's truck. An oldie by now, it was still right on time. The ladies went crazy but not as crazy as Pete. He started tossing bills like he was a true boss, and in true hood-rat fashion, they all started twerking to see who could get the most of his attention.

I couldn't help but cheer my homeboy on. Instead of joining him, the flock of chicks, and a few of the guys who'd surrounded them for the free show, I sat back, giving Pete his room to shine. Although he was a hustler who always kept a bankroll in his pocket, females didn't usually give him any play because his brain wasn't put together correctly and he'd only last for two minutes, per his own admission. None of that mattered with dollar bills getting tossed in the air. The ten I lost in the *Madden* game to him was the first to fly.

"'I'm throwin' all this money. I'ma fuck around and buy her,'" Pete Rock sang along to Slim Jimmy's verse.

I puffed on the spliff, then looked down at my phone. Porsha was blowing me up by text, but I chose not to even open them. I'd get at her ass after I checked out of the hotel room I wasted my money on. Had I known I wasn't going to get some hours in to wear her out, I would've brought her back to the trap or maybe copped a cheap motel room down on the boulevard instead. I'd spent $200 plus dropped a $100 deposit for twenty minutes of stroke and a couple of nuts.

"Well, well, well, look who's over here acting stingy with his cash." Jamika walked up on the porch, talking smart. "Why aren't you over there with your boy getting wild? Mack's murder got you twisted?"

"Naw, that dude wasn't on my team, so I'm straight. I like to do my thang with the ladies solo-dolo. The real question is, why aren't you over there trying to make a few extra dollars? We all know how you get down," I cut into her. There wasn't any reason to pay her respect if she didn't pay herself any.

"Being that you know how I get down, why haven't you pushed back up on me? I'd be willing to do my thang with you solo-dolo," she cut right back into me.

When I didn't answer fast enough, she used her finger to make a trail down from my chest to my manhood, then tapped on it gently. It was time-out for throwing innuendos. Jamika was trying to drop her panties quick, fast, and in a hurry.

"What's up, Street? You already know what tip I'm on. I've been trying to see what your work is all about, but you be shading a bitch."

Already worked up from banging Porsha's virgin walls a short time ago, I didn't need to flick Jamika's clit for my dick to get hard. I was like an adolescent boy in heat. My manhood was jumping to explode.

"Fuck it. That's on you if you wanna be sore for the next nigga, 'cause I fa' damn sho' ain't about to wife you." I kept it real with her about my intentions. "You gonna suck, fuck, and then be gone. Are you good with that?"

"I wouldn't be over here if I weren't," she nonchalantly replied, shrugging her shoulders.

Picking up my cup of liquor, I led Jamika between the trap house and the vacant house next door. I wasn't about to take her in the spot with money, guns, and product all around, stashed or not. Not only was shorty known around town as a jump-off, but Jamika's reputation also included whispers of her being a setup girl. A few cats from around the way had come up either tied up, randomly targeted, or robbed for their riches. The last nigga she fucked around with got his chain snatched off his neck right after she grabbed the Cartier frames off the bridge of his nose. I was none of those lames, though. I didn't give two fucks about bodying a bitch. The loaded pistol on my hip wasn't for decoration.

As soon as we got between the houses, I ordered her to her knees. The garbage cans were blocking us from being seen by everyone, but it was dark out here anyway. She didn't waste a second proving to me she'd rightfully earned her reputation as a ho. She unzipped my pants, and my hard dick was down her throat and hitting her tonsils before I could finish my joint. She was slurping on a nigga so sloppily that I almost passed out. Resting my head on the brick wall while grabbing hers, I held her still and damn near choked her with all the inches I was feeding her.

Although I had not called Jamika in spite of me throwing her name and probable willingness up in Porsha's face, I was glad she'd shown up in rare form. The petty nigga in me wanted to take a picture of her doin' her thang and send it to li'l P's phone. I was feeling myself.

First, I'd gotten into some virgin pussy, and now I was getting some head from an all-American. Jamika didn't even flinch behind the aftertaste of Porsha's cum. She wasn't gagging, pulling back, or the least bit intimidated by my force.

"You want some ball action, baby?" Jamika questioned, tickling my sac with her fingertips, then running her tongue up and down my shaft.

Before I could answer, she had them in her mouth and was humming. She was gonna end up suckin' the dollars outta my pockets with her skilled ass. Jamika had me shaking. I was anxious to shoot a few babies down her throat.

"Let me feel it inside of me, Street. Pretty please," she begged. "I wanna cum too."

Mind spent, I pulled my cock out of her mouth and slid a rubber over it. As anxious as I was to shoot my semen down her throat, I took Jamika up on her offer. "A'ight, fuck it. You want it? You've got it. Brace ya'self against the wall and hike ya skirt up."

"Oh, hell yeah. Give it to me, daddy," she freakily moaned, holding her juicy cheeks apart.

"Take this meat with ya thirsty ass." I rammed it into her rough and raw since she wanted it that way.

She gasped loudly. I knew she was exaggerating because her pussy was wide, sloppy, and wasn't fitting my manhood like a glove. I might've been coming down too harshly on her since I'd just come out of some virgin-tight pussy, but my dick kept slipping out and softening up.

"A'ight, drop back to ya knees so you can swallow this nut."

She smacked her lips, then got her mouth real juicy before swallowing my dick whole again. I damn near choked her when I braced the wall and stuffed myself as far down her throat as I would go. I was trying to stroke

Jamika's esophagus. When it was all said and done, it took me a few seconds to regain my composure. I had to look down to make sure the skin was still there. I peeled her off $100 before I zipped and buckled my pants up.

"So, what'chu got up when the block starts drying up?" I questioned, plotting on taking Jamika back to the hotel room so she could put me to sleep with her mouth and mouth only.

First counting out the money with the light from her phone, she then responded as sarcastically as she could, "Um, from the tally of these bills in my hand, 'bout to shoot a move with my girls to the Zone. I'm on a mon- eymaking mission, and this here ain't enough money. Them niggas over there gettin' it like I thought you were."

I chuckled, always amazed at how tough chicks acted when they were arguing with men. "Hey, ya better watch ya mouth with ya cum-thirsty ass. Real talk. If you keep talkin' cocky, not knowing ya place with a nigga, I'ma snatch them bills I just blessed you with back out of ya hand and shove this dick back down ya throat. Whatever suck and fuck get-rich plan you've got mapped out within your li'l mind, I suggest you not plot me on that muthafucka again. Get at me when you know how to act."

With that being said, I pushed Jamika to the side and left her between the houses with her jaw dropped while I looked to the sky for a full moon. For these hoes to be out here talkin' reckless like they were, both Jamika and Porsha, it must've been a full moon.

"Yo, Pete. I'm 'bout to shoot a move back to the telly. I'll get at you in the a.m. Hold it down."

CHAPTER 17

TRINITY

"Hooty-hoo." The incoming drug call from outside disturbed me from doing a little bit of dirty work.

Since I had not been able to find any incriminating messages between my husband and his ex-mistress, I backed out of all the applications I was snooping through and slid his phone back into his pants pocket before answering the drug call. Had I found what I was looking for, though, the custo would've been a witness to me catching a body. Cal and I had not gone to sleep on good terms, and I was still in my feelings, ready to rev back up with him once he rose to hustle.

By the time I reached the window, the custo was whistling up and calling out again.

"Yo, it's early as fuck. Give me a sec to wipe the crust out of my eyes," I snapped, uncaring of the twenty-dollar bill he was waving up at me.

"S . . . sorry, Trin," he stuttered, knowing I'd clown in less than two seconds. "I tried last night, b . . . but Porsha said no credit. I've been hustling all night. Please."

I backed down, not having a reason to trip on him anyway. "You good, I got you. Hold on a sec."

Calvin was snoring when I walked out of the room and downstairs to the trap. Had I not wanted some solo time to smoke and sort my thoughts out, I would've thumped him in his head and made him rise to serve the custo. I usually didn't care about slanging. But this morning, the morning after fist fighting with his ex-mistress and her sidekick, and then him all throughout the night, my body was aching. The pain started setting in as I treaded down the stairs to the trap. Before grabbing a baggie to serve the custo, I found Calvin's stash of Norcos and popped one. I wasn't about to be slowed down.

"Sorry again, Trinity," he apologized again as soon as I swung open the door.

"It's cool. Do ya thang." I served him.

Porsha was right for not giving him credit last night. I'd never been too fond of freebies, not even if I was on the receiving end. Because free shit always comes with strings.

Back upstairs, I walked into the kitchen and saw that the milk was out on the counter, along with a container of Benzie's oatmeal. My kids had been up in the wee hours of the morning without me even knowing. To myself, I thanked Porsha for being a good daughter to me. I didn't know what I would've done without her for the past year. I never thought I'd have one child, let alone two, and Porsha was making it a breeze. She cared after Benzie like she birthed him, kinda like how I was the one who looked after my siblings as their protector. I looked at her knowing the apple didn't fall too far from the tree.

Anyway, if it weren't for her getting up with Benzie in the middle of the night for feedings, he'd probably have been trained by now to live off air and his imagination. I was gonna miss her when she broke up outta here to whatever apartment I knew Calvin was gonna hook her up with. I hoped I'd miss Benzie, too, from being over at his big sissy's house so much.

Putting the milk into the fridge and the oatmeal back into the cabinet, I pulled out a gallon of orange juice along with a bottle of wine. I was about to make a morning mimosa to help shake my hangover. I had a hustle to manage.

On the porch, I lit up and started my private wake-and-bake session. Whether it was the Norco or the sips of mimosa I'd been taking from the kitchen to my seat, I was becoming numb to the aches and pains. One thing was for sure if nothing else: if I was feeling the way I was feeling, Cal's li'l groupie and her flunky had to be feeling ten times worse. My woes were because I was out of shape. Not because I got my ass kicked. It was God's job to show mercy on muthafuckas, not mine. I'd smashed both of them. And just in case they came back lookin' to get at me for revenge, I was going to get my ass in the gym and tone it up.

Ring, ring, ring.

Answering before my phone woke anyone up, I wasn't in the mood to talk with my sister but didn't have a choice. I wasn't about to hang up in her face. "Hey, Trish."

"Good morning to you too, your dryness. I didn't sleep with you last night." She caught on to me not being thrilled to hear her voice.

"I know. We haven't had to do that shit since we were kids in that cursed-ass house you better not be calling me about." I was blunt with my little sister.

See, within my clan of sisters, nothing was a secret, and all news traveled fast. Tanya was probably texting Trish our conversation word for word as she and I were having it. *Naw, naw, that ain't like Tanya.* She was probably recording the call so she wouldn't get any of my slick remarks misconstrued during translation. She'd always been the sister with the big mouth.

Out of our sibling clan, Trish and I were the most similar. We might as well have shared our mother's womb at the same time. My first day home from the hospital as a newborn was the exact same day Trish was conceived. My father had not given two fucks about giving my mother a six-week vacation from sex to heal. She popped me out, brought me home, and was on her back against her will but willingly. Ruby ended up telling me, Tanya, and Trish about that night once we were old enough to understand. Being the oldest, she was the quietest of us all. Ruby went through her own bid of hell all alone until Tanya came along. That was why the two of them were the closest.

"Ahhh! Oh my God! Between you and Tanya, I don't know which one of y'all works my nerves the most," Trish complained.

"Well, since I didn't call you, I'ma put my money on Tanya being the winner of the one who works your nerves the most. Don't put her shit on me."

"I can't with you." Trish was laughing. "You're not gonna let your baby sister catch a break, huh?"

"Yes, I am, baby sister." My response was loaded with sarcasm. "I'm gonna give you a break and tell you that I'm not paying the taxes on that house for our mother before you ask me to and get cursed out behind doing so."

"Ha-ha! Girl, bye! I'm not worried about you." She blew my threat off, laughed hysterically, and then started going off in Spanish.

Trish was slanging Spanish slang words at me like Cal and I slanged dope: effortlessly. Ever since she started dating this Mexican cat, living *la vida loca* with him and his family, she'd become fluent in the language.

I heard *puta* about two or three times behind my name and Tanya's, which I knew meant "bitch." Trish had called me that before. And *egoista,* that meant "selfish," and Trish was calling me that too. Funny thing was, though, in my opinion, I was the least selfish of all my siblings. But whatever.

"La-la-la, boom, pop, ta-muthafuckin'-da," I mocked her, not being able to argue with her fairly. "You're wasting your time, because I don't know what you're saying, girl."

Taking a deep breath like she was getting her bearings, Trish responded with emotion. "Look, all jokes aside, what I'm saying is that you're not right for leaving the rest of us hanging. We've always stuck together. We've always held each other down and watched out for one another. You know how this goes, Trinity. It's fucked up that you're breaking the code. You're breaking our pact."

The conversation between Trish and me took another turn, an emotional one. I didn't show many people that side of me.

The more puffs I took and the more mimosa I sipped, the clearer my head became. I'd drunk damn near a whole liquor store last night. It was starting to make sense why Calvin was so upset at me for fighting those women instead of going outside. It was fucked up to feel like this, but I was relieved the bullets struck Mack and not my man. I might play the coldhearted role, but I'd probably fall apart if I had to bury Calvin. *I'ma make sure to throw some cash and gift cards to Mack's baby momma to help where it might.*

Once my mind is right, I'll count up all the money Porsha made last night. Drunk or not, I'd heard Porsha tell Calvin that she'd sold out. Plus, that a young nigga came through and dropped hella chicken. I woke up with money on my mind, wanting to know how much. The quicker we could stack, the quicker my husband could get the peace he needed from this dope game.

I wasn't saying I loved living and trapping at the same time, all the time, but I'd gotten used to it and good at it. I'd excelled within my element. And although I was gonna move to where the grass was green and flowers bloomed year 'round, I couldn't imagine my ghetto ass uprooting myself from this house and this hood. I loved sitting on the porch and smoking a fat blunt without being worried about my neighbors or the police fuckin' with me. I appreciated the li'l things of the hood, like getting a beer for Calvin at nine in the morning using food stamps. And unlike a few of my homegirls I grew up with who were only fuckin' trap stars for enough cash to get some money to move up outta the slums, I made a trap king wife me so I could live like a queen in the hood.

When I was backed against a wall to give all of this up, it'd seem like I was giving a piece of myself up, too. Yet and still, wherever Calvin and our family ended up, I fa' damn sure wouldn't be making playdates with Beckys and Billys for Benzie to play with. The thought of conforming made me sick, and not wanting to fall into another crabby mood because of Calvin, I took a big gulp of my mimosa and a few harder hits of my blunt.

Nobody is perfect. I've got my skeletons. So I've gotta quit trying to judge my man. That was what I kept telling myself.

I was like the banker of our trapping operation. It was my job to count up and keep track of every dollar and dime that came into this house, as well as find stash spots for it. I had our wealth hidden in heating and cooling vents, electrical sockets, duct work, various holes in the wall that I'd patched over, and even within some of the nonworking pipes within the basement. I had to get creative with so many people running in and out of our spot. To be honest, I prided myself on being crafty, witty, and outsmarting even the most intellectual muthafucka. If a cocky muthafucka ran up in here, they'd be dead and up in these walls with our riches. I swore to that word if no else did. *I might give up living in the hood. But I won't give up what I've made in the hood.*

In this case, all it took was for me to watch a few YouTube videos and take a three-hour trip to Home Depot for supplies and a tutorial from one of the workers for me to become a regular ol' handywoman. It might've taken me a minute to catch on, a few more trips to the hardware store to replace some misused supplies, and even a hand from Calvin, but those were small hurdles to my independent ass. Although Calvin was a great provider and protector, I'd never waited for a man to show me how to survive. Cal met me already in survival mode. Growing up around a weak mother made me strong. Porsha, however, would be strong because I wouldn't have it any other way.

"G'morning, babe. You got up this early to cook ya man some breakfast?" Trying not to laugh, Calvin knew I wasn't about to burn no bacon or biscuits.

"Boy, bye. All I'm burning is this blunt. I'll pass it after a few more puffs. As far as a meal goes, I suggest you go back to sleep and dream up a dish. If I get in that kitchen whippin' anything up, it'll be a hot pot of grits."

"Don't start with that shit, damn." Calvin got aggravated. "You went to sleep talking shit, had the nerve to babble some bullshit in ya sleep, and don't think I didn't hear you mumbling about how you should suffocate me with a pillow before you tiptoed out of the bedroom earlier."

"Oh shit, I was talkin' in my sleep? And you heard that this morning but still didn't rise to serve ya custo?" I laughed until my side hurt.

"Yeah, I did. You've gone far enough, and you've talked enough shit. Game over, Trin. I ain't trying to hear nothing else about ol' girl."

"You know what? Fuck it. You're right. Let me start over." I chose to take the high road, a route I hadn't traveled often. "Good morning, bae. Naw, I ain't cookin' up nothing this morning but some crack if you need me to. I can call in some Coney Island for you to pick up, though."

His mood lightened as he realized I wasn't antagonizing him, but making a truce. He fell in line. That's what couples do: argue, then get right back to lovin'.

"You fooled a nigga with all that cooking you used to do back in the day, Trinity. Had me thinking you was gonna burn for me every day and shit."

"Nah, I ain't never have no plans of slaving over a stove all day every day. You're absolutely right. You did get played."

Pulling me up out of my seat and down onto his lap, he then rested his chin on my shoulder and began kissing on my neck. I ignored his morning breath. What I couldn't ignore was his thick dick sticking me in the back. What I'd always loved about Calvin was his ability to calm me down. His ability to stroke my feisty fire out, lighting a whole new one between my legs.

"I love you, Trin. You know that, right?" he questioned, kissing my earlobe.

"You better love me, Cal. What happened with ol' girl better not happen again." I wasn't finished talking, but he put his finger on my lips.

"Shh, bae. We said we weren't gonna do that. I fucked up then but haven't since. I was foul, but you can't keep punishing me. You can't keep putting yourself through that, plus reliving all the emotions I shouldn't have had you feeling anyway. I'm sorry. But I swear I'ma do right by my family. I've been showing you that, and I'm not done. Everything I do is to make sure y'all are straight. Believe me, Trin." Calvin was just as apologetic today as he was the day I pulled up at his jump off's house.

I wanted to tell him that we were all good and all was forgiven, but we weren't all good on that tip, and he wasn't 100 percent forgiven. I wasn't sure any woman got over her husband having an affair, especially when they're pregnant. I was a rider for Cal, but I had a heart and a helluva fear. I didn't want to be a weak fool for a man like my mother was. Being too far gone in love and accepting will make you do some crazy things.

"Calvinnnn," I heard Robin's loud mouth screaming. I cringed. "Morning, Trinity-boo."

Of all of our customers, she racked my nerves the most, and not because she begged. Robin didn't ask for anything, ever, but to be treated equal. She wanted to sit and kick it with me while she smoked the dope I sold her. No. She wanted my kids to call her Auntie Robbie. Hell no. She even asked if me and Cal could fund one of her fly-by-night decisions to get rehabilitated at a clinic. "Me no speak no muthafuckin' English," was my response to that question.

"Where do you think you're going?" Calvin was playfully trying to hold me down while I was trying to muscle my way off his lap. The moment had passed. He knew how irked I was by Robin.

"You better stop and let me go." I was just as playful with him but put a little more weight into breaking his grip.

Then Robin interjected, "Aw, ain't y'all so cute? Calvin, you better not have my girl fighting over yo' ass no more. Other than Mack, I heard what went down at the cabaret last night."

"Her big-ass mouth always got some drama coming from it," Calvin complained, releasing his grip, knowing Robin might've stirred awake the napping beast in me.

"Don't blame her, Cal. Your ass is the one who gave these peasants something about me juicy enough to gossip on," I snapped. "Hurry up and get rid of her. I'm going to do the morning count from what Porsha made last night."

Calvin rushed to serve Robin as I made my way into the kitchen. Shaking my head, I was mad as hell about my name being on any of their tongues. I prided myself on waving to the little people from up top on my throne. Calvin's indiscretions had not done nothing but knock me down a few levels in their eyes, plus made these thirsty hoes of our hood think there was a chance for them to creep with him. *I know how it goes. Calvin is the one who doesn't. He can't think like a bitch because he's not a bitch. Me, however, I'm that one. I'm already prepared to take a bitch shopping for her funeral outfit. Anyone can catch a death date behind trying to break up my family. Anyone.*

CHAPTER 18

PORSHA

Wide awake and staring at the ceiling, I was lost in my thoughts and low-key having a panic attack behind everything that happened last night. I could not wait until Nikola got out of school so we could talk. I needed her advice. Imani's inexperienced ass would not know how to advise me or how to make me feel better. There was so much that happened that I wished I could change and take back, and I was devastated that I could not. I'd texted Street all night without getting a response even once. My feelings were all over the place. I didn't care how pissed Street got about my dead-end threats about telling my daddy about us. He knew I was too desperate for there to be an "us" to expose us and the truth. I felt played and rejected, and for that, I felt regret and resentment. I'd gone from happy to mad to sad all within a few hours.

In the middle of the night, when I'd gotten up to get Benzie a bottle and change his diaper, I'd taken a hot shower and played with my pussy the same way Street did before stroking my virginity away. I'd wanted to see how it felt to him, if it was still tight, and if he had a reason to come back for seconds, thirds, but first to accept my apology. I also had to cry my pain out in peace. The running flow of water made it so no one could hear my light sobs. I now knew how it felt to get played. I'd never wanted to be "that girl" in "this position." But here I was.

As I rolled over, my eyes hit the back of Imani's head as well as the flicker from the television. We'd been watching reality shows all night. Imani was trying to cram as much cable in as she could before having to go home. And me, I was trying to keep my mind off Street as well as drown out my mother and father arguing. The shit they were saying to one another was embarrassing. Especially the part about my dad cheating. I was still thinking of something that would be worth Imani's while to bribe her with. I couldn't have my parents' secrets floating through the hood.

Come to find out that while my mom was carrying Benzie around in her belly and being a raging bitch, my dad was busy being a creep. He'd actually risked breaking up our family for a random piece of pussy. In between Trin tossing threats his way and jumping up on tables and onto him like a championship wrestler, she even cried. As much as she and I bumped heads, I was actually on her side and mad at my dad. He couldn't get a pass from me for being the man he'd always told me to stay away from. Yet and still, I couldn't help Street double-cross him anymore.

Rolling over, I plugged my dying phone into its charger and deleted the entire thread of risqué messages between me and Street. I didn't have another dude I was talking to who could find the messages and get jealous. He probably wouldn't have been shading me right now if I did. But what I did have was a nosy momma who'd go through my phone whenever she felt like it because she paid the bill. I knew better than to leave incriminating messages around. When the phone was finished doing its thang, I slid it underneath my pillow and closed my eyes to get some more sleep. I felt queasy and lightheaded, a sign of me having a hangover from last night.

TRINITY

"I take it Robin's got her crack pack and has gone on about her way," I spoke up, seeing Calvin walk past the kitchen doorway. I was stalking ol' girl's Twitter page to see if she'd said anything slick or out of the way since last night. Like with Calvin's phone, I'd come up dry.

He doubled back. "Yeah. I told her to start getting served around at the trap house on the block. I ain't got time for her starting no fires here." Calvin was trying to avoid his jump off continuously becoming a topic for us to discuss.

"Good idea not to let an outsider burn ya house down." My statement was loaded. "Anyway, are you picking us up some Coney Island or not? My stomach's been growling ever since you mentioned food," I grunted, rubbing my belly and poking out my lip.

"Yeah. Call it in, and don't forget to order Porsha's little friend a breakfast special, too," he said, reminding me of our daughter's friend, who needed to wake up and get home immediately.

Not only had Imani heard too much last night between Cal and me, but I also didn't like people lounging at my house or freeloading all over my furniture and in my space. As bold and vivacious as I could be, I liked my privacy.

After ordering everyone's food, I took another sip of my mimosa, then went and sat on the floor of one of our lounge rooms. This room was reserved for counting money. There were a lot of rooms in our house since it used to be a four-family flat. Besides a clock to tell the time, there were no electronics in here. Distractions weren't allowed. Focus was a must. We didn't fuck around when it came to making sure our money was right.

Untying the knot from the grocery store bag containing last night's profits, I dumped all the cash onto the floor. Bills of every denomination except a two-dollar bill fell from it. We didn't see a lot of those floating through the hood. I was getting ready to give Porsha some accolades and praise for a job well done until I got to the bottom of the pile. That was when I lost my muthafuckin' mind. The hundred-dollar bills she'd bragged on collecting last night couldn't buy the Jackson family nothing but property on the Monopoly board. Every last one of them was fake. My daughter had been played. Which meant I got played.

In a haste to grab the fake bills off the floor and my phone to call my husband, I knocked my glass over and soiled my carpet. I was pissed as hell, but not enough to slow down to clean it up. I had a stupid-ass child to snatch up outta her sleep.

"Yo, bae. What up? You want me to stop at the store or something?"

"Hell naw! Fuck the store and that food. Hurry up and get ya ass home. Porsha . . ." I commenced giving him the short version of what happened and what was about to happen.

CALVIN

Ring, ring, ring.

My phone was on jump. Naw, scratch that, my morning was on jump. It was like the craziness of last night had poured into my morning. Even ol' girl called while I was grabbing our Coney Island, talking about she was in

urgent care behind Trinity's beatdown. I'd hung up and
called the phone company to change my cell number but
got sidetracked when Trinity called me, screaming about
Porsha. I'd grabbed the Coney and come straight home
but got stalled twice by a couple of custos.

Finally, as I was two steps from hitting the upstairs
front door, my cell rang again. I stopped and pulled it
from my pocket, knowing Fame's ring tone.

"Yo, what up, bro?" I answered, glad he'd called. I knew
I was gonna need his famous "attention" when it came
time to follow up on whoever scammed my baby girl.

"Shit, not a muthafuckin' thang with me, chief. It's
you who seems to be in the middle of a war zone. You
good? Trin good? What about li'l P and my big body
Benz?" Being a concerned friend and godfather, Fame
questioned me without hesitation about me and mine.

"You must be outside," I assumed.

"Yup, yup, in the driveway. I called myself falling
through to get a wake-and-bake session going with some
cookie so we could kick it," he responded. "Do you need
to hit me up later? It kinda sound like you tied up and
whatnot with the fam."

"I am, but you straight. I could actually use your help.
Do me a solid and make ya way to the door so you can
hold the trap down until I finish trying to figure out what
went left here last night."

"One hundred, I've got you covered. Open up."

I rushed to let Fame in so I could kill two birds with
one stone: trap and handle family business. There were
junkies lined up and more coming up the block, all
chasing their morning hits. I wasn't about to miss out
on sales behind a petty-ass argument about a grand. A
nigga of my pedigree was more concerned with beating
the brakes off whatever brave li'l nigga robbed me. Fuck
trying to recoup my product or the cash. I'd spend a

grand on McDonald's in a month for Benzie. I was pissed off principle alone.

I heard Trinity screaming from all the way downstairs. She was cutting Porsha up with her tongue, and I understood why. She didn't want anyone in the streets to take anyone in this family as a weak link, all the way down to Benzie. I was sure my baby girl was gonna do all the research she could once her momma got up off of her ass for not recognizing counterfeit cash.

"Bro, these rollies out here heavy. Where the stash at so I can get to serving 'em?" Fame got straight to hustling as soon as he stepped foot into the foyer of my house.

"Underneath the floorboard in the bedroom. Good looking, Fame," I thanked him in a hood way.

"Chill. It ain't no thang. You and ya squad is live as hell upstairs. I heard y'all all the way in my car, so I know you got shit to get settled."

I went to speak, but he cut me off.

"Don't shit need to be said, bro. I already know what it is."

Giving him dap, I went back upstairs and got ready to get my house under control. My family wasn't about to be dismantled over no petty-ass cash.

PORSHA

"Porshaaaa." My mother's howling voice shook the house.

Before I had the chance to question what was wrong or to panic, my bedroom door flew open, and my face got hit with a wad of cash.

"You don't know fake money when you see it, stupid?"

My heart stopped, and her yelling continued.

"What in the fuck is wrong with your stupid ass?"

I see the word of the day is "stupid." Looking down at the crayon green money sitting in my lap and on my bed, I felt my stomach doing flips and bubbling. I really did feel stupid. I'd been checkin' for ol' boy last night 'cause I thought he was a baller. But the joke was on me. He was a bum who was about to have me knocked upside the head.

"I swear they didn't look like this last night." I regretted saying the words as soon as I said them. I knew they sounded dumb. I blinked, felt my momma's hand slap me in the mouth, and then heard Imani scream.

"Shut up before you get some too," my mom snapped at Imani, not caring that she was innocent and terrified.

Imani leaped up, not wanting no part of the wrath I was receiving. She didn't have to be told twice. Trinity had a way of making people wanna piss their pants. Me included. My momma wasn't nobody's joke, so you'd better believe I wasn't laughing. I'd have done anything to turn back the hands of time or simply get her off my head.

"Ma, I swear to G, I'm sorry. It was dark." I tried giving her another excuse.

Trinity's eyes stretched wide. She was looking like the devil himself, with horns and all, as she stared at me in disgust.

"Why does she keep talking? Huh? Please send me an answer down for once! Lord, please tell me this child of mine ain't as stupid as she's trying to act like she is," she shouted to the ceiling as if she were talking through it to the high heavens.

She then started pacing back and forth while punching her fist into her other hand, acting like she was possessed. I sat quiet and still, not knowing how else to respond. The last thing I wanted was her fist attacking my face.

"Yo, chill the hell out, Trin." My father's voice rang over my mom's.

She jumped to answer first. "I told you I was gonna get your stupid-ass daughter together for giving our product away."

"But like this?"

"Uh, yeah. Did she get the dumb gene from you?" My momma flipped the script on him.

"Don't get choked up on the muthafuckin' wall, Trin." My dad rose his voice again.

"Yeah, yeah, yeah, whatever. When you're done choking me out, make sure to choke ya daughter out next. She's the one who let a nigga scheme her with some fake hundos."

I gulped hard, not knowing what reaction I was about to get from my father.

CALVIN

Stepping into my daughter's bedroom, I swooped Benzie up and gave him to Imani, then sent her to the living room. I tried keeping as much of our family business private as possible. Once Benzie was old enough to understand street politics and the dangerous life I lived, he would be a part of family meetings as well.

"Listen up." I commanded my wife's and daughter's attention. "All this arguing and shit over a petty-ass grand ain't nothing but a waste of time and driving a wedge between the two most important women in my life. This bullshit is stressful and unnecessary. Trinity, I need you to quit beating a dead horse when we spent double that last night on liquor. And, Porsha, I need for you to break down a full description on that scamming-ass nigga so I can go speak to him. Although I ain't trying to go upside yo' head like ya moms, I agree that you were too busy being all in his face to peep that he was hustling you. I won't lie and say I am not disappointed in you, baby girl."

"I know you are, and I'm sorry. I swear to God I'll never be fooled like that again," she apologized, but I needed her to understand it was bigger than her getting got for $1,000 of product. Ol' boy had not popped up at our house for a band of weight when I was not home by chance.

"You better not," Trinity added her two cents in. "Matter of fact, if you do slip up again, you better fear me more than God. You have too much responsibility in this family to be fucking up, and if this is how you are going to be out on your own, I will be burying your gullible ass sooner than I'll be throwing you a baby shower. Do you not know or understand how thirsty these young muthafuckas are? Do you not know how jealous they are of your father's longevity in the game? If you are weak and create a pathway for one of them to get to my husband, me, or even Benzie, then what? You have got to think with your head."

Threatening our daughter like she was the creator of mankind, Trinity then turned and stomped out of the room without looking back. She knew her word was bond and it had better be respected.

"I'm sorry, Daddy." Porsha's voice cracked as she apologized to me again. Now that we were in the room alone, she was trying to soften me up, knowing I hated seeing her punished by my wife.

"Don't be sorry, and quit saying that you are. There's a difference between being sorry and being apologetic over a mistake. Got it?" I schooled her, ignoring her puppy-dog eyes pleading for me to take it easy on her.

She nodded, realizing my firmness. "Got it."

"Good. Now I'ma need you to think back to last night and tell me everything that happened when ol' boy came to cop some weight."

Porsha started breaking down the rotation of fiends throughout the night, including one I gave credit to on a regular basis who she sent away. She'd followed each direction I'd given her to a T and was on her A game as far as I could tell, until ol' boy came through and scammed her.

The hustler was light skinned, wore long dreads, was a little bit shorter than me, and had a deep voice. She also said he had a tattoo on his hand of a skeleton's face. I chose not to ask her how she got to see a skeleton's face so clearly in the dark. It was obvious she was paying closer attention to whoever the dude was than to the transaction.

"Look, Porsha, as much as you run around here reminding me and ya moms that you're about to be grown, you sho' in the fuck dropped the ball last night when it mattered. Age doesn't mean shit if you ain't got wisdom to accompany those years. That rookie mistake didn't cost your friend, you, or Benzie any harm, but it could've. Just like me, ya moms, and my crew have run up on niggas and their families, they'll do it to us if the right opportunity presents itself." I lectured her with the raw truth.

Sitting on the edge of her bed with her elbows propped on her knees, Porsha was holding on to every word I spoke like there was going to be a quiz afterward. "I get it, Daddy. I didn't think about all that, but I should have. I swear I've learned my lesson."

Usually a firecracker like her mother, Porsha was completely docile and apologetic. Trinity probably knocked all the spunk up outta her.

In spite of her seeming like she'd learned her lesson, I continued drilling my point into Porsha's membrane. Last night's bullets might've not been meant for us, but they very well could have been. It was time for all of us to tighten our shit up around here.

"Make sure that you have. I ain't coming down on you about the money, because you know that's nothing to me, Porsha. It's about you moving maturely and knowing another man's move before he makes it. These young bucks coming up with you don't operate how me and my gang did back in the day. They don't abide by the same rules, morals, and street codes you've grown up witnessing with me, ya momma, and Fame. I'm trying to move all of y'all to the suburbs and turn this crib into the Carter, but until then, you gonna have to keep your hot ass outta these slum niggas' faces, grinning and shit. I don't want no more pitiful excuses why your brain didn't work."

"There won't be another excuse. I swear." Her voice cracked like she was about to cry. Even as a little girl, she hated for me to discipline her.

Trinity could spank on Porsha, curse her out, and dish out jail-like punishments better than a Republican warden in wingtip shoes, yet nothing crushed Porsha's spirits like me telling her I was disappointed in her. There's something about girls and their fathers. My daughter hated disappointing me just as much as I hated being hard on her. Even still, she needed some lessons the hard way to ensure the same mistake wouldn't be twice made. The Jacksons weren't known for living a hunky-dory lifestyle where our mistakes could be forgiven.

"A'ight, I'ma chill. Your word is all you have, and I'm expecting nothing less." She was let off the hook, for now at least.

"Thank you, Daddy. This is the last time we'll have this conversation, I promise."

I nodded, then continued, "Just so you know, I'll be taking care of the dread-head nigga, and you can erase him from your membrane." Ol' boy was as good as dead. Digging in my pocket, I gave her the keys to my Benz, which was a rarity. I usually chauffeured Porsha around.

However, since she'd just gotten her license and was about to turn 18, I was trying to treat her more like an adult and less like an adolescent. She needed to know how to handle herself on her own, which she was only halfway proving to me she could do so far. "Drop Imani off at home, and come right back. Take Benzie with you and give ya friend one of those breakfast specials out of the kitchen. Make sure you heard every word I said, and take it to heart, Pooh Bear."

She smiled at the nickname I had not called her since she begged me to stop when she turned 16. Jumping up, she ran up and gave me a hug as tightly as she did when she turned 8. That birthday, I'd come home with a Barbie DreamHouse and one of every doll in the aisle. "I love you, Daddy."

"I love you too. Now g'on and do what I said the way I said it. I've gotta go calm yo' momma down. Your carelessness done fucked around and ruined everyone's morning." I was truthful as I walked out of her room to find my wife. The heat may have been off of me temporarily, but the fire was still hot and going fa' sho'.

CHAPTER 19

PORSHA

"I swear to God, I cannot wait until I turn eighteen. I do not care if I've gotta go to a shelter. I am going to be out of this jailhouse," I muttered under my breath as soon as I heard him and Trinity talking and the focus was temporarily off me.

Moving with purpose around my room, I hurried up and got dressed before Trinity found out Calvin was letting me drive Imani home. I was rocking a tight pair of denim capris, a fitted shirt that had my name on it and was studded out, and a pair of customized Chuck Taylors. I could not chance seeing Street in a dingy pair of pajamas. As irked, confused, and sad as I was about Street not reaching back out to me after all my attempts, foolish or not, I was itching to see how he was going to act once I was in his face. My ego had taken a swift blow in less than twenty-four hours. It felt like a million butterflies were swarming through my stomach.

Scooping Benzie up on my hip, I waved for Imani to follow me, then flew to the car.

"Wow, I thought I had it bad at home." Imani broke the silence between us once we got out the driveway. She called herself pitying me, and I thought that shit pissed me off worse than Street not hitting me back.

"You do." I rolled my eyes.

"That might be true, but you have got it hella bad. Trinity came through like Storm from *X-Men* on yo' ass."

"The apple does not fall too far from the tree, I heard." I gave Imani the side-eye. "And you can save your jokes. Trin was on your head too, and you were speechless. You did not utter a single, solitary word or barely breathe after she told you to shut up. Keep it real, please. We both know you ain't tough."

"Girl, bye. You wouldn't know if I was keeping it real or not. You ain't out here spotting real ones," Imani clowned me, then burst out laughing. Her bad joke was a direct reference to me accepting counterfeit bills.

"Okay, you've got me. That was too easy. I quit," I gave in, laughing as well.

It didn't take long to get to Imani's house. That was probably why my daddy let me whip his Benz. I got to run simple errands every once in a while, but never with my homegirl in the passenger seat. It was a shame that I could not bend corners and floss with her, but I was not about to take the chance of pissing my parents off twice in the same day. My plan for today was to stay under the radar with Benzie, my headphones, and my phone.

The block and the field were both dry as hell. Even the trap house was dead. Driving past, I looked up in the driveway as hard as I could, trying to see if Street's car was in the back.

"Wow, Elvin must have dumped some helluva dick off in your guts," Imani called me out.

"Hell yeah, he did. That nigga's dick was so big, it was in my stomach. I cannot wait until we hook back up again." My shattered ego would not allow me to tell her the truth about last night.

"Damn! Say word up?" She started celebrating for me in the passenger seat. "Why didn't you tell me? I am going to need all the details once you get home and have Trinity off your back. I want the story blow-by-blow of how that nigga's sex game works." She seemed too eager. We'd both made out with boys, but I was the first between us to have gone all the way. Nikola had been fuckin'.

"I'll see what I can do." I popped my collar. "I might be too busy texting him after giving him all this good-good, but I'll hit you up and probably be over later with a blunt," I laughed, feeling myself. I was stunting hard, but it was true that I felt different since my V-card was cashed in.

She burst out laughing. "Girl, you are funny as hell. That nigga is not about to be checking for you no harder than he been doing. If it ain't Jamika's hot-and-ready ass popping up over here cum chasing, it's between two other girls. Your man is for everybody."

I was not trying to hear Imani's rundown of Street's playboy antics when he'd been telling me he was trapping twenty-four hours a day. "Ugh, why are you being such a crabby bitch about my glory?" I questioned with my nose flared and my face twisted.

"It ain't hating when you are keeping it real. I thought that's what real friends do."

"Yeah, yeah, whatever. You are being a hater, but it's all good. I ain't worried about you or any other trick out in these Detroit streets who are jealous of me." It was not my intention to snap on Imani, especially since she was only keeping it real with me as her best friend, but my ego could not handle any more blows. It was bad enough Street had been ducking me. I was not trying to hear about him entertaining other females. In my mind, he was my man, so I was territorial.

"Wow, Porsha. Of all the years of us knowing each other and being best friends, I never thought you would get dick dizzy. Especially after your first dose," Imani snapped.

"Come for me one more time and I'ma pop you in the mouth," I half-jokingly responded, kind of feeling some type of way about her calling me dick dizzy. I was mad about it.

"Okay, well, I think that is my cue to get out of Calvin's car before we get into it for real."

"That's the realest shit you have said since you started talking."

She looked at me like she wanted to clap back but chose not to. Making the right decision, Imani got out of the car, retrieved her bag of hand-me-downs I blessed her with along with her Coney Island breakfast, and then gave Benzie a kiss goodbye. I was wrong and I knew it, but I was stuck in my feelings and refused to humble myself. She and Nikola were used to me being a bitch and apologizing later for it. I went to grandstand and pull off, but I heard her mother call out my name before I got the chance to shift the gear into drive.

"Excuse me, little girl. What's up with you getting this wig of mine together?" She pointed to the hair standing wild on top of her head.

There was a lot of stuff on my mind, to say the least. I had totally forgotten about the arrangement we agreed upon for Imani to come over. "My bad. I know we had a deal, but I've gotta get right back home before my momma be 'round here snatching me up outta ya head. I've got strict directions to bring my ass right back home. Excuse my language, but that's what she said. Do not worry, though. I've got you." I was only temporarily blowing her off.

"Aw hell naw, heifer. You promised me yesterday a hairdo when your best friend came home. She's home, so you owe me. If you cannot make good on your promise now, you are gonna have to add on another free hairdo." Her mother was trying to play me.

"Fine, whatever. I will call Imani so she can tell you what time I'll be back around here." I did not wait for her to respond before I pulled off.

Riding back past the trap this time, I saw Street's car parked in front. I started getting butterflies until I pulled on the side of the car and saw Jamika in the passenger seat. Being a drama queen, I rubbed my eyes then popped them open as wide as they could go. "I know my muthafuckin' eyes be playing tricks on me," I shouted.

"Porsh say a bad word," Benzie cooed from the back seat.

"Dang, I forgot you were back there, little brother. But cover your ears. I've got to be a superhero for a second." I wasn't about to go smooth on Street.

I looked back over at Street, and he had the nerve to smirk at me and then mouth to Jamika for her to sit still. That got me even more heated. If Jamika wanted all the smoke, I was hot enough to give her third-degree burns. I was so mad that I could not contain myself. I leaped out and acted like my momma. I went hard in the paint on that nigga. I called him every liar, deceiver, manipulator, and fake-ass hustler I could think of. When none of those words dragged him from the car, I started pounding on the window like a police officer with a warrant.

Finally, Street got out and put me in my place quicker than Trinity and Calvin ever did. Yanking me up by my shirt, he backed me up to my dad's car and slammed me across the hood of it. This was the second time in less than twenty-four hours Street put his hands on me. According to my dad, it only took three times to make something a habit. *Hmmm . . .* I couldn't think about how I was gonna handle the future 'cause I had to defend myself in the now.

"Yo, like I told you last night, you better quit mutha-fuckin' testing yo' limits with me. I ain't one of them niggas you take notes next to in class, so you better do some more studying on how to handle a nigga on my level."

I heard Jamika laughing at our interaction. I couldn't wait until he let me go. Instead of trying to tussle or fight back with him, I calmed down and manipulated the situation. I might've not been able to win a battle with him. But I was gonna fa' damn sho' claw Jamika's face up. With the foul intention in my mind, I thought the next time Street looked at Jamika would be the last.

After I agreed to quit tripping, get the hell off the block, and answer my phone later when he called, Street finally let me go. I took a few seconds to massage my neck and stomach from where he'd been applying weight and pressure, then ducked past him toward ol' girl anyway.

Jumping in the driver's seat of his car with my fist in front of me, I landed a mighty blow between her eyes and temporarily disabled her and gave me time to climb over the console. I was going for the trick's jugular.

"Snap out of it, bitch, and take this ass whooping." I slapped her face a few times, then felt her muscling up to defend herself.

"Fuck you, little girl." She grabbed my ponytail and snatched my head back.

Before she could get another good hit off, I threw up my arm to shield my face, then headbutted her. I instantly thought about Benzie and knew I needed to hurry up and get this beatdown over. So I started scratching the skin off her face. I literally felt her dirty, clogged skin underneath my nails as I clawed away at her beauty. I was giving her a makeover that A&D ointment would not be able to fix. It felt like an eternity before Street finally opened the door and pulled me off of her.

"You's a dumb ho. You see how long it took him to get me off you? He cares about this outdated-ass Impala

more than he cares about yo' trifle-life ass." I bullied
her even more, then spit directly in her face. Street was
barely holding me back. And when I went to run back
to my dad's car, there was not a fight to breakaway. I
had called it right. He did not care about Jamika. She
was simply a convenient jump off because I was not old
enough to be on call. But even still, he'd proved I was not
worth the wait.

"You already know I'ma blow ya shit up, nigga. If it's
fuck me, you already know it's fuck you!" I shouted.

Benzie's face was covered in tears as he screamed and
cried. I instantly felt bad for having him out here witnessing all this drama. I needed to get off the block so I
could grieve in peace. I had given a lot to Street's disloyal
ass, and he was playing me the whole time. He'd been a
cancer to me, and I hadn't recognized the symptoms.

I slammed my foot on the gas pedal and recklessly flew
up the street like a rocket. It was only by the grace of God
that I did not get into an accident.

CHAPTER 20

CALVIN

"I know you've got different parenting techniques than I do, but you're way too fuckin' soft on Porsha." Trinity stood across from me, complaining, gripping the neck of the Tito's bottle like she was two seconds from slinging it at me. "All the years we've gone without being crept on, and these young niggas see her dumb ass for a fool and make a move on us. I swear to God, Cal, that precious daughter of yours is going to be our downfall."

The more I tried ignoring Trinity, the more she went off. I understood her point of rage, but I wasn't with taking my anger out on my daughter.

"Look, Trinity, for the hundredth time, I'm not advocating for Porsha to fuck up or be a weak link. Fall the fuck back so I can think."

"You better be thinking about how you're going to make sure that dread-head nigga knows not to fuck with mine again." She stood in front of me with her arms folded.

Part of me was irritated with Trinity's pushiness, but the other part of me was turned on. She ain't never not been in the mud with me, and it was her loyalty that made her stand out among all the other hood girls who were throwing coochie my way. Despite me creeping, I knew I was lucky to still have Trinity riding dirty with me.

"Baby, rest assured that muthafucka won't ever fuck with our daughter again. You can send his mother a black dress right now if you want something more productive to do. I got this family, Trinity."

"Goddamn, nigga! You know you turn me on when you start talking like a Mafia man." She leaned in to peck my lips, but I grabbed her neck and held her close to me.

"You have been with me for over twenty years, and you are still doubting if I'm going to protect you, Mrs. Jackson? What the fuck a man gotta do for you to trust me?"

"I trust you, Calvin. It's these young and thirsty hustlers I don't trust. If you don't make a lesson out of ol' boy, that will give someone else the green light to try Porsha, me, or even you. Look how they shot Mack down."

"Well, baby, I'ma come back with blood on my hands, so you can stop worrying." I swiped my pistol off the nightstand and tried pushing her out my space. "Lemme me move, Trin. Back up."

"Nope. You know I like it when you talk all rough and shit, baby." She slipped my gun from my hand and then put her hand into my pants and wrapped it tightly around my manhood.

Whenever Trinity was in a giving mood, I took advantage of it. My dick hardened up on instant because I was about to get the chance to do some damage to her juicy pussy. Last night had been a total bust, but with Porsha and Benzie gone, we had a second chance to get buck wild. I wanted some sloppy head and some freak-nasty sex. It had been a minute since Trinity threw some juice on a nigga, and I was hungry for a nut like a teenage boy who just hit puberty.

I'd never been attracted to submissive girls who turned into puppy-dog women. I was the type of nigga who desired a bad bitch just as gritty as I was. Trin was undeniably that with her sexy, bullheaded ass. Regardless of what we went through or what we may have said to each other in the heat of the moment, she was gonna be my happily ever after. That ring wasn't never coming up off of that finger. I put that on my kids and my life.

Trinity stood on her tiptoes, gripped the back of my head, then kissed me deeply. I returned the kiss, tasted the champagne, and then slapped her on her booty hard as hell. I wanted her to drop to her knees and blow me off, but she jumped in my arms, making me fall back onto the bed instead. Either way, I was about to cum, and that was good for me.

Trinity was just as sexy as the day I met her. Her thick li'l frame had all the right curves in all the right places, even after giving me two kids. My dick thickened up as I felt all over her body.

"G'on and get some of this dick so you can calm the fuck down. I should have broken yo' ass off in the bathroom last night at the cabaret." I hoped me bringing up last night didn't put my wife back into a sour mood.

It didn't. Matter of fact, she threw the pussy on me like a porn star. In her mind, she was probably making sure ol' girl I'd cheated with never reappeared in my life. I left Trinity in bed, blowing on a blunt when I walked out the door on a mission. Sometimes you've gotta put it down to shut a chick up, ya dig?

Porsha was walking up on the porch as I was coming out the front door. I'd forgotten all about her being gone since I'd been busy banging her momma.

"Put my keys on the table. Why is Benzie crying?" I asked, seeing his face was red and hearing him sniffle.

"He wanted some McDonald's, but I did not want to stop and chance being gone too long," she responded, stumbling over her words. "I was planning on giving him some ice cream out of the freezer."

"Oh, a'ight then," I responded to Porsha, unsure if she was being straight up with me, but I did not have time

to micromanage her the way Trinity did. That nigga
Dread had a death wish by showing up to my house, and
I had a role to play as a genie. I was strapped to shoot a
bullet straight through his skull. "Chill out, junior. Daddy
will bring you back some McDonald's when I come
back." I kissed his forehead and got in the car with my
number-one shooter.

"I ain't never been as eager as I am right now to get my
hands dirty," I said to Fame as soon as I climbed in his
hooptie. He had pulled the 1993 black Grand Prix out of
his garage, so I knew he was down for the same murder-
ous mission I had been laying out in my head all morning.

"You know I stay in the mud, my nigga, so I'm game for
whatever. But what's on tip? Something happen on the
block at the trap?"

"Naw, something much more personal than that." I
gritted my teeth with anger. "Some dread-head buster
copped some weight last night from Porsha with some
fake hundreds. She did not know any better, of course,
but Trin's trained eye caught it on instant. I gave Street
his description, and he got with some broad with a J
name to see if it sounded familiar to her. That tramp
must bang niggas from set to set, 'cause that nigga called
me back within three minutes with the rundown on ol'
boy."

"Word? I'm in rare form to give a nigga some celebrity
attention, so don't be slow on the draw pointing him
out. Them niggas shooting at Mack still got me wired. It
ain't nothing but a word from ya mouth and I'm on one."
Fame was going crazy.

When Fame rode up on a nigga giving them some of
what he called "celebrity attention," that meant he was
on some massacre-type shit. His nickname was earned.
He was famous for murder.

Fame was one of the realest men I knew. Once I met him, I quit begging my momma to have another li'l bastard for me to play with. I did not need a brother because me and Fame were street-made brothers. If ever my shoes needed to be filled, I knew without a doubt Fame would hold my wife, kids, and trapping business down. Fame was more than my right hand, chauffeur, and godfather to my children. He was my muscle and my muthafuckin' ace of spades.

"You know how I do it, bro. I ain't wanna say shit about what went down until I was sure about how to play it."

"And you know how I play it, so say no more." Fame pulled his gun off his hip and placed it on his lap. "I'm blasting the block up when you say let 'em rip. Know that. It's time we start teaching these li'l young bucks that there's going to be fatal consequences for coming at one of us or our families. I might not fuck with Scooter's crazy ass half the time, but she is off-limits, too." Fame was ready to kill upon command.

Whoever this dread-head li'l nigga was, he was about to reap severe consequences behind underestimating my thug pedigree.

CHAPTER 21

CALVIN

As soon as Fame crossed over Hamilton into Highland Park, a block across from Detroit, my trigger finger started itching, looking for a dirty, dread-head cat. This scheming-ass cocksucker was about to get dealt with, and I put that on young Benzie. I wasn't in the game to make other families rich. Fuck that! My risks were for me and mine only. With Mack getting murdered last night, it was more crucial than ever to send messages loud and clear.

We rode around HP for a few minutes, paying extra-close attention to the liquor stores and a closed-down hospital that used to have more patients than they could heal back in the day. Matter of fact, it was the same hospital I got my first gunshot wound stitched up at. Nowadays, though, with it being abandoned for years, it was a melting pot for drug addicts and dealers alike. Even the most inexperienced hustler could make sales around there.

When those spots came up dry, we bent a few blocks more before finally striking gold. Simple-minded criminals were always easy to find.

Whipping up in front of a porch full of niggas, Fame was ready for war as he hopped out with his pistol in hand. "Sup? Y'all li'l niggas know where I can find a dread-head cat at? 'Bout my height?"

"Naw, nigga, we don't." One of the guys mugged Fame, then looked over in the car at me, mugging me as well. He had no idea what he was asking for.

Pop! Fame's trigger finger sent fire into the air. "Don't muthafuckin' let the next one rip ya face open, li'l homie. Do I look like the nigga to test?"

With the same attitude he'd just answered Fame with, he licked his lips and flared his nose. He obviously didn't give a fuck about the warning shot, and it showed. Once again, Fame was quick to make a move. He ran up on the porch, parting the boys like the Red Sea, then cockily snatched ol' boy up by his collar. The boy's chest slid down each stair before landing on the pavement. That was when he finally uttered that the chump we were looking for was inside.

"A'ight, all y'all niggas can break on about y'all business," I commanded, pulling my shirt up to expose that I was strapped as well.

Making the right decision, they all broke off, running in different directions.

Fame finally took his foot off the dude's neck and allowed him up. "Open the door and shout inside for that nigga to step out. I don't think I need to warn you about trying to play that tough-guy role again." Following him as he carried out his orders, Fame kept his pistol pointed at the boy's head just in case he tested him again. It wasn't a problem, though. He'd learned the first lesson hard enough.

Finally, the man of the hour stepped outside. I was assuming he was just as arrogant as he was last night approaching my house as he was at this moment, 'cause the young nigga addressed me like it wasn't shit to it.

"Sup, Cal? Shorty must've told you I slid through there last night and dropped a few bills on her. That must be why you're over here in my neck of the woods, lookin' for a nigga." He was talking like he'd slept with my daughter.

"Say what, li'l fella?" By the time I made it onto the porch to check him nose to nose, he'd pulled out his gun, which looked like a Walmart toy. "You draw to shoot, ya li'l ho ass nigga. I see you're too used to posing for Instagram pictures and shit."

I snatched it from his hand. He had not even loaded one up top while he was waving it around like he was about to bust a cap. I pistol whipped him like Fame did his friend. Too bad for him that wasn't the extent of the punishment he was about to endure for playing Porsha and ultimately trying to play me.

"Enough of the games. Where's my money at, li'l boy?" I questioned, looking down on him.

"In the crib," he answered through his gritted teeth, still refusing to swallow all of his pride.

"Then get yo' muthafuckin' ass in there and get it." I spit on him.

Dread-head was hesitant to go in the house, which made kicking him in his back through the front door even better. I was greeted with the pungent smell of filth, that stale, musky, bottled-up shit smell. The trap house wasn't set up like mine. It was a run-down house that should've been abandoned. Besides the tattered furniture they'd probably dragged in from the curb and fifty-inch TV screen to play the Xbox on, there wasn't shit else in here to accompany the horrid smell.

"Down, boy." Fame addressed the other hustler like a dog, pushing him down onto the couch.

I swore I saw dirt poof up in the air when his behind hit the cushion. *Trifling-ass trappers.* I felt even more disrespected that he'd copped from Porsha with fake money but couldn't pay a basic broad to clean up.

"Is anyone else in here?" I questioned, looking around in the places I could see while keeping my gun aimed on the dread-head.

"Naw," he answered, shaking his head with worry in his eyes.

"Your word better be realer than that cash you passing around," I threatened, rubbing the tip of my gun across his lips. "Or you gonna be sucking on a straw to get fed the rest of your life."

He gulped, and his breathing intensified. "I swear we're alone, Cal," he stuttered. The thug amour he'd been draped in minutes ago had completely vanished. Left before me was a punk.

Fame left the three of us in the front room while he checked the rest of the house. I knew we were all good even before he returned because gunshots had not rung out.

"Cal, dog. Please." His teeth chattered through each word. "I just had a little girl. I swear on her that I'll never come for you again. I fucked up, Cal. My bad."

"Yo, yo, yo, yo, naw, chump. I ain't no state social worker paid to give two shits about ya problems. You can swallow that sob story you trying to spit out 'cause I ain't trying to hear it. On the real, I don't give a fuck about ya daughter, just like you ain't give a fuck about mine. I can't feed my family off them phony-ass bills you tried passing my way, now can I?"

He shook his head no, agreeing that I couldn't.

"Exactly. Good answer. Now that we've proved you know better, I really ain't about to cut ya no slack."

Ol' boy kept fidgeting, twiddling his fingers, and looking back and forth to his homeboy on the couch, which raised a red flag with me. Thinking back to last night when some shit was going down behind my back and I was oblivious to it, I refused to be the last one shooting again.

"Oh, what? Y'all muthafuckas got something to say to each other that I can't hear?"

Feeling froggish, I leapt.

Pop! Pop!

I wasn't about to get plotted on. Aiming ol' boy's beginner pistol at the other hustler, I unloaded two bullets into the chest of the one on the couch. Reason being, I knew he was probably strapped, and the dread-headed nigga wasn't.

Pop! Pop! Pop!

Fame came in busting bullets without asking a single question and then shouted on the follow-through, "Who want it?"

Ol' boy's body jerked up and down on the couch cushions from all the extra bullets Fame sprayed into it, finally resting permanently. He'd been sent into a permanent slumber.

Pop!

One single bullet zipped past me and landed in the dread-head's neck. The shit was like a cartoon the way blood squirted up and out of the arteries that kept him living.

"Straight the fuck up, nigga? Damn!" I addressed Fame, not expecting him to murder two men in less than thirty seconds.

"Yeah, homie. Straight the fuck up and just like that. I heard shots being fired and came up blasting. The fuck else was I s'pposed to do? Come up looking for clues? Nah, never that," he nonchalantly responded, leaning over ol' boy's body on the couch to make sure he was dead. "Never that."

Each of us picking up a body, we pushed them down the basement stairs, then followed down behind them. Fame found baggies, cash, and the equipment they'd been using to make counterfeit bills when he'd been searching the house a few minutes ago. Real talk, they had one helluva makeshift operation that could've gone far had they fucked with a simple nigga.

We took it all except for the stacks of phony hundreds spread across the table. I wasn't gonna be the one responsible for flooding the street with 'em. Either you could afford to eat or you couldn't. Period. Bending over Dread-head, I pried his mouth open, stuffed in a few of the bills he tried feeding my family with, then lit a flame to one of them.

"See you down below, nigga."

Turning around, Fame led the way out of the house. I didn't feel the least bit of pity or regret for what had gone down. I had not made it seventeen years in the game by having a heart. Fuck them, their family, and any bastard seeds they had brewing inside of some basic bitches. All I'd ever care about was my family 'til the day I rocked up outta here.

Feeling my stomach grumbling, I was hungry as a hostage. I had not gotten a chance to smash my breakfast special this morning. "Hey, I need you to swing through the McDonald's drive-through before we get home because I promised Benzie a Happy Meal. But first, I'm about to call some Coney in. Do you want something?" I questioned, digging my phone from my pocket.

"Hell yeah! My stomach over here bubbling like I ate one of them rotten-ass niggas back there," Fame sickly joked. "Get me a twenty-piece wing-ding dinner with chili and cheese on the fries. Fuck a pop. I'ma stop at the store for a two liter and a beer."

"Legends. May I help you?" the Coney Island worker answered.

Sounding like a runaway slave, I ran down our order, getting hungrier with the words of food coming from my mouth. I couldn't wait to get home to wash my ass and have my grub. After I let Trin know the problem was handled and there was blood on my hands, she'd surely get off my back and give me some peace. If all went as a nigga wanted it to, I'd be trapping from my man cave for the rest of the day.

CHAPTER 22

DAYS LATER

TRINITY

Blowing out a stream of smoke, I felt my chest rise, fall, and burn from the strong green Kush buds of weed. My personal batch was hitting hella strong, giving me an out-of-this-world head high.

As I raised the window for some fresh air to blow into our bedroom, the cool morning breeze felt good and refreshing. Cal and I had been going at it like teenagers for the last two days, and the scent of sex had built up more than the clouds of gray smoke. Every free moment Calvin got from the trap, he was between my legs apologizing for ever straying from our marriage, breaking our vows, and weakening our bond as far as trust was concerned. I was hurt behind his infidelities but still very much in love and addicted to my husband, and for that, I chose to stop punishing him and only punish her. Petty or not, someone had to keep paying, and it might as well have been a bitch I didn't have any ties to.

Retrieving my phone from the nightstand drawer, I turned the alarm off before it started beeping. As usual, my nightmares had me awake earlier than I had to be and before everyone else. Unless there was weed and liquor in my system, I'd probably never get any rest. The downers put me down. And when they wore off and my body sobered up, I was back up looking for mood depressants.

"Wake and bake, Cal," I yawned, shaking my husband awake while at the same time blowing a cloud of good-good into his face.

"Morning, bae." His voice was raspy. Inhaling the smoke I blew out, he reached for the blunt to get his first hit of the day out of the way.

Thankfully, since two days had passed, we were back in a good spot. Sometimes he'd be the first one up, especially if the night before was a long one, but usually, I was the early riser in the morning. Today, for example, I'd already walked around my entire house, making sure things were exactly how I left them when I went to sleep. I'd peeked in both Benzie's and Porsha's rooms, watched the limbs of trees shake outside, and timed how many seconds it took for Calvin's chest to rise and fall as he breathed in his sleep.

I'd roamed in the night since I was a kid due to my terrible sleep habits. Mainly because I was tormented in my sleep with nightmares all ending with my mom dying by my dad's hand. The psychiatrist told me to keep that shit to myself 'cause it sounded like I'd committed premeditated murder when I killed him. I did exactly as I was told because there was truth in her words. Keeping it bottled up, however, didn't stop me from living with the truth.

"What are you thinkin' 'bout, Trin? I can tell the levers in that wicked mind of yours are cranking," Calvin questioned me, sitting up in the bed, still puffing.

"Nothing but a whole lot." Choosing not to weigh our morning down with the heavy drama I'd been carrying since I was a young'un, I spoke only about the lighter tasks for my day. "I've gotta go meet up with Porsha's guidance counselor about her grades and graduation, then meet up with my sisters for lunch. What'chu got up?"

"I'll get to that in a second," he nonchalantly responded. "Did you get that care package together for Mack's baby momma? I dropped a few bucks in her donation bucket but told her you'd be falling by."

Not having any money to bury Mack, his baby momma was doing shit I'd never heard of to come up on the cash. She started a GoFundMe, stood on the corner begging for change a few times with a bucket, and even posted flyers all throughout the hood saying she'd even take things to help support her and the baby. Mack wasn't the type of nigga muthafuckas cared about, so in addition to the $100 me and Cal gave her, she'd only raised $200. Wasn't nobody giving for the dead when they themselves could barely live.

"Yeah, I got another few hundred dollars for her, plus Porsha bagged up all of Benzie's old clothes and toys. After this donation, the Jackson family contribution has been maxed out. Agreed?" I might've felt sorry for Mack's baby momma, but sympathy only went so far. And hopefully she didn't get to acting ungrateful and make me snatch all this shit right back.

"No doubt, agreed. You didn't have an argument coming from me about that."

"Good. Now tell me what you've got up for the day, and don't tell me 'in a second' again." I let him know I'd heard his li'l blowoff.

"Me and Fame got a meeting with the connect, and then we gotta lock it in for a few hours to cook up. The numbers from yesterday were short because they ran out of product. Street hit my line late last night trying to get a re-up, but I told him I'd get at him after three. I need to be up and outta this bed and making moves." Taking another hit of the blunt, he finally passed it, then made a move on me instead of out of the bed. "Let me get some of that good-good to wake me all the way up first." Leaning over, his big body covered my entire tiny frame.

"Um, naw! You know I can't get wet if I know we're missing out on money. Get up and to work," I snapped, pushing him off of me. As bad as I wanted an early morning fill-up of Cal's dick, I'd get a dose of it after he got some bundles back on the streets. Out of the bed and leaving him disappointed with his dick in his hand, I trotted out of the room and toward Porsha's. It was time for the Jacksons to get their day started.

PORSHA

Saturday and Sunday had been long, rough, and gruesome for me. Trinity had me on the punishment from hell. I hated school, but I was anxious to get there today. When I'd gotten back with my dad's car and a blazing hot attitude about seeing Jamika with Street, Trinity slapped me with a chore list and my first set of printouts about counterfeit money. Not only did I have to familiarize myself with the topic, but I got tested on the sheets once I told her I was done studying them as well. Trinity was always the last one laughing when it came to money.

On my hands, my knees, stepstools, and ladders, I'd cleaned the entire house from top to bottom and every room. Trinity had me up by 6:00 a.m. and working in three-hour shifts with an hour break in between until I passed out from exhaustion. Until well after the sun set, I did late spring cleaning inside and outside. My mother didn't believe that girls should be excluded from manual labor. I'd cut the grass and painted the porch rails a fresh coat of chocolate brown. One thing was for certain—I'd never need a man to hold my own.

In contrast to most of the times when my father took up for me, he'd allowed my mom to do what she wanted with regard to my punishment so he'd remain in her good graces. That was if you asked my opinion. The more Trinity focused on me, the less they argued. My dad was sacrificing me so he could get some peace. All weekend long, for the first time ever, I'd been wishing out of my window on the few stars above the hood that they'd get into it. This hell of a weekend must've been my karma for helping Street scam my dad.

Without a phone, computer, or tablet, I'd been banned to only reading about counterfeit money during my spare time. I couldn't even daze off and daydream, because every time I did, the visions were of Street, and I'd get mad. I couldn't wait to get my fiery ass back on the block. I knew I threatened to tell my dad about him and me, but my dad couldn't deliver the pain I was carrying for gettin' played. I had to battle for my bitter heart on my own.

"A'ight, it's morning time and time for school! Wake up, Porsha." My mom burst into my room.

"I'm up," I yawned. Today marked the day I was getting off punishment, getting all my stuff back, and getting from up under her evil ass. She should've known I'd be awake and counting down the minutes. Hell, I knew how many hours there were until I turned 18. 'Cause on that day, I'd dare a muthafucka to speak the word "punishment" to me.

"I bet you are," she said, handing me back my electronics. "You better hope you don't find yourself back being my little slave without all this shit and locked in this room until you're grown. I've got a meeting with your counselor at eleven thirty."

I rolled my eyes, wishing the next few weeks would fast-forward by and be over. School was definitely becoming an annoyance for me. "I know, and Dad already told me to have my behind in every class every single day until graduation." I paraphrased what I'd heard, halfway giving the topic my attention. I was too busy powering my phone back on. Forty-eight hours out of the loop had driven me straight crazy.

Trinity noticed me half giving her my attention and brought me back to reality real quick. I mean, real, real, quick. "You ain't learned shit over this weekend and must still got me twisted. I'll break this muthafuckin' phone off in ya ass before taking it a third time." She snatched it out of my hand. "When I'm talking, put it down and pay attention. Do you understand me?"

I quickly nodded, thinking that my birthday would be here soon enough, setting me free. "My bad."

"Good. Now let's try this again. Is there anything you need to tell me before the counselor gets a chance to? Don't let me get up there and be embarrassed or caught off guard when you can come up off the bullshit now." My mother wasn't holding me up this morning.

Making sure I didn't fidget with my gadgets, I set them down and kept my eyes fixed on hers. "You won't be surprised, Ma. I ain't did nothing more than what they've already sent a million notices home about. And after today, I promise you won't have to see another administrator from my school." I made a promise I was for sure I could keep. Trinity didn't want to go to the school. I didn't want her up there. On that topic, we agreed.

She laughed. "Okay, Porsha. You can save all that bullshit for them counselors and teachers you've gotta impress into not making you attend summer school. I couldn't care less one way or the other if you don't waltz ya ass in here with a degree on time. That's money I can save from spending on your party, a prom dress, and a graduation outfit." She was bluffing. My mother wanted me to get my diploma and wouldn't accept anything less. That was why I had not been pulled out and home-schooled.

"Anyway, you can go ahead and get ready. We're walking up outta here in an hour so I can drop you off, then go pay ya granny's house taxes before it gets too crowded downtown. If I'm running late to our little meeting with ya counselor, tell her I'll be there and what I had to do."

"I thought you weren't paying Granny's taxes." I was shocked hearing my mother say she was going to do something she'd cursed against for so many months. She and my aunties had argued and damn near come to blows over my mother refusing to help my grandmother save her home.

"Stay in a child's place," she snapped. "The only worry you need to have is making sure that counselor doesn't say a word I haven't heard. Be ready in an hour, Porsha."

Not willing to take Trinity to a level of rage, I rushed to get dressed. Being that I'd been on punishment with nothing to occupy my free time, I'd organized my closet and bagged up all my old stuff for Imani. I'd also picked out the perfect outfit to return to school in. Girls and dudes alike were always checkin' for the threads I was draped in. I stayed rockin' name-brand clothes on my ass and legitimate jewelry in my ears, on my wrists, and around my neck. My daddy kept me in diamonds, and my momma taught me how to rock them. I was a spoiled brat, but what dope man's daughter shouldn't be? Hands down, I was the best dressed kid in the entire school, and I was barely there.

Once I made sure my look was on point, my purse had a few pads in it for the period I was expecting, and my book bag was dusted off and sat by the door; I finally gave my phone some attention. It was almost full to capacity but still loading up with notifications. I'd missed a helluva' lot being on punishment and unplugged. Sitting on the side of my bed, I clicked on the message icon, ready to read through all my text messages first.

Bang! Bang!

"What was that?" I murmured to myself, caught off guard by the sudden noise coming from downstairs.

Bang! Bang!

When it came louder than before and closer, I got a bad feeling. It was like time stood still, but not for long enough.

Boom! Boom! Boom!

I then heard my mother scream out bloody murder.

"Detroit Police!"

"Y'all dirty muthafuckas better not touch not one person in my family. I swear on my life," my dad shouted right before he squealed out in pain.

"Check the house, and clear it out from top to bottom. Go." A cop's command sent an army of footsteps treading through my house.

Leaping up, realizing we'd been hit with a raid, I dropped my phone and ran for Benzie's room. Over all the loud commotion and everyone shouting, I heard him screaming and crying. I needed to get to my little brother. I needed to soothe and protect him. Not because I'd been taught to protect family. But because I was all Benzie knew outside of our parents.

As soon as I swung the door open, my heart sank deep into my stomach, and I pissed on myself. A long stream of hot pee. I'd been to the bathroom this morning and had not felt a sensation to go since, but I guessed instant fear had taken over. The big, masked white cop scared the shit out of me. I couldn't see any part of his face but his beady blue eyes.

"Got another one," he called out to his cop friends, throwing me face-down onto the hallway floor.

Within seconds, my hands were handcuffed behind me, but I wasn't allowed to sit up. After he ran and checked the rest of the places in our house that his buddies weren't, he came back to me. The whole time I'd been on the floor, I'd been looking side to side, watching the policemen's every move and calling out to Benzie that everything was going to be okay. I couldn't even feel bad for myself for feeling terrible for my little brother.

When the cop finally peeled me off the ground and walked me into the living room, tears immediately began streaming down my face. The man I thought of as a superhero was cuffed, beaten, and bleeding from his head.

"Y'all are dirty as hell! I wish death on all y'all muthafuckas." I spat venom, meaning each cold-blooded word.

"I see you've got a live one," a lady cop smartly commented, looking just like the cop who roughhoused me out of my room, with the same set of beady blue eyes.

I ignored her, more concerned with my bloodline. "Daddy! Dadddddy," I cried out, wanting the protection of my father.

I was scared for myself, but my fear for him was tripled. He was the kingpin, the dope pusher, and the head of our drug-rich family. He was also the murderer who'd just gotten blood on his hands behind cleaning up my slipup.

With a black cop's hand over his mouth, he couldn't respond. He looked like he was ready to bite the pig's hand off, though. Even beaten up, he still had a spark of spunk in his eyes. If I had known that Monday arriving represented all of this mayhem and these unfortunate circumstances for my family, I wouldn't have wished it here. My mother's punishment, yeah, I'd take that ten times over right about now.

"Where's my momma? Where's my brother? Y'all better answer me and let my daddy go, you dirty-ass pig muthafucka." I was going absolutely crazy with my mouth.

"Ya daddy gonna get let go of, all right. Right into the jail system for the rest of his life," the cop who was covering my dad's mouth spat. "We've got a couple of witnesses in protection saying he killed two men, mutilated a dead body, and then committed arson. And with all the drugs and illegal weapons my partners are finding, ya momma gonna be locked up as a co-conspirator."

"Fuck you. That'll never happen." I was cocky, believing that my parents were untouchable even with us in the middle of a raid and cuffs on my wrists.

The cop chuckled but didn't respond in any other way to me. He didn't move his hand from my dad's mouth, either. I was piping hot, especially when I heard glass breaking, things hitting our walls, and them continuously tearing our house up. There were cops running from upstairs to the trap downstairs, collecting everything illegal they could find. I wanted these intruders out, but I knew they weren't leaving without my dad.

"Instead of me breaking your daughter's heart, I'ma give you the pleasure of letting you do it, Calvin Jackson. You might as well tell her whatever it is ya need to say before we haul ya ass up outta here. It's gonna be a long time before you two get to communicate. You already know what happens when we raid and break up families." The cop then took his hand off his mouth.

My dad hung his head low. It was like his soul died a hundred times within five seconds. He ignored the cop's devilish laugh and responded to me with a cracked voice.

"Listen up, baby girl. Life is about to get a whole lot harder for you before it gets easier. If I get out of this, it'll be a miracle I probably don't deserve. Do your best to stay tough, and remember what I taught you about taking care of Benzie and all the shit I've drilled in you as far back as you can remember. Less talk and more thought. Tell me you understand, Porsha."

I knew exactly what he meant. And that was to keep my mouth closed about everything. "I understand, Dad,"

I barely responded, in disbelief that this was happening. I wanted to wake up, but everything around me was a reality.

My dad's words began sinking in as they pushed him out of the front door of our home, leaving me feeling emptier and more lost than I'd ever felt in my entire life. As the sirens of the police car he was in got fainter, my meltdown couldn't be contained. I cried, screamed, begged the cops to bring him back, and even asked God to deliver a miracle my dad didn't think he deserved.

"Mommmyyyyy! Benzieeeeee!" I screamed out for the two family members I had left in the house, realizing that my brother wasn't crying anymore and I had not heard my mother but once earlier.

My hands were cuffed but not my feet. I ran toward the lady cop like a football player. I threw my head in front of me so it would lead the way and tackle her backward by the gut. She moved in time, making me the only one to fall. I was in panic mode, anxious, terrified, uncertain, and any other word that described petrified.

"You've earned a quicker trip to the group home, li'l bitch. I was gonna give you a few minutes with ya momma and brother, but ya fucked that up," she spat. "See, your mother is going to jail behind ya dad's murders. Which means you and your little brother will be transferred into the system until their cases are over. We always give the kids a little time with their parents before splitting the families up, but since it was just fuck me, fuck you!"

Sounds familiar.

I growled, pissed that I was handcuffed. If I had been free, I would've tagged her ass worse than I'd done Jamika. "I hope you suffer the same pain I'm feeling. And a li'l bitch, I'll be that. When I get out of juvie, you'll see just how much of a bitch I really am," I warned her.

"You people always have bigger dreams than y'all can achieve. Now turn around and let's go. Try another stunt on the way to my squad car and I'ma shove this joystick up your asshole and get you prepped for juvie," she mocked me, totally amused.

I was escorted out the same way my father had been escorted out a few minutes ago. The bottom had fallen out.

"You don't know me! Keep yo' mafuckin' hands off me," I yelled at the lady cop, squirming and trying to get free from her grip.

"Shut up, little girl, and keep still. You don't scare me. Just like your wannabe-thug-ass father doesn't scare us," she hissed with a smile on her face. "Do you think I was playing upstairs when I told you I'd shove my nightstick up ya ass?"

"You're gonna regret talking to me like this once my daddy gets out of jail. Trust and believe that," I screamed at her as loud as I could.

She grabbed me by the arm, twisted it until I squealed, then pushed me into the back seat of the government-plated Crown Vic. "You better learn how to say fuck ya daddy just like the world has done. He ain't getting out of jail, like you've already been told, so welcome to the life of an orphan. You'll be in good company of the rest of these li'l degenerate bastards in ya city." She slammed the door. The car rocked, and so did I.

Tears ran freely from my eyes, down my cheeks, and off my face. All I could envision was my father getting dragged out of our house, handcuffed, and badly beaten. I was in disbelief that our hood-royal family was going down. Leaning my head on the window, I now knew how caged beasts felt.

The white lady cop berated me the entire ride to the police station in an attempt to break me down mentally.

She verbally abused me, calling me names like "a stupid nigger" and "a waste of good tax dollars." Although I tried turning my ears off to her evil and gut-wrenching words, I knew I'd have to transform into a gutter girl in order to survive. My dad might've raised me to trap, but he'd failed to tell me how to survive in police custody. Probably because he hoped I'd never get here. Quick, fast, and in a hurry, whether I wanted to or not, it was time to grow the fuck up.

When the car stopped and the engine cut off, my stomach sank as far as it could go. We were inside a garage surrounded by cameras, which moved when my pupils did. If I couldn't be honest with anyone else, I had to be honest with myself. I was scared. My whole body was trembling, and I was nauseated, overtaken with fear. It was no secret what cops did to innocent people, so being that I was part of a guilty family, who knew what their handling of me was about to be like.

I squirmed around in my piss-soiled panties, in no rush whatsoever to take them off. Maybe if I reeked loud enough, whatever deviant waiting inside the jail for me would leave me alone. I was nervous. I'd grown up in a trap house, not back and forth to the county jail. My dad's words flooded back to the forefront of my memory. *"Life is about to get a whole lot harder for you before it gets easier."*

So far, Calvin had not been wrong about any of his advice. Everything he'd told me when I was a child had come to pass. If only I wasn't learning this lesson now, after it seemed to be too late. If only I had not been so busy grinning in the boy's face who passed the counterfeit money off, I could've prevented my father's anger, therefore preventing the vengeful murder they'd come and arrested him for.

Squeezing my eyes as tightly as I could, I pushed the rest of the tears out of my eyes that were built up for me. It didn't feel right dwelling in a pity party when I was the reason for all of this madness.

The lady cop got out of her seat and marched around to the back passenger side door and swung it open. "Get ya ass up out of the car, you little piece of shit," she whispered coldly before gripping me by the arm, trying to yank me out.

The image of my dad was replaced with the face of Sandra Bland. If they'd killed an advocate, they'd surely kill me. Now I saw why my social studies teacher dwelled for almost a month on police brutality.

"Stop! Get off of me! Take me back home," I cried out, fighting with all my might against being detained.

I might've not wanted to be in a squad car, but I fa' damn sure didn't want to get out. Going inside of a jail seemed so permanent and irreversible. I was having a panic attack, like once I walked in, I'd never walk out. I couldn't go down like that. I tried kicking, screaming, and nudging her off me with my shoulders, but it was no use with my wrists cuffed behind my back.

"Back up! Back up! I need help in here," the officer called out.

Her lying ass didn't need any help. She was only trying to make it seem like I was resisting her more than I actually was. Hearing the voices of officers telling her to back off and they were there to save the day, I couldn't let her go thinking she'd broken me down. Her pig ass was already walking away with the trophy award of breaking up my family. Moving my head back, I snapped it forward against her forehead with as much aggression I could muster up with her weight on top of me.

Crackkk!

"Ahhh! This little nigger headbutted me," she yelped out in pain.

In spite of my head pounding, feeling like it was going to split into two, I felt ten times better for causing the supposed protector some pain. My grin was ear to ear. I'd never forget her, so I hoped she'd never forget me.

"I told you to get your hands off me," I screamed out again, then spit right into her face. "Fuck you and your oink-oink-ass friends!"

I'm Porsha Jackson, daughter of Calvin and Trinity Jackson. I wasn't bred to be a wimp. The world will eventually see. Once I turn 18, I'ma be walking up out of juvie with a chip on my shoulder, ready to set shit the fuck off.

But I had to get through the system first.

LOCKED UP

The interrogation room of 1300 Beaubien rocked from the inside out as two officers of the Detroit Police Department badgered Calvin Jackson about the murders of Vincent Belmont and De'Mario Cooper. The cops had been going at it for hours strong, starting at the hour they met at the station and suited up for the raid of his home. They felt cocky, unstoppable, and superior to the drug-dealing kingpin, as Calvin sat slouched at the table, seemingly defeated.

Calvin Jackson's wounds were fresh from taking an ass whopping of a lifetime from the gang of cops who'd snatched him out of his sheets, including the two before him. Calvin's lip was busted, there were several lumps on his head, and his rib cage was bruised from one of the brazen officers stomping him in his chest. They'd shown no mercy toward him, and he planned on doing the same when his chance of revenge presented itself.

Raging like a bull on the inside, Calvin wanted nothing more than to be free from the cuffs and chains that secured him to the table. He felt the pulse of his heart speed up with every threat, derogatory insult, and fist the cops threw his way. Even the veins in his arms and hands were enlarged. Each deep breath that Calvin took was an attempt to calm him down. However, the only solace he found was in the thought of mapping out the murders of each Detroit Police officer who raided his home.

CHAPTER 23

PORSHA

Being yanked down a dreary hallway by a buff-body, man-looking woman guard, I was then tossed into another windowless room like a piece of trash, before being cuffed to a bench. I'd gone through this sickening experience three times already, and I was sure this one wouldn't be the last.

"Ahh," I yelped out in pain when the metal of the cuffs cut into my wrists.

"Shut up before I make 'em tighter," she growled, using her power to control me. "Whatever you get, you deserve. Especially for that li'l stunt ya pulled in the garage. Now, what ghetto-ass name did your mother give you? I need your first, middle, and last."

Grunting, struggling to sit up on the bench without cutting my wrists more, I still managed to speak up smartly. "Don't speak ill about my mother," I huffed.

"Or what? Huh? What do you think you can do to me that I won't do to you and call it self-defense? I'll be in the shower washing the backsplash of your blood off me while your body is lying here waiting for the state-paid medical examiner to write up a report releasing the system and their employee of any wrongful doings. I'm not my comrade. I'll shoot a nigger like it doesn't matter in a second."

I was quiet, stunned, and in shock.

"Yeah, exactly what I thought. Now, like I asked you for, what's your full name?"

"Porsha Shanae Jackson."

After making a judgmental face, she asked for the spelling of my middle name before typing it into their system. Following that, she keyed in my date of birth, address, and the name of my high school. Though I wasn't being a bitch, I still took my sweet time giving her all of the information. If being here was uncomfortable and unfair for me, I fa' damn sho' wasn't about to make her processing job simple.

"Take your shoes off and step up on the scale," she ordered, giving me the same attitude I'd thrown her.

Oh, she's mad? Ain't that a bitch? The audacity. "I ain't putting my feet on that nasty thang," I rudely responded, twisting my face up in pure disgust.

She shook her head like she pitied me, but I quickly learned that wasn't the case. "Your problem is not mine. Get up on the scale so I can log your weight, Jackson." She called me by my last name only, a true sign I'd crossed over into some real rough shit.

I thought about pushing her limits like I'd done to her buddy, but I didn't. I had enough problems on my plate. Whereas at first I was only facing a few hours with a state social worker until one of my aunts showed up to get me and Benzie, I was now facing charges for assaulting an officer of the law.

I might've been standing tall and acting tough, but I was scared as hell. I've never once had a run-in with the cops without Cal or Trin being around. So having a bunch of them barking at me that I'd be going to prison terrified my soul. I wanted my mommy and daddy, and I didn't care how juvenile that sounded. I wasn't sure of what to do.

Trying my hardest to be compliant, I slid my shoes off and stepped onto the filthy scale. I was grossed out but stood still. This wasn't shit but the start of my transition into a group home. After the digital numbers bounced around, they finally landed on 123.4 pounds.

"See? That wasn't so hard," she mocked me. "Now, after you put your shoes back on, stand right behind that black line. When you get there, say cheese." She was being sarcastic, rubbing my face in my misery, and trying to piss me off all at the same time. She had the same condescending tone the other cop had before I split her cranium open.

Biting my lips to keep them from flapping and talking shit, I did exactly as I was told except for smiling. My expression was ripped, set to kill. If only my mom had been here to put the processing officer in her place for talking to her baby girl so recklessly, I'd be grinning instead of frowning. But they'd already told me my parents were going to jail before hell when I'd first thrown my bloodline up.

With my back against the wall, I wished I could chuck my middle fingers up at her in all of the mugshots. She took my front picture, exposing the huge unicorn knot I had on my forehead from headbutting her partner, then my profile shots. I was usually camera thirsty, but I wasn't feeling the flash today. I knew my face was roughed up and bruised from battling it out with that lame-ass cop who was gonna catch these hands for real whenever I got free.

"If you hated taking off your shoes, you're surely going to hate the next part." She found joy in antagonizing me. I stared at her with tight lips, afraid to ask what was next, but she killed my curiosity quickly. "The strip search."

"Aw, hell naw! Y'all already searched me in the garage," I complained, pulling my arm back before she could grab it. "I'm not taking my clothes off, so you might as well

back up off me. Your perverted ass ain't about to see me
naked." Being compliant, yeah, that was now a notion of
the past.

Instead of attacking me like the other lady did, this
officer chirped her walkie-talkie on and called for backup,
saying I was refusing to leave the processing area for a
strip search. With a grin on her face, she leaned against
the wall I'd just taken pictures on, tapping her foot
and picking the dirt from underneath her nails. "You
can make it as hard on yourself as you want to," she
said to me nonchalantly, shrugging her shoulders. "I'm
scheduled to go home after processing you, which means
I won't be stuck here a minute longer having to fill out
paperwork behind an incident."

"Blah, blah, bullshit, yap, yap. Unless you're about to
take these cuffs off, which we both know you're not going
to, then shut the fuck up," I simply responded, more
concerned with the officers who were getting ready to
barge into the room.

She rolled her eyes, knowing I'd pulled her card. Then
she hit me with the same line all uppity people said when
they'd be hoed. "I wouldn't dare stoop to ya level, ya li'l
bitch."

I was shaking mad, and my legs were trembling uncontrollably. I wanted to get up and handle her without
reaping a consequence. It was hard as hell bowing to
someone who wasn't Calvin or Trinity. Closing my eyes, I
took a few deep breaths, because I heard voices and shuf-
fling coming from the other side of the door. The last tag
I ever wanted attached to my name was the one of a punk.
The voice of my momma kept playing over in my head
to *take my punishment like a woman*," so I planned
to. This might have been my karma for creeping around
with Street. Until I went against family, everything about
everything had been all good.

CHAPTER 24

ELIZABETH

I called my assistant over the speakerphone into my office. "Excuse me, but I need you in here."

Within seconds, she was in the doorway of my office with a notepad and pen. "Yes, Mrs. Hines? What can I do for you?" She was always prompt and ready to serve. I was glad to have an assistant working as my second pair of hands.

"Call the courts to see which judges are scheduled to hear the cases of Calvin and Trinity Jackson. If the list isn't favorable for us, see if you can get the clerk to shift a few things around it becomes favorable. Then call Katie to see if she can meet me for bagels in an hour. And finally, let Mr. Heagenbon's assistant know that it's urgent for me to see him upon his arrival."

"Got it," she said, still penning notes. "Anything else?"

"Yes, a fresh cup of coffee. Put on a new pot, because this case is kicking my ass." Without saying thank you, I waved her from my office and dove right back into trying to prepare myself for Mr. Jackson's jail consultation. He'd given me way too much upfront money for me to come out of the gate choking the first time he needed representation.

Pacing back and forth in front of the windows of my office, I stared out across the waves of the Detroit River into Canada. The sun was shining, and the water looked blue and calm, but the Zen-like view wasn't putting my mood at ease. I wanted so badly to take another bump to relax my nerves, but I couldn't risk meeting with my associate high. He didn't indulge but should have.

Gregory Heagenbon was on the firm's roster as the go-to guy for straight and narrow cases because he was a straight and narrow guy. He was the friendly face of the firm. Gregg didn't break rules, make deals with the devil, or cut a person's throat for wins. He was the perfect guy for the plan I'd concocted. That was why I had to be on the up-and-up when I asked him for the favor.

I'd been diligently working on the Jackson case, Calvin's record in particular. I was trying to find loop-holes, incongruent stories from witnesses, if the cops violated his rights as a citizen during the raid, and whatever other factors I could legally argue in his defense if the case went to trial. The evidence stacked against the trapping family was insane, but they wanted Calvin's head on a platter in particular. It was my job to change his foreseen circumstances. That was where Gregg would come into play.

Besides Calvin being charged with the murder and mutilation of two bodies, the DPD also recovered large amounts of cash, drugs, and a few pistols from his home, referenced to as "an operation." Working Calvin out of the system was going to take a little more than magic. However, that was why all the big dogs paid me the big bucks. I wasn't above making cruddy deals. It's not always about what you know, but who you know. Oh yeah, and how you work the system. I was willing to do all of the above plus things unmentioned to win a case. My resume was far more important than my reputation.

"Mrs. Hines?" my assistant chirped over the intercom.

"Yes, what is it?" I snapped at her, irked that she was interrupting me with a call instead of the cup of coffee I'd requested.

"Um, sorry to disturb you, Mrs. Hines, but Mr. Heagenbon's assistant just called and said he's on his way up."

"Oh, okay. Thanks. Make sure that cup of coffee is in my hands before he's in my office."

CHAPTER 25

TRINITY

"If you wanna walk up outta here with your baby boy and not have him lost in foster care somewhere, you better write some juicy shit on this notepad about your husband and his drug operation," the police officer said, trying to intimidate me, slamming a yellow notepad and pencil down onto the table in front of me.

"Tah! You got me fucked up, Mr. Officer. I ain't writing shit on that paper but my food order, because I'm starving." I set him straight, picking weed flakes from underneath my acrylic nails.

"Do you think I'm playing with you about the powers I have, Mrs. Jackson? My partner already hauled ya daughter away to the group home." He thought his news was gonna make me shit.

Both of the officers were coming at me from left and right with what they'd do, what they had on my husband and me, and how our family would be completely dismantled if I didn't at least give them some pertinent information against Calvin that would stick. They kept advising it would be best for me to take their deal, allowing me to go home and keep the kids out of the system, especially Benzie. That sour deal, however, meant my husband would do all of the time for all of the crimes.

If I were dumb, which praise God I wasn't, I'd have actually believed the deal they were giving me was the best one available. I couldn't wait until the attorney Calvin had been paying strutted her high-heel-wearing ass into this precinct and escorted me out of here. Them trying to coerce me into snitching, making a deal, and incriminating myself meant they didn't have a helluva case against me anyway. I continued holding my own.

"White boy, please! You ain't said nothing that'll make me blink. My daughter is built just as sturdy as I am. We ain't frail, feeble, and trained to bow like the Sallys, Sues, and Beths you mingle with. We're some muthafuckin' brick houses," I said confidently, leaning back in the seat and crossing my arms.

Something I said struck a nerve in the cop, because he leaped in my face and growled. Had we been on the streets, I would've gotten right back with his coward ass. Being that I was cuffed, I settled for using my tongue, which was sharp as a blade.

"I don't care about that badge in ya pocket or that muthafuckin' toy gun on ya hip. You better back up outta my face." I spoke in a cool and collected tone, although firecrackers were spewing off inside of me. My fuse might've been short, but I knew when and how to play my position. I'd been practicing being in control since I sliced my dad's neck.

My chilled demeanor was intentional, and I manipulated my moves to antagonize and piss them off. Cops hated when they couldn't make a muthafucka shiver. They thrived off power, but they weren't about to stroke their cocks off my weakness. They'd cuffed the wrong chick if they thought I was the type of bitch to bend and buckle at the knees.

"Ahhhhh! Let me go! Please, Travis! I swear I'm sorry for not having the food ready. It's almost done. All it needs is a few more minutes," my mother cried out.

"You didn't do nothing all day but take care of these mismatched, funny-looking-ass kids you done trapped me with. Even if I was tired of dogging ya ugly ass out, Bee, I couldn't leave ya, 'cause my whole check'll still boomerang back to this miserable-ass house."

"If you wanted to leave, Travis, I wouldn't put you on child support," my mother sobbed.

Wap!

Wap, wap!

"Ahhhhh! Travis! Noooo!"

"You better close that door like Momma told you to keep it," Tanya said, sitting in the middle of the twin bunk she and I shared. She slept at the head, and I slept at the foot, although there wasn't a headboard or footboard to denote which side was which.

"But Momma is crying. That nigga just slapped her in the face with his open palm, the same way he hits us on our bare asses," I told my elder sissy like she wasn't familiar with my dad's attacks.

"You better quit worrying about Momma and hope Daddy ain't heard you curse, let alone call him the N-word," she warned, wrapping her arms around her knees while rocking back and forth. Tanya was scared. She was always timid, quiet, and obedient when Travis was home.

"I ain't scared of him." Making a muscle, I was the toughest li'l sprout around.

Tanya started giggling. When she hiccupped and snorted, it made me laugh too. These were like the silly moments all of us shared when my mean poppa wasn't home. It was like he sucked the life out of the whole household when he finally dragged his feet through the front door. Not only was his face always twisted into a scowl, but he always smelled like sweet perfume that made my mom sob. Ruby, my eldest sister, said *that was because the fragrance woke the sleeping fool up in her. The sad part about her comment was that I wasn't far enough removed from the sad situation to not understand exactly what she meant.*

Every time I heard my mom cry or saw her put makeup over bruises or practice in the mirror a lie she'd eventually tell us about a gash on some part of her body, a huge chunk of my innocence evaporated. I loved my mom but not enough to wanna be like her. Early on, I chose to break every rule she enforced because I figured her path could only lead to me marrying a mean man and living miserably.

In the meantime, Momma tried her best to give her five daughters a normal childhood. My dad had a well-paying job at the plant that could've had all of us spoiled, but he cheated with his check and spent it on the children of those home-wrecking hoes. Me, Trish, and Tiana shared clothes and shoes, while Mom, Ruby, and Tanya shared the same. We all did our best hustling up money doing odd jobs for our neighbors to help bring in the dividends my dad so easily withheld. With all of us working together as a team, I couldn't understand why my momma didn't leave the bastard who served as Lucifer in the household.

He always broke our spirits whenever he was home. I didn't know how, but we'd even turn on each other when his presence lingered for too long. Travis brought out the worst in us. All of us acted differently, not like family but like strangers. The only reason this moment was unfolding between my sister and me was because it was going on behind a closed door. Had even my mother known about the joyous occasion while my dad was home, she would've whipped the smile off our faces herself. She'd rather beat us than have our callous, heavy-handed father do it.

The more Tanya and I laughed, the funnier laughing became, so the louder we got.

Then all that shit stopped because the devil himself barged into the room. I should've stopped thinking about his evil ass long ago and enjoyed the happy moment.

"Shut up in here! I don't want to hear all that loud noise in my house! Do y'all think y'all outside? In a zoo? On a playground somewhere?"

Sweat was pouring from my father's face as he yelled into our faces. When he pulled his thick leather belt from the loops of his pants, Tanya's shrill cry filled the room like he'd already struck her. Seeing my sister completely terrified made me want to protect her.

Instead of hiding in a corner hoping my spanking wasn't coming next, I tiptoed up on my father while he taunted Tanya with the belt, and I yanked it from his hand. I didn't snatch it completely from his grip, but I did divert the attention from my sister.

With her hand covering her mouth and tears running from her eyes, she backed farther back on the bed, awaiting my dad's reaction. I didn't expect her to have my back and come to my rescue as I did for her. Tanya wasn't cut like me, though we were cut from the same cloth. She acted more like my mom, and me, yeah, my mannerisms were more like my pop's. That was why he and I were looking at one another like equals. That was why his nose flared and his reaction slowed. He knew there were more of his characteristics within me than he'd ever noticed or cared to stick around long enough to learn.

Knowing what was coming my way in spite of his epiphany, I took a deep breath and tightened my lips so a scream wouldn't release from them when he struck me. Travis knew what I was doing because it was the same thing he would've done, so that was why he tried beating the spunk out of me.

On my father's third swing, my mother burst into the room, begging for him to stop. On her heels were

her other three daughters, who she pushed back out
the room. She slammed the door so they wouldn't
see the madness.

My father's attention shifted from me to his wife.
And so did the attention of his belt. He whipped her
mercilessly, slanging the belt wildly until damn near
every exposed part of her body was welted. My sister
and I hugged each other tightly, fearing what he'd do
next. Her face was buried in my neck, but my eyes were
glued to the horrific scene before us.

"Tra . . ." She tried speaking his name but couldn't
finish it. Her voice was soft and low. "Plea . . . st . . . go . . ."

The more she begged, the crazier he got. I blacked out
for a lot of him whipping her. I might've been stronger
than my sister, but seeing my mom almost lifeless made
me cringe. I blacked out, and when I came to, my hands
were bloody and my dad was dead.

Bang!

One of the cops slammed his fist down on the table,
stirring me from the gruesome flashback of my childhood.

"Hey, you! You ain't got all day. Either write something
on that pad for my partner and me, or you can find
comfort down in ya holding cell. It doesn't make me shit
'cause I'ma walk up outta here and eat my fat ass a juicy-
ass steak either way." He continued being an arrogant
asshole.

I took a deep breath and picked up the number two
pencil. As I hit it on the table a few times, the sound
of the taps triggered tears to stream from my eyes
uncontrollably. I was pissed as fuck that I couldn't stop
myself from breaking down in front of two pigs who were
beaming at me crumbling in my seat, but I was making
myself stronger with each sob and tear. These shit bags
didn't know my struggle, the grief I'd carried on my heart,
or my evil intentions.

Without weed or alcohol, I was lacking the vices I'd been using to cope. I started hearing my daddy's voice, who I heard haunting me every night, telling me he was going to get me for what I did. I always whispered back, for no one else to hear, that I'd meet him in hell with an even bigger piece of glass. That was why I could never sleep.

Slouched down, I slid the notebook closer to me and gripped the pencil to write my first word. I couldn't go home unless I gave the cops what they wanted.

CHAPTER 26

PORSHA

On the outside looking in, this alternative home didn't look as grim as it actually was. The green grass, full trees, and beautiful landscape of flowers were strategically placed to hide the gated windows, guard towers, and multiple fenced-in buildings that I was now learning all the girls were categorized and separated between. My eyes and ears were wide open and alert for every word spoken or look shared between cops, social workers, or anyone dressed casually. I wanted to know what their intentions were with all of us newbies dressed in what looked like pink nurse scrubs but were really prison getups.

Every hour on the hour, a cop or child protective service worker marched in here with an at-risk teen they swore needed a safe haven and around-the-clock therapeutic intervention. Kicking and screaming, like me, none of us wanted to be locked away within a baby jail that was dressed up as a place of healing. We all knew what this was. We all knew what we were in for. Pure hell.

The holding room was more like a sweat box. I ended up pulling my shirt off like many of the girls and was down to my bra. I decided not to do so, but I really wanted to strip down to my panties. Had I not spotted a few questionable chicks, I might've stripped naked altogether. I felt delirious, lightheaded, and woozy like I was about to pass out. Plain and simple, it was scorching in here. There was absolutely no ventilation or circulation of the hot air all of us were breathing. And though many of the girls complained, screamed, and pounded on the door for someone to have mercy on us, none of them did. We'd already been tagged as kids who would never amount to anything. The guards were completely numb to us, our issues, and our behavior.

When the backup guards came in to take me for the strip search, they were accompanied by a nurse who gave me some type of muscle relaxer shot. All I could do was blink. The whole time they undressed me, then clothed me back in the pink getup, I was alert but couldn't move or cover myself up. This whole experience was one I'd never forget.

Finally, one of the guards called for me and a few other girls. Our small group was escorted out and to a different part of the building while they explained some of the rules they didn't show leniency for when broken. It was a long fuckin' list. I swore I heard the guard call off smiling as one of the things we weren't allowed to do.

Whereas we'd been locked up in a stuffy cage that was hot as hell, we were now in a chilled room ventilated by an air conditioning unit. It wasn't for us girls, though, but for the administrators present. This was our orientation into the alternative home, although we'd already been improperly introduced. The room had about ten folding chairs, a podium, and a long table that had papers spread across it. After being handed a packet each, we took our seats one by one and listened to the director of the home. We heard crap about how they'd make us better citizens of society and how to make better decisions that would better our future. They claimed that once we got transitioned and stopped fighting, the healing could begin. They meant brainwashing, but healing sounded better. Still, bullshit.

If I were coming here homeless, neglected, or abused, this alternative solution for teenage living might've been a miracle for me. This situation, however, was nothing but a downgrade from what I was accustomed to. Of the eight girls in the group I was in, three of them were genuinely happy about the services offered. Me, however, I wanted out of this dressed-up dungeon with a one-way ticket back to the trap.

Right out of orientation, we were led to our assigned counselors. My therapist was a middle-aged woman with skin the color of mine. I thought she was gonna be cool, maybe on that black power or sister-to-sister shit, but nope. It was like the melatonin in her skin made her meaner. She was short, blunt, and direct about what she expected and wasn't going to tolerate from me. The whole intake process was grueling, and that was putting it lightly. Every time she twisted her face up at me, I wanted to spit in it to show her the type of cloth I was cut from.

After I refused to spill the beans about my upbringing, thoughts, and what brought me into the group home, she labeled me a problem. I didn't give two shits about her label as long as she left me alone, so I didn't fret or shrug. Even with my family already being broken up, ain't nobody affiliated with the cops could manipulate me and use my therapy session as testimony against my father. I wasn't stupid. These cock-sucking judges would never understand what it meant to grow up in the trap anyway, which meant them and me would never relate.

Calvin didn't subject me to a crappy-ass lifestyle. In the hood, it was better to grow up with pushers instead of the poppers. The State might not have felt like Calvin made the best decision as the leader of his family, but he'd already schooled me that Blacks weren't mighty or powerful enough to ship the shit overseas anyhow. They were charging my dad for the dope they wanted him to poison his community with.

Calvin didn't just slang drugs, he slung knowledge, although he'd really been a puppet in all of this. I saw the way the cop's eyes smiled as he held my father's mouth shut and his head up to face his own demise. He'd been happy in his point of power and cheerful about our misery. Whenever my dad got out, though, I already knew the cop would get two untraceable bullets to the head. Hopefully he had kids who would get to witness him broken down as well. I hated seeing my daddy like that.

Once the grilling sessions were done, we were tossed into the general population of teens within the group home. I was assigned to building C. Building C came with hella restrictions and housed all the girls with deviant backgrounds. You had to be either serving out juvenile sentences, waiting to have your case heard as I was, or waiting to age out of the system to be transferred into a state prison. The latter was what I feared.

Sitting on the side of the bed they'd assigned to me, I bowed my head, trying to gather some mental strength. Tears were at the brim of my eyes, but I didn't wanna let the other girls see me crying. I'd never been to a group home, but I knew enough to know that crying would get me tagged as a weak link then bullied every day after.

I was honest enough with myself to say I didn't want beef because I was too inexperienced with fighting to survive. However, I'd also taken too many beatdowns from Trinity to not know how to handle myself. If a bitch came for me up in here, they'd get twirled on their head.

For every time I couldn't hit my momma back, I'd be laying a fist into their face. Fighting fair wasn't an option.

Finally coming out of my temporary living quarters, I posted up in the recreation room. A lot of the girls were in here either watching the fuzzy-picture TV screen, playing a 1990s board game, or throwing some cards around the table either in a game of spades or tunk. I didn't wanna partake in none of the so-called recreational activities but really didn't have a choice since there was nothing else to do. We weren't allowed to have cell phones or electronic devices. I was going crazy not being able to log into my social sites. And unlike when I'd been on one of Trinity's punishments, I didn't have the foolishness of the hood going on outside my bedroom window to entertain me. I'd have given anything to hear some scrappers stealing the pipes from the house next door right about now. I'd have given anything to serve a fiend up right quick for a hot ten-dollar bill to take Benzie to the corner store with. The thought of my brother almost made me buckle at the knees.

I went the whole morning and part of the afternoon without getting anything but curious stares from the other girls. I didn't know if it was because of my long but now sweated-out curls, all the bruises on my face from the police roughing me up, or the basic fact that I was one of the newest girls there. I expected them to want to know my story, yet I wasn't up to making friends. To help pass the time, I found myself thinking about what I'd tell Imani when we finally talked. The more hours that passed by, the more miserable I became.

After walking down every hour of the depressing day to group therapy gatherings, counseling sessions, and even a visit from a State-appointed lawyer who was allegedly going to help me fight the charges of assaulting a cop, I

skipped eating and retired to my bunk. I couldn't wait
to start the job they'd give me within a couple of days
so I could have money to make a call. Shit was crazy! I'd
helped my dad count up thousands made in one night by
hand before, but I was on craps tonight without a measly
dollar.

"So, what's your name? You've been here all damn day
and ain't said shit to none of us," a girl addressed me.

"That's 'cause I don't have much to say," I responded,
keeping it real. I'd gone the whole day sulking to myself
and wanted to keep it that way.

"And why don't you? Everybody up in here has a story
to tell." She pressed the issue.

"Okay, well, that's the first lesson in learning I'm different from everyone else. I ain't no damn Teddy Ruxpin
bear. If you trying to get a bedtime story told, cuddle up
to some other bitch."

She burst out laughing like a deranged crazy person
then ran up on me in an eye blink. "Naw, I've got the right
bitch."

Wop, wop!

Her fist connected twice with my face, right underneath my eye. She'd knocked me into shock, temporarily.
As soon as she got cocky enough to open her mouth to
talk shit, I threw my fist down her throat. I went in her
grill like a homeless hungry man, knocking her two front
teeth out in the process. "Naw, baby girl, you ain't got the
right bitch."

Wop, wop!

Wop, wop, wop!

I wasn't going out without a helluva fight. Brianna
should've stayed the hell out of my space. Fighting her
like I'd seen my mommy throw fists at chicks, I kept
hitting her in the same exact spot each blow I served. As
soon as I cracked the skin above her eye, I moved my

hand lower to target the skin beneath it. I was trying to make her eye pop from its socket. Since she wanted to look funny, she could. Her muthafuckin' wish was my command.

I knew without a doubt this wasn't going to be the last of these girls to try me, so I went in on shorty, making sure whoever saw our fight knew I'd be a helluva competitor.

CHAPTER 27

CALVIN

"Say what? She's where? And what happened?" Growling like a beast and yelling at the top of my lungs, I didn't give a fuck about Elizabeth just sucking me off.

Listening to the news she was delivering about my baby girl, I was foaming at the mouth, and it wasn't from the coke. I now knew why she'd come in giving me a taste of the mind-altering drug and moistening my rod with her spit. Wouldn't no man feel at ease, not a real man, while hearing his offspring was in a damn near no-win situation. I wanted every muthafucka up in this jail feeling my pain as I felt it now, especially the stankin'-ass pigs. They wanted the freedom of every immediate family member except for Benzie.

Looking back and forth between the door and me, she tried getting me to lower my tone. "Calvin, please calm down. The guards you've already made enemies of are itching to drag you down into solitary confinement." In spite of her being the voice of reason, I ignored her and attacked.

"Quite frankly, if you can't tell, I don't give a fuck about them or you." Slamming my fist down onto the table, rattling it, and knocking papers to the floor, I was ready to choke the nut she'd just swallowed back up from her stomach. "The person I give a fuck about is Porsha. With that being said, I suggest you pack ya briefcase up, straighten out ya wig, and hurry up outta here to get her case thrown out." Hearing that my daughter was detained in a group home with charges pending against her for assaulting a cop had me enraged. Not even the woman I'd paid a hundred grand to was on my team at this point.

One of the COs who'd dragged me down here opened the door to see what the commotion was about. I eyed his ass like I could serve him death if he wanted it like that, but Mrs. Hines threw her hands up, intervening so he'd back down. She knew my resume well.

"Officer Baker, please back off some to give me and my client a little space to work over this case. You know I can handle myself, honey," she sweet-talked him, making his chubby ass drool at the mouth. She was working her sexual magic on the CO as she'd done to me months ago.

"That I do." He blushed. "But if for any reason you need me, I'll be right outside this door. And I won't hesitate to put the cuffs back on him if need be."

"Thank you, Officer Baker. That won't be necessary, but I'll keep that in mind."

After adjusting his hard-on, the CO slammed the steel door, and Mrs. Hines's eyes repositioned themselves on me.

"Calvin, look, I can't sugarcoat shit. Porsha is in a lot of trouble behind headbutting that cop. I'll be going over to the group home to counsel her later today, but until then, I hope she stays quiet. They'll hold anything she says against her, and you."

I sat still and silent. I'd never been in a position where I couldn't protect my family. Being helpless made me feel crazy inside. I sat back, listening to all of what Mrs. Hines had to say, then advised her to make sure Porsha didn't get stuck with any charges. For my sanity, I didn't even ask about Benzie. Knowing my son was out in this world without his dad was fuckin' with my sanity.

A few minutes later, I was itching to conceal the pencil I was holding from Mrs. Hines's briefcase so I could use it as a weapon to stab a nigga out later. From the police officer's report of my "volatile attack" against him—his words and way of spinning shit, not mine—I was about to be resting my head up in here longer than I'd anticipated. That meant my team on the outside was gonna have to step it up to hold me and mine down. During this time was when I'd see who was real, who was fake, and who deserved death in return for disloyalty.

"Calvin, you're going to make it so my hands are tied. If you want me to work my magic on the judge presiding over your case, you've gotta do a complete three-sixty up in here and start keeping a low profile," she advised me straightforwardly. "That means no fights with inmates, no additional ones with correctional officers, and please withstand from having sexual intercourse with any of the women COs. The last thing you need is some bitter-ass guard trying to keep ya dick locked up. Do you understand?"

I snickered, truly amused with Mrs. Hines's bossy demeanor. On the low, she wanted to make sure she was the only one getting dick served to her since Trinity was locked up. "Look, with all due respect. I'll handle my time up in here how I need to in order to survive. And you, well, you better make sure you're worth that hundred grand I've invested into ya polished ass that you probably jacked off on your li'l habit."

Elizabeth sat across from me in a pleated pants suit, red-sole Louboutin heels, and a fragrance floating off her skin that smelled like flowers. She was classy, sophisticated, but a coke head on the low. Pretty messy white girls usually were. *Shorty better not let that habit be her downfall.*

Visibly taken aback by my comments, she snickered while scratching her head before responding. "Mr. Jackson, don't let the polish, gloss, or coke I do fool you. I'm intelligent with degrees to prove it. Please don't insult and belittle me again." She was firm. "And yes, you paid me a hundred grand. Not only is it my business what I do with what I earn, but I gave you a discount. My services aren't cheap, subpar, or what any other attorney within this region can offer you. Being that you have them, take advantage of them and know I will walk you out of here personally if you do as I say." Not batting an eyelash, Elizabeth confronted me and my thuggish demeanor head-on. She didn't even blink an eye.

It didn't matter if I believed her little spiel. I couldn't do shit but fall back. Like I was in the process of teaching Porsha and had already taught Street, everybody has a role in life to play. "Yeah, a'ight. Let's just move on before your fat-ass cop comes back in here lookin' to get his ass beat."

She rolled her eyes, then got to work.

She placed five manila envelopes in front of me. I flipped each one open and viewed what the boys had on me. Two of the folders had the information on the young dudes Fame and I killed and all of their personal information, including addresses. Both of their murders were pinned on me. I made a mental note of that information before opening the third folder. It was the biggest of the five and contained info on all of the suspected illegal items in my household, the paraphernalia from the trap, and all the seized cash. The folder also contained all the charges pending against Trinity and Porsha. My heart sank seeing the letter Trinity wrote in the interrogation room right after they arrested her.

The fourth and fifth folders I looked in contained pictures, reports from private investigators, and testimonies.

I tried memorizing everything in the snitch files, but Mrs. Hines told me the pertinent information within the files would be given to Fame later at their meeting. Off the rip, I knew he'd take care of anything dangling between me and my freedom.

Mrs. Hines sat across the table from me with her eyes glued to my face the entire time I sorted through the papers and pictures in the files. She gave me the silence I needed to process everything, yet watched for twitches and expressions that hinted toward my inner thoughts. I gave her nothing to work with, though. Her job wasn't to pick me apart, but to get a judge in my back pocket. I was expecting her to go above and beyond doing that, too.

Closing and then stacking the manila folders on top of one another, I slid them back across the table to her. "So, what's your plan? I'd tell you what I'm thinking, but I don't wanna insult your intelligence again." I was being facetious but serious at the same time.

"Nice joke, Mr. Jackson," she replied, wearing a half smirk. "But with that pencil you're about to snap in two, write down what you want relayed to Mr. Famous instead. While I'm working on a few technicalities and slipups made by the DPD, your right-hand man can clean the streets up on your behalf." Her words were weighted.

I knew exactly what she meant. Mrs. Hines might've been well-off and reserved, but her desperation to stay on top made her equally cut-throat. At the end of the day, she was down for anything, just like I was.

CHAPTER 28

FAME

Standing outside of the Greyhound bus station, I pulled on a Newport, wishing it could've been the blunt I left in the car. The nicotine I was inhaling wasn't hitting on shit to settle my nerves. If I wasn't on the cusp of downtown, I'd be blowing my dope of choice out in the open without question. In this area, though, there were too many cops surveying and monitoring. I blended in the best I could, hoping my big black ass didn't stand out too much.

"Hey! Yo! What's up? Ask the driver when he's timed to pull in. I've been posted up outside of here for the last twenty minutes," I barked into the phone to my cousin Cricket.

"I ain't gettin' up askin' that old white man shit, cuzzo. I don't give a fuck how emancipated niggas is up here. Where I'm from, we still fear the pink-power piglets."

"Nawww, I know I didn't send for ya ass from all the way down in the boonies of Tennessee for you to come up here on some scary shit," I half teased and tested my cousin. I wanted to see how far he'd go.

"Fame, you got me fucked up. I'ma pass the phone to my brother because he's better with his words than I am. I don't know what other way to tell you hell no, so hold on." Cricket was the boldest, silliest nigga I knew, but you better not meet him at night.

More reserved and the thinker of the two, Adam was also the oldest. He was the brother that monitored, kept his mouth closed until necessary, and made his first move the best one possible. I respected that, but he'd better respect me, my resume, and the street credentials it was loaded with.

"What up doe, cuz?" Adam got on the cell phone, cool, calm, and collected.

"Shit, a nigga ain't doing nothing but trying to find out where y'all asses be at. According to the text message ya bro sent, that muthafuckin' driver was supposed to be pulling into this station thirty minutes ago." I was aggravated and antsy. With the amount of chaos unfolding in the hood, I needed to be in the thick of thangs, not puffing on a Newport, watching travelers go to and fro.

"Chief, are you serious right now? I'ma need you to take a Xanax or whatever it is y'all up-north niggas pop and swallow to chill out. I'm riding with my bro on this one. You iggin' out on some shit none of us can control. We ain't whippin' the Scooby-Doo van." He referred to the automobile they did missions in at home.

On the last trip I made down to Tennessee, I bounced around in the back of the seatless van as they kidnapped and beheaded a white boy who'd racially disrespected their momma, my auntie. It wasn't that they owed me one for my involvement in the gruesome murder. We were family, and that was how I showed my love. Cricket, Adam, and I were like brothers split from the same rib.

Anyway, Adam was speaking the truth. They weren't controlling the steering wheel. When I placed the call to them a few days ago to come up here, I already had bus reservation information on hand along with the code they needed to scoop up some cash from Western Union. I paid them niggas five grand each just to make the trip, and I promised boss statuses on arrival.

The only thing I could promise as of now, though, was a lot of dirty work. With Calvin being knocked, wasn't none of us sitting on the thrones we'd been plotting on protecting. I needed my goon-ass country cousins to help me shake these Detroit muthafuckas up.

"Be ready to work, fam."

"I stay ready. You know what it is. But I'll get at you when I get there. You know I can't stand nosy muthafuck-as, and I got a bunch of faces in my mouth tryin' to be a part of my conversation and shit."

"A'ight, no doubt. Holla."

We disconnected the call, and I flicked the finished cigarette to the ground. Shit was all the way wrecked. I'd yet to hear from Calvin. I didn't know why he'd been knocked, but I did know the Carter was still surrounded by cops and the trap spot on the block was completely dry of product.

I couldn't wait to get back into my element so I could start making moves. If shit worked out the way it was supposed to, I'd have some weight for Pete Rock to move before the sun set. I might've not communicated with my ace yet, but I knew not to stall when it came to making business moves. Lighting up another Newport, I saw a few buses bending the corner to whip up in the station. I hoped one of the three was carrying Adam and Cricket so we could be out.

Bzz! Bzzzzz!

Thinking it was one of my cousins calling back, I dug my vibrating phone from my pocket to answer it but hesitated, seeing the Michigan suburb number. I ain't fuck with too many muthafuckas outside of the 313, and if I did, I fa' damn sho' had their numbers saved. I started not to answer, but something told me to.

"Yo," I answered, being short on purpose. If the person didn't catch my voice to know me, they shouldn't have been calling anyway.

"Hello, may I speak to Mr. Famous? This is Elizabeth Hines." The proper voice made me stand straight up.

"Yeah, hold on, ma." Flicking the cigarette to the pavement, I put it out with the sole of my shoe, then walked up the block where there weren't a lot of people around listening. Elizabeth Hines was Calvin's lawyer, among other things. I'd been waiting for her to call. "My bad, I'm back. What's the word, Liz?"

She sighed. "Meet me at my office in about an hour or so. There's a lot we must discuss. It's going to take a lot of magic to get your friend home." She was vague, then ended the call.

Attorney Elizabeth Hines didn't have to go into detail. Her saying the word "magic" to me was all I needed to hear to know I was about to make some bodies come up missing. Walking back toward the bus station, I lit another square up. I couldn't wait to start making moves so my manz could get back on the streets. *If magic is what Calvin needs, magic is what he'll get.*

My cousins were standing in front when I walked back up. With two big, stuffed duffel bags each the size of a grown body, I knew their asses were about to be pissed they were gonna have to walk a few blocks down and then catch a city bus a mile down to my car. I had not parked nowhere near downtown Detroit with dirty tags on my license plate and dope in the car.

"What the fuck, fam? Real talk, if you was any other nigga or we ain't have the same blood running through our veins, I'd lay these country hands on you for getting me up here under false pretenses," Cricket barked from the back seat.

I chuckled like a crazy man. "Naw, muthafucka. You're the one who's lucky my auntie May raised ya ass to know better."

"Damn, y'all two niggas arguing like some females," Adam complained. "After that long-ass bus ride, I ain't trying to hear shit but the crackle of this blunt wrap burning as I inhale the weed within it."

"Then hurry up and hit it so you can pass it back here. Maybe I'd be on chill if I could get a few puffs in with ya hogging ass."

The three of us had been going back and forth on petty shit since I told them we had to catch the bus to my car. Wasn't none of our threats serious though, just three cornbread-fed cousins linked back up. Me, Adam, and Cricket, whose real name is Christopher, were raised like brothers. There wasn't shit neither of them could've done that I wouldn't be willing to excuse.

On the ride to the hood, I revealed to them all the turmoil my crew was involved in. They knew Calvin and respected him, so past all the jokes, they were willing to body whoever it was gonna take to get him out of jail. Me and Cal might've served as each other's right-hand men, but there ain't no better feeling than having ya fam covering ya back. One hundred.

CHAPTER 29

PORSHA

One of the staff members popped her head into the private room they'd transferred me to. "Hey, Porsha. Your lawyer is in the conference room."

With a cold rag on my head, I was trying my best to keep the swelling down. It was also helping to keep me sorta cool, too. Though this room wasn't a sweat box, it was hot as hell in here. Ol' girl Brianna rightfully earned bragging rights when it came to the lump on my forehead, the cut on my chin, and the sore jaw I kept hearing pop when I moved it. She'd landed some helluva haymakers to my face even after I'd knocked her teeth out.

After putting my shirt back on, I slid off of the cot I'd been resting on and shuffled my feet out the door and down the hallway. I was right behind a guard. We had to be escorted everywhere. I wasn't in a rush to see whatever lawyer the State paid to represent me. From the stories Street had told me about a few of his associates who'd fallen in the game and were in jail, state-appointed attorneys weren't shit but fillers put in place to get more evidence to help the prosecutors fuck you with. I wasn't helping no man or woman work against me. *I ain't no fool.* I knew all the lawyers were friends and made deals with one another. I'd watched *Better Call Saul* and *Law & Order.*

I walked into the conference room with my face screwed up and my mouth twisted into a frown. I wasn't a nice girl. I was a mean girl who missed my mom, dad, and brother. The quicker this meeting was over, the quicker I could get back to my cot and plot how I was going to square up with Brianna if she ran up on me again.

Since the time they'd walked her up outta here all bloody but still trying to talk shit, I'd been thinking about all the times Trinity had left me with bruises from beatdowns. I was gonna be ready to take ol' Brianna all the way up outta the game the next time she tried me. I'd been trained by the baddest bitch in the game to box hoes out.

Being a crab and as difficult as I could be for no reason at all, I leaned against the wall and folded my arms with an attitude. I looked straight into the attorney's face, and she didn't blink, fret, or look even the least bit amused by my behavior. Her boldness was what made me step outside of myself, being so self-absorbed like I was detained without human rights, and take note of her. There was something about her.

"Look, your father's not the only cash cow paying me. I have a lot of cases to work, so please save your teenage attitude for the girls in this group home. Of course I'm versed in your record, so I know you've had a rough start."

I didn't know how to take her last comment, but I let it fly over my shoulder. It was the first statement from her mouth that had a smile plastered on my face.

"My dad sent you? You work for us?"

She smirked, rolling her eyes to the side like there was a pleasant thought running through her mind. "Yup, you are your father's child indeed."

"And my mother's." I put emphasis on the word "mother's." For some reason, I felt the need to throw that obvious point out there.

Batting her eyelashes, she looked like she took pride in what she was about to say. "Porsha, my name is Mrs. Hines. I work for your father because he's the one paying me to make sure you walk out of here with a clean name and a fresh start. Your mother is your mother. Let's not have that misunderstanding again."

If she wanted to be a smart ass, I'd jump petty to meet her on her level. "My daddy always said a winner proves themselves and a loser announces their accolades. Verbiage doesn't make me shit, Mrs. Hines." Cockily speaking, I sat across from her with my arms folded and my bruises exposed. I also had my lips twisted up and my eyes rolling each time I blinked them. Whether she was paid by my daddy or not, I wasn't feeling this Mrs. Hines chick, and I wanted her to know it.

She shook her head and rolled her eyes back, seeming completely unmoved by my posture and tone. "I bet being transferred to a woman's correctional facility like ya momma would make you shit," she clapped back, then made a facial expression I read as "bitch, what."

I shouldn't have been thrown off my square, because she was hired by my daddy, and he only associated with thugs, but this lady had me fooled with her dressed-up ass. It only took a few seconds for her words to linger to have an effect on me. No matter how hard I thought I was, or might've been when throwing my fists on Jamika, I wasn't ready to be locked up with no real-deal Holyfields. This baby jail I'd been put in was too much.

Mrs. Hines picked up on my silence and even the uneasiness in my body language. I knew she had to have, because I was no longer being bold, being disrespectful, and spewing bullshit her way. Instead, I was slouched in my seat with my head hung low, worried that I'd already gone too far to redeem myself.

"Oh, okay. It looks like you're ready to be a big girl and get down to business." She snuck in another diss, purposely antagonizing me. "I'm glad it doesn't take you long to catch on."

Ain't shit about life sweet right now, I know. I've told you since birth I was gonna protect you, and I'm sorry to have failed you. I fucked up. Ya old man fucked up, P, but that shit ain't on you. You can't carry my years. You ain't ready for my walk. Your place is out in the world, being the daughter I raised you to be. Point blank, you can't be swaying on the po-po. Not in a lifetime. Chill ya feisty ass out, and let Mrs. Hines walk you out of there when it's time. Do what I say or I'ma fuck you up, P. Don't think ya dad can't touch you from in here. If I don't come home, I need you home for Benzie. You know how I feel about family, our family. Don't let me down. Don't let me down. I meant to write that twice, baby girl.

I love you. Word is bond.

Dad

"Whatever you say, with every fiber in my body, I swear to God I'll do it," I said over my tears. I was crying so hard that my head ached. Because of my father, I was now a compliant client for Mrs. Hines.

"Aww, the little girlie pooh been crying? Found out shit ain't sweet and you're going to have to get comfortable making new friends up in here?" A junior counselor who wasn't nothing but a few years older than me at most was mocking me.

Biting the inside of my jaw, I marched beside the employee of the group home, wishing I could trip her to the floor real quick and swiftly. Per the advice of Cal and Mrs. Hines, I couldn't lift a finger or raise my voice to an administrator; and the fight with Brianna was already one more altercation than recommended. I had to play by the rules and stay off their radar. I wasn't about to be pushed to failure only two minutes after being instructed to stand strong.

I let the junior counselor berate me and attempt to pump my mind up with worries all the way to the kitchen without flinching at her once. *Whatever anger management classes I'm supposed to be taking, for her sake, they better hurry up and start. I ain't trained to be acting church on these chicks.*

Ms. Stubbs was the lady who oversaw the kitchen. She greeted us as soon as we walked into the eating area. Unlike the rest of the overseers and cops I'd encountered, she seemed nice. Hell, if she wasn't, at least she faked it and smiled. My tough-acting ass low-key felt a little better when she did.

"Call me over my walkie-talkie when you've completed your interview, Ms. Stubbs. I'd appreciate it," the junior counselor said, then excused herself.

I sighed, and Ms. Stubbs giggled. "Hold your head up. She won't be around long. Trust me."

"Good, because if she is, I swear to God I'ma go to real jail in a few months instead of going home." I regretted being brutally honest as soon as the last word left my mouth.

"Oh, no! You don't want to do that. No, no, no." At that point, her head fell into a small stack of papers attached to a clipboard. After flipping through them, she pulled a sheet out and held up her index finger, requesting my patience while she read it over.

I knew she had to know about me popping off on the officer, but she didn't mention it. If I did get hired to work in the kitchen, I'd try to mimic her grace. She might've not been dressed as classy as Mrs. Hines was, but her aura was much more calming. I found myself crossing my legs, hoping to get the job, which was weird since I wasn't the type of teen to take to folks.

After seeming only somewhat flabbergasted by my inappropriate comment, she stopped speaking about anything outside of the questions on the interview sheet. She asked me about my work ethic, what I might've had allergies to with regard to food I could handle and cook, plus how I would handle confrontation if one of the other girls tried bringing heat my way. I was honest with her, all except the answer about keeping my cool if a chick wanted to get set straight. I thought Ms. Stubbs knew it was bullshit, but she nodded and smiled at my response anyway.

"Well, Porsha, I'll be happy to ha—" Her sentence was cut short unexpectedly, and our heads turned toward the door.

"Oh shit! Ms. Stubbs! You better come to the kitchen now." A girl burst into the room we were sitting in, completely hyped and frazzled.

"Um, Maxine, I'm in the middle of an interview. What's going on?" As frantic as this Maxine person was, Ms. Stubbs didn't seem fazed or moved.

The Maxine girl must've picked up on how cool and nonchalant Ms. Stubs was acting, because the urgency in her voice was now just as cool, calm, and collected as Ms. Stubbs. "Oh." She shrugged, like what she was about to say meant nothing. "My bad to interrupt you or whatever, but Tiffany just threw a pot of boiling hot water into Alicia's face."

Yup, Ms. Stubbs lost it.

She damn near fell out of her seat as she scrambled to get out of the room. I fought to hold my laughter in, while Maxine didn't care. She kept wiping tears from her cheeks, saying she couldn't stop crying, at the same time as holding her crotch like she was holding in pee. My group home experience was gonna be one to write about for sure.

"I swear, I don't know why they put her old hag ass up in here with a bunch of firecrackers." She spoke out loud, but it was more like she was talking to herself. "She's gonna end up croaking one of these days." After having a conversation with herself, Max finally addressed me directly. "Anyway, excuse my ratchet manners. I'm Max. Are you about to work in the kitchen too?"

"Uh-huh, so they told me." I kept it short and sweet.

She picked up on my standoffish air and chuckled. "Slow down, slugga. We ain't got a problem unless you really want one. I'm just asking. And real talk, so you'll know I ain't trying to pop off with you, I'ma give you your props on tagging Brianna. I wasn't there to see it, but I didn't need to be." Putting her hand up to give me a play, I extended my hand and dapped it up with her on some "we cool, my bad" type shit.

"Thanks. Birds have been chirping like that?" I questioned her about what rumors were spreading about my fight with Brianna.

"Girl, bye! Did you forget where we're at? You ain't gonna be able to change ya tampon without these nosy heifers telling the next nasty heifer."

Just as I thought and wasn't looking forward to.

"Max, girl! What are you doing? You're missing all the drama! They can't detain Tiffany's crazy ass." Another girl burst into the kitchen just as amped as Max had come in for Ms. Stubbs.

"For real! I live for the drama up in this muthafucka." She spun around to run behind the girl. "Oh, Porsha, wanna come?" she asked me as a quick afterthought. "If you're interviewing here, you'll be working here. That's how this place operates, so you might as well get acquainted with who you'll be slaving beside."

Pausing for a second, I gave Max the impression that I was thinking about tagging along, but I knew the answer was no before the question was fully formed. These girls could mind each other's business all day long. Around the clock, if they wanted to. Me, though, I'd be busy working from the pages of my own agenda.

"Naw, I'm straight on that. Given all the bullshit I've dealt with over the last twenty-four hours, I'd really enjoy a moment of silence over a turned-up one."

"Shit, I can respect that. I'll holla at you when I see you around." As quickly as Max had darted into the room, she scurried out. I heard her loud mouth laughing when she reached the drama that was unfolding.

I wondered how many days were like this in the kitchen. Working here might've been harder than I'd anticipated. I listened to the drama for a few seconds, then crept to the door to see if Ms. Stubbs was coming back. When I saw the coast was clear, I darted behind her desk and snatched up the phone. I couldn't help myself. I had to talk to my best friend, if only for a second. With my eyes watching the door for an unwanted surprise, I waited for Imani to pick up.

"Hello," she finally answered.

"What it do, girl? What have I been missing in the hood?"

"P? Porsha? Is that you?" she questioned, sounding shocked to hear my voice but not like she was still upset over us beefing the other day.

"Yup, yup. It's me. I'm calling you from the kitchen of the group home on the sneak tip. So don't call this number back," I warned her.

"Oh, okay. I've got you," she agreed. "So ummm, what up? I really don't know what else to ask or say." Imani was honest.

"It's cool. It ain't like either of us have been in juvie before." I cut her some slack. "But to answer your question, shit ain't straight this way. Not only did my dad's lawyer say they might make me stay up in here until my birthday, but they might send me to real jail for headbutting a cop."

She gasped. "Oh my God, P! That's crazy!"

I sighed, "Yeah, tell me about it."

There was an awkward silence on the phone between Imani and me. I didn't want to state the facts, and she probably didn't want to piss me off by saying the wrong thing. Since I called her to get a moment of freedom from all the monitoring and escorting going on within the GH, I changed the subject.

"Welllllll, what's been poppin' on the block? Tell me something I'd like to hear."

"It's been kinda slow since y'all—" She paused, knowing she'd put her foot in her mouth and it was too late to backpedal.

"G'on and say it, Imani."

"My bad, Porsha. I ain't mean no harm or disrespect." She was quick at taking a cop.

"No problem. It is what it is." I cut her apology off. "Since you're keeping it one hundred today, tell me what Street's trifling ass has been up to." I had not spoken to Imani since exchanging a few words with her about Street. I figured she had a mouthful to tell me.

"Girl, girl, girl! Don't ask questions you really don't wanna know the answer to." That meant she was about to drop a bomb on me.

"Look, I've dealt with so much shit since the cops raided my house that I've lost track of time. Whatever you tell me can't compare, and trust when I tell you I can handle it," I said, pushing her to continue.

"You always want it yo' way, but whatever. Here you go." She took a deep breath before continuing. "Ain't nothing new with Street but that he might be burning. I heard Jamika's germy pussy is hotter than fish grease."

The room started spinning, my stomach sank, and my lungs started constricting. "What?" I stuttered. "I . . . can't breathe." I was wheezing and grabbing my chest like Fred Sanford in an episode of *Sanford and Son*. This wasn't a joke, though. I really thought I was about to pass the fuck out.

"Yeah, girl. And the burnin' bitch got the nerve to be down at the trap house right now." Imani threw salt into my wound.

Click.

That was me disconnecting the call. I'd heard enough from the middleman. I needed to have words with the source.

STREET

"Why are you rushing out of bed? It ain't like the trap got some work to move. Everyone knows Cal is in jail and y'all are dried up over here," she giggled. "The way your toes were just curling up, do ya'self a favor and lie back down on that pillow so I can earn a few more dollars."

If I did want to shoot another nut down her throat, she'd cancelled that thought with the other way she used her mouth, which was smart and unattractive as hell. Jamika, although good for news, could never ever get wifed up. Turned off, I pushed her over to the other side of the bed, not wanting her dick breath in my face. I had to admit, she did a much better job pleasing a nigga this time around.

"Yo, ya place ain't in my business or my money. So watch ya mouth, ma."

Taking my heater off the waistband of my pants and setting it on the dresser, I then stepped in my pants and drawers just as I'd left them. I knew when I'd gotten in the bed with Jamika that it was gonna be a quick sex session. I always had to think about Porsha when busting a nut. Her tightness, perkiness, and spunk to please a nigga had me open and thinking I should've appreciated her a little more. I knew she'd come back to a nigga when she got to be 18, though. The best part about it was that her coochie was gonna be just how I left it. I knew li'l P wasn't about to get down with another girl.

Smart-mouth-ass li'l P. Yeah, I missed the shit out of her. The way her juicy, thick thighs wrapped around my body when I popped her cherry had me trying to figure out how many days there were until her birthday so I could hit her up the day she walked out. I had not spoken to Porsha since the day she went wild on me for having Jamika in the passenger seat, on the strength of her dad. That's some knowledge shorty didn't know.

Jamika brought the focus back on her by smacking her lips. "Well, you think we can go to the mall later?"

I smacked my lips back the same. "Fuck naw! Why would I want to do that?"

"Because I know something you wanna know. That's why," she said boldly like she planned on using that same line time and time again.

I had to stop myself from grabbing her ass by the throat. "Oh, so this meat I just shoved up in you wasn't enough to get ya mouth to tell me what's up? Just enough for you to swallow nut?" She'd come at me like a rat, so she was getting treated as such.

"Um naw, don't play ya'self, Street. The dick is good and all but not no different from all the other dudes I let hit. You gotta come with something like you did that hundred. Dread-head I snitched on, he routinely copped me a few pairs of shoes once a month. Maybe you can take his position doing that."

She was straight giving me a role. A job. Making me her employer. To hell with that thought. And her. "Whatever, here." Going into my pocket, I tossed her about $500. "You better grab them bills up, make 'em work the best you can, and stay the fuck up off this block until I have a heart and let you stroll back up and down it!" Wasn't no thotting-ass trick getting ready to put me in a box, corner me up, or make me do what they wanted. I had not conformed to my momma's rules and wishes and still wasn't close to giving a fuck.

"Straight like that, Street? Over some gym shoes? Some whack-ass sneakers? Damn, I guess them pockets are bleeding worse than I thought," she huffed, thinking her mouth was gonna keep running with no repercussions.

Ring, ring, ring.

Ignoring my ringing cell, I moved around the bed with speed, grabbed Jamika up by the jaw, and muscled her onto the bed. "Who in the hell do you think you talkin' to? Do you need me to yank ya tongue up outta ya mouth? Huh? Speak up, li'l squeak." I roughed her up, putting her back in her place as the hood rat she kept proving to be.

She squirmed underneath me and tried prying my hands off her face. The more she fought, the tighter my grip got. Her face was turning red, and her punches were becoming weaker and weaker. When I felt my point had been proven, I aggressively pushed her head into the mattress and mushed her face one last time before letting it go. I started to take another round of head, but it wasn't even worth it.

"I can't believe you put your hands on me," she said in utter shock and disbelief. Swooping up the money off the bed and the bills that fell to the floor, she stuffed it in her tattered bootleg purse and tried rushing for the door. "Fuck you, Street! I hope something happens to you out here. Something real fucking bad." She called herself putting a hex on me while rushing out of the room.

"If it does, it won't be by yo' hand, ho! Na get the fuck on up outta here before I do it again."

Wiping the sweat I'd built up from fighting with Jamika off my forehead, I pulled out my cell to see who I'd missed a call from.

Damn! Fuck, fuck, fuck!

I had not missed the call at all. During my scuffle with Jamika, it was apparently answered. I saw the counter at a minute and nineteen seconds. The caller had not hung up. They'd just been completely quiet. Plus, they'd heard everything said between me and that hood ho I should've chased up out of here for threatening me. After a second more, the silence was broken. I knew exactly who the caller was.

CHAPTER 30

TRINITY

"Sit your ass all the way up and stay at attention, Jackson," the prison guard shouted. She blew her hot breath in my face, then slammed her wooden baton against the steel bench I was sitting on, sending waves of vibrations through my nerve-wracked body.

I was sick within my gut that I was restrained. It had been more than seven hours, and the only time I got to stretch my legs and arms and relieve the pressure from my cramped stomach was during the five-minute bathroom break they allowed me to go on over two hours ago. My body barely had enough energy to take in oxygen, let alone keep a perfect posture. I tried sitting up but ended up slouching to the right again.

"Inmate, you better get up before I get you up," the correctional officer growled again, making me ball my fists up. "Down, girl. Before I have you processed into max." She played against my vulnerability.

"Whatever will make you feel safer," I couldn't help but mutter.

"What was that, inmate?" She got down into my face, antagonizing me while abusing her power. She knew exactly what I'd said but was testing me to say it again.

"Whichever you can get me to the fastest, I'll take it so I can sleep. I'm tired as hell of you and these bullshitting-ass circumstances." I reworded my response, yet with the same attitude as before.

Compliance was not my strong suit. I didn't have much experience knowing how to walk a fine line with people or rules. I was well aware that I was gaining a bad reputation with the detectives and guards, but I'd never been a breakable bitch. I wasn't sure I could even look myself in the mirror if I cooperated with the law against my husband. I was Calvin's anchor and his muthafuckin' accessory. I'd take those titles to my grave, and I knew it was the same way with him. He would never allow me to be the fall guy. Just like I wouldn't ever fold.

The correctional officer was still in my face, saying li'l slick shit to get a rise out of me, when another inmate leaped up and did some gangster shit that even my gangster ass could not fathom doing. Like dominoes, every single guard and detainee began sounding off. Even I couldn't help but dropping the common hood response, "Hell naw."

"CO Tindal, we've got a live one," another CO yelled to get the attention of the guard who'd made herself my personal tormenter.

"What in the fuck? Yank that degenerate up." Her command echoed throughout the room.

The detained chick was turning red, looking like she was about to pass out, yet she was smiling like a joker in excruciating pain as she attempted to bite her tongue off. As if I were watching a movie, I witnessed blood pouring off her lips and from the corners of her mouth. Even with two guards trying to pry her lips open, they couldn't stop the young girl's suicide attempt. My eyes had seen some cold, ruthless, and sick shit, but this right here was mad psychotic. Li'l momma's charges must've been mighty helluva and coming with a possible life sentence for her to be so driven on taking her own life.

When we caught eyes a few hours ago, both sitting here waiting for our fates to play out, I thought about Porsha and sized her up as the same age. I was now forced to think about what it would be like to get the news while I was a prisoner that my daughter got murked or killed herself in jail. Even with me raising her rough and around some of the grimiest cats of Detroit and the surrounding hoods, I didn't prepare her for jail.

"Let her go and stand back." CO Tindal's voice sounded like a screeching siren. "Arm up."

Before I got to question what was about to happen, Tindal pulled out the same nightstick she'd rattled me awake with and slammed it straight across the girl's lips.

Silence and stillness fell over the room as the young girl's lip, nose, and forehead split open. It wasn't until her limp body collapsed to the floor that someone started squealing and crying.

"Oh my God! Oh my God! Get me out of here. I don't wanna die," another inmate yelled out, terrified and in shock.

"Shut up before you're next," CO Tindal warned the girl. "You cannot test an officer of the law. You all's little friend was told to follow an order, and instead, she made the conscious decision to march by the beat of her own broken drum. Now before you is her consequence and what could be your consequence if you dare to test me or any one of these fine officers within this facility." She ended her speech with her eyes on me.

I dropped my head and bit my lip. It was about to be a hard muthafuckin' time walking down my days until trial.